A STING IN HER TALE

To my favourite cousin!
Mark

A STING IN HER TALE

MARK EZRA

NO EXIT PRESS

First published in the UK in 2025 by No Exit Press,
an imprint of Bedford Square Publishers Ltd,
London, UK

noexit.co.uk
@noexitpress
info@bedfordsquarepublishers.co.uk

© Mark Ezra, 2025

The right of Mark Ezra to be identified as the author of this work has been asserted in accordance with the Copyright, Designs and Patents Act 1988. All rights reserved. No part of this book may be reproduced, stored in or introduced into a retrieval system, or transmitted, in any form or by any means (electronic, mechanical, photocopying, recording or otherwise) without the written permission of the publishers.

Any person who does any unauthorised act in relation to this publication may be liable to criminal prosecution and civil claims for damages. A CIP catalogue record for this book is available from the British Library. This is a work of fiction. Names, characters, places, and incidents either are the product of the author's imagination or are used fictitiously, and any resemblance to actual persons, living or dead, businesses, companies, events or locales is entirely coincidental.

ISBN
978-1-83501-244-4 (Paperback)
978-1-83501-245-1 (eBook)

2 4 6 8 10 9 7 5 3 1

Typeset in 11.2 on 14.25pt Minion Pro
by Avocet Typeset, Bideford, Devon, EX39 2BP
Printed and bound in Great Britain by
CPI Group (UK) Ltd, Croydon CR0 4YY

The manufacturer's authorised representative in the EU for product safety is Easy Access System Europe, Mustamäe tee 50, 10621 Tallinn, Estonia
gpsr.requests@easproject.com

For Jenny

'If I be waspish, best beware my sting.'

William Shakespeare,
The Taming of the Shrew

1

West Sussex, May 2019

Entering the world is easy. Other people do all the work: a mother with a cry, a midwife with forceps, a surgeon with a scalpel; it is the leaving of it that is hard: the bitter bite of poison, the breathless leap from a clifftop, the point-blank blast of a handgun – if you know where to get one, and I most certainly do – or a high-speed crash without a seat belt. I've weighed them all and found them all equally repulsive. When you have steeled yourself to carry out the deed it is not the pain, though one should take that into consideration, but the indignity and inconvenience to others that rankles. I was never one to make a scene.

A fresh breeze had sprung up and made the new green leaves of the elm tree outside my bedroom window shimmer in the sunlight. It brought promise of warmer weather and bluer skies, a hope, for some, of a new love and a new life. But not for me.

I slipped my final letter into my faded escritoire. It was unsealed and not addressed to anyone in particular. Somebody would find it, read it and deliver it to the relevant authorities. If they chose to pass it on to my middle-aged children, well, it would be their first written communication from me in years, other than the odd Christmas card. I never sent birthday cards. The memory of carrying my twin boy and girl for nearly nine months and their subsequent birth was unwelcome, for good reason. This had led to resentment. On both sides.

I forced my way through a thicket of brambles and nettles to reach the river. The last time I had scouted the area they had not been so dense. Old habits die hard: check the lay of the land, observe the angle of the sun, ensure you are not being watched.

Brambles slashed my bare legs. I tore myself from their grip and ploughed onwards. I slipped and slid down the muddy bank, landing hard on my bony backside. My bunioned feet in open sandals struck the water. It was colder than anticipated, even for May. I had endured far worse. All I had to do was take a few steps into deeper water. The stones weighing heavily in my pockets would do the rest.

At my first step the water rose to my waist. My skirt trapped air and ballooned around me. A ridiculous sight, but there was nobody to see me. In any case I did not care. I glanced up river to my right, then left, then right again, the way I had been taught as a child to cross the road. There would be no lorry bearing down to crush me here. But what about a family out in a pleasure cruiser, or a couple enjoying a romantic punt? I could not afford to risk rescue. I took another step forward and prepared for the water's cold numbness to wash over me.

A flash of black and white caught my eye: something caught in the reeds upstream. As I watched, it worked itself free and drifted towards me. It caught in my skirt and, in that moment, I saw it for what it was: a baby's car seat with a handle and, strapped into it, a sleeping baby. The seat was sinking. As it passed I reached out and grabbed the handle. Its weight almost pulled me over. I had not expected so much resistance.

I kept the baby's seat raised as I waded back to the riverbank. The stones in my pockets nearly had me over more than once. I scrambled up the bank and grazed my knee on a sharp flint. I lowered the seat between tall tussocks of grass and dropped to the ground. I checked my knee. Blood flowed freely down my shin, but when you've witnessed your lifeblood gushing from a bullet wound onto cold snow you know when you've got nothing to worry about.

I am more than seventy years old – I won't tell you exactly how much more, there are limits to what a woman is willing to disclose. I can still walk a brisk few miles across country and keep pace with people half my age. But the exertion involved in holding the baby in its sodden car seat above the fast-flowing current and getting us both safely back to dry land had knocked the stuffing out of me.

I lay flat on my back for a full minute, counting off the seconds, catching my breath and wondering where the baby had come from, where its parents were, and why it wasn't crying.

In my experience, babies spent most of their young lives wailing, puking or soiling their nappies. I rolled over and peered into the seat. The baby's eyes were shut, but it breathed. I woke it. That is, I gave it a prod. Its eyes opened. Blue, unfocussed eyes, pupils dilated. They closed again. The child had been drugged.

What kind of person would drug a child? An addict, breastfeeding while high on heroin? Questions swirled around my brain. I undid the straps that held it tight and felt soft, full flesh. The child was well fed, healthy. How had it come to be in the river? Why was nobody out looking for it?

A breeze blew up. I hugged the ground to absorb what remained of its warmth as I puzzled what to do next. Then

I saw him: a man, striding swiftly along the path on the far side of the river. He was pretending he was simply out for a stroll, but his darting eyes revealed that he was searching for something, in all likelihood a missing baby. His lack of distress bothered me. That, and the meanness of his slack mouth as he chewed his gum.

At that moment he glanced in my direction. A non-professional might have ducked down, but I had had too much experience in the field. Any sudden movement would be noticed. When you've stalked human prey, as I have, you know these things. I simply narrowed my eyes to cut down their reflection and swayed ever so slightly with the grasses. With luck he wouldn't have glimpsed my wisps of grey hair. A cloud came over and he turned away. He headed back the way he had come, whistling 'The Miller of Dee' with studied casualness as if he was off for a couple of drinks in the local pub before lunch.

I waited a few minutes. The nearest crossing was more than two miles away, so there was no risk of his coming up behind me. If he had seen me he would return, threading his way back through the trees lining the path. A pair of kingfishers nested there. He could not avoid disturbing them. When I was sure he had gone for good I took hold of the baby seat by its handle, hauled it through the brambles and strode home. In all this time, the baby had made no sound at all.

2

It was a different matter when we got back to the house. The moment I shut the back door the baby opened its eyes, took one look at me and howled. Well I wasn't surprised. I can look a fright at the best of times. After plunging into the river and dragging myself backwards through the brambles – which is how the nuns described my appearance when they caught me scurrying down late for breakfast – my grey hair stuck out like a Halloween witch's wig.

It was a long time since I had had to deal with a baby. My own had been sorely neglected. Not through any fault of mine, I liked to remind myself, but because of the demands of my work. I was often away for much longer than I would have liked; but in my day children were considered tougher, more resilient and were expected to take care of themselves at a far younger age.

I cleared the kitchen table of the box files and envelopes which I had prepared in a neat and orderly fashion. They summed up the last years of my retirement: bank statements in one, utility bills (all paid) in another, passwords to some – but not all – of my electronic devices (those containing evidence and details of my past career had been buried in a box deep in my garden, along with my MBE medal for special services). The final envelope contained my last will and testament, together with a short list of wishes which my children would almost certainly ignore.

I sat in my sodden clothes and made a list while the baby screamed. I was fortunate that my nearest neighbours were elderly and deaf, and inclined to mind their own business. In any case the walls of my house were so thick that few sounds could penetrate. Besides, the houses either side of mine are second homes. They are occupied less than six weeks a year and I hardly ever see the owners.

My list was short: milk, feeding bottle, nappies, baby wipes. That was as far as I got. Baby wipes were not available in the 1970s when my children were born, but they are in the news every day as a major cause of blocked drains. I considered adding some sort of sedative to my list, before deciding that such a thought was uncharitable.

Why did I not simply call the police and report that I had rescued a baby from drowning? That had been my first instinct, but when I thought back to the man on the riverbank, searching with such little diligence for the baby, I felt that he, or whoever had sent him searching, did not deserve to have this child back. Not until I had done some research. I was going to have to find it a safe home and, until I had done that, I was perfectly capable of providing one myself. There was another reason, of course: the publicity. I knew how this might develop and I could imagine the increasingly hysterical headlines: 'Granny Saves Baby' could so easily morph into 'Recluse Snatches Tot' or worse – and this wasn't out of the range of possibilities – 'Old Witch Lures Innocent Babe into Gingerbread Cottage for Satanic Ritual'. The last would be once the press had talked to my neighbours. I keep to myself, but I've heard the rumours they spread about me. Water off a duck's back, in normal circumstances, but when the gossip goes nationwide, one can get a lot of unwanted attention.

Mind you, it wouldn't be the first time I would hear my house described as gingerbread. It was one of a row of five detached labourer's cottages in Sussex Georgian vernacular. The front is of blue-grey knapped flint set in yellowing mortar in a 'snail-creep' pattern. Brick quoins support the corners, with jutting hand grips running all the way up to the roof, while ancient oak beams (from an earlier construction) create a frame for the flint and broken brick, or 'bungaroosh', as they call it in this part of Sussex. From across the street the chunks of brick look like large pieces of orange peel and the sprinkles of dark flint resemble currants, all set in a marzipan mortar. No, reporting myself to the police was out of the question.

I warmed a little milk in a pan and scoured the pantry until I found what I was looking for. A small bottle with a yellowed teat. I had helped an old friend with lambing on his farm a few years back, and somehow this bottle had remained with me. It was dirty and the teat had stiffened and cracked with age, but I soaked it, then poured boiling water into the bottle and gave it a good scrub. A few minutes later the child was sucking contentedly at the teat. If it caught anything and died, at least it would have died content.

It was a girl. I had checked of course, though there was something about its soft skin and ready smile that had already given it away. It was a pretty girl at that. Bright blue eyes, not so harsh or piercing as mine, and lips like little rosebuds. She gurgled merrily as she drank the warm milk. When she had had enough I hid her in the larder, still strapped into her seat, and locked the door.

I changed out of my wet clothes, took a hot shower to get

my circulation going, and put on a pair of corduroy trousers. I needed something to cover up the bramble scratches. The trousers had been meant as a present for Dennis, but I never had the chance to give them to him. I had had them shortened by a couple of inches and taken in at the waist, so they fitted well enough.

I drive a 1982 Volvo. It was only three years old when I got it, so I've had it a long time. It is solid and reliable and though it's got more than 100,000 miles on the clock, it still does the job. I drove out of the village and took the bypass as I headed for the largest town, a good twenty-five minutes away. Of course, I could have got all the items I needed at the village corner shop, but that would have attracted attention.

I parked at the out-of-town Sainsbury's, positioning my car up against the large sign advertising their two-hour free parking policy which masked me from the supermarket's CCTV cameras. I headed in and made for the pharmacy. But when I got inside I saw that they had remodelled the layout and the pharmacy, which had been tucked away in a darkish corner, was now in the heart of the building and of a brightness that Gabriel and all his Angels would have found garish.

My hopes of a quick 'pop in and out' dashed, I found it took longer than I had imagined to find the items on my list, and I had to resort to asking a young lady assistant for help.

'Disposable?' she asked. I had no idea what she was talking about. I looked at her blankly.

'Disposable nappies,' she said loudly, as if I were deaf, or stupid. 'Single. Use. Only.'

I hadn't heard of these. After my time I suppose, not that I ever spent a great deal of my day changing my children's nappies. 'Don't you have the other sort, the ones you wash?'

She looked me up and down. 'Yes, we do,' and pointed out a small and neglected pile on the bottom shelf. 'But most customers haven't got all day to spend washing them out.'

'I can assure you that I do not have all day available either,' I replied. 'I shall take five packs of disposables.'

'Age?'

'What's my age got to do with it?'

'The – age – of – the – baby,' she explained in a patronising tone. 'One year old? Two year toddler?'

'My grandson is one year old,' I answered, more positively than I felt. I could have been out by a few months either way. But I was pleased with my quick-witted change of its sex.

'Okay, anything else?'

I reeled off my list and let her find the items for me. I followed her to the till and she rang up my purchases.

'Two hundred and fifty nappies,' she said. I had not realised that each pack contained fifty. I had not intended to keep the baby more than a day or two before deciding what to do with it.

'Do you have a loyalty card?'

'No, I don't.' I did, of course, but I had no wish to leave a record of my presence or my purchases.

'That's a total of £87.13. Pop your card in the machine.'

I resisted the urge to pull out my debit card and instead held out two £50 notes. The girl sighed. It took her three attempts to count out the correct change and even then she was twenty pence short. I was happy to forgo it. If I made a fuss she would remember me.

'Disappear into the crowd, don't stand out'. That's what we were taught.

As I headed out I lowered my head and let a shock of grey hair fall over my face. I was wearing a faded lilac anorak that

I only used for gardening and would ditch before I got home. As I passed the main bank of security cameras I sped up a little. If they ever checked, they would only have three or four frames to work from, and my face was completely obscured.

I was thinking 'they', but who were they? Figments in my tousled head? No, not with a missing baby involved. At some stage people might be checking CCTV cameras and so I followed my training. I drove out of the car park and headed north along a minor road, away from home. About five miles out of town I glanced in my rear-view mirror to check that nobody was following then suddenly swung off onto a farmer's track that led through a hundred metres of private woodland and out onto the A road. I followed it south, wrapped a scarf tight around my head to cover my hair and was back home in half an hour.

As I entered the village I had to slow down – there's a cattle grid set to rattle the frame of even the best-sprung motor. I noticed two strangers coming out of the newsagents. One was opening a packet of cigarettes, which he offered to the other. The one with the cigarettes was my friend from the riverbank. I fixed his features in my mind. He was dark-haired, with a low brow, a broken nose skewed sideways and a weak chin. His prominent teeth gave an uneven aspect to his mouth as he took one of his own cigarettes and flicked it in. There was nothing clearly defined about his face – he seemed devoid of cheekbones. Either that or they had been rearranged for him by some larger opponent. I felt I should give him a name. I settled on 'Igor'.

His companion, who refused the cigarette, possessed better defined features: a broad brow, intelligent brown eyes, a fine patrician nose over full lips and a heavy chin, which doubled as he lowered his head. His thick hair was sandy and he wore a Loden coat. I have always loathed those things: green shapeless sacks at the best of times. God knows I haven't worn stylish clothes for more than twenty years, but anyone who thinks he looks good in Loden is labouring under a sad misapprehension. Unconscious of my disapproval, the man held himself straight and proud, as if he were being photographed for some magazine cover. I named him 'Fashion-Plate'.

These descriptions, based on their appearances, were what Dennis would call 'prep-school' nicknames. Easy to remember and, more importantly, not immediately recognised by those who earned them.

I carried on at a slow pace – there's a 20 miles-an-hour limit in the village – and as I glanced in the wing mirror I saw Igor staring intently at me and my car. I knew that look. He was memorising the number plate. I was relieved I was wearing a scarf that covered my mop of hair. I could not guarantee he had not spotted me in the tall grass. If, as I suspected, he was a professional, he might easily have done so and given nothing away. Instead he turned to study the occupant of a car being driven in the opposite direction: Phyllis Price, a nosey old busybody about my age and with similar grey hair, though hers was coiffed weekly at Chez Doris, the little hairdressers at the far end of the village. How Doris makes a living in such an out-of-the-way place is a mystery. It's probably a front for money-laundering, though a lot of ladies come in from all over the county to have her 'do' them, so she must be getting something right.

I carried on along the road, going way past my house, then checked in the rear-view mirror. There was no sign of either Igor or Fashion-Plate. I took a left, then turned into the track that ran around the back of the cottages. I parked on the gravel stand and carried my purchases in through the back door.

I found the baby just as I had left her, asleep. To my shock I realised that the baby seat was damp from its immersion in the river and the baby was quite cold. Water must have soaked up from the base. I boiled the electric kettle and half-filled a hot-water bottle. I topped it up with lukewarm water from a tap. I laid it on the kitchen table and covered it with a towel.

I unstrapped the baby and laid her on the warm towel. She woke drowsily and gurgled happily as I changed her nappy, wiped her down and wrapped her in a new disposable one. It was easier than I had expected. I had bought several items of baby food, some of which could be served straight from their jars and others which had to be mixed with water or milk. I tested a few sample batches and was gratified that the baby took to them all without complaint. This was the most delightful child I had ever encountered and, now that I felt we were safe, I was able to take the time to study her.

At a rough estimate she was around nine to eleven months old. Up until then I had thought she might be younger, because she was so small, but now that I looked into her bright eyes and felt her grasping hands, I saw she was older than I had imagined and more alert. I don't think I had ever seen such a beautiful child. If she had been drugged, as I suspected she had, the effects had now worn off and her true, cheerful nature surfaced. I decided that I could not keep calling her The Baby, even in my own mind, and decided on a name for her: 'Alice'.

She soon fell asleep again and I realised I had made one major omission in my purchases. I needed a cot for her to sleep in. I placed the baby seat on a radiator for it to dry out overnight. Then I went down the concrete steps to the cellar, unlocked the heavy oak door, and brought up a large wicker trug which I used for flower cuttings from the garden. I lined it with a soft blanket then took it up to the spare bedroom. I placed Alice gently inside it, the full bottle within easy reach, and switched off the light. I could honestly say I had never known such a peaceful baby.

I felt differently at two in the morning. Alice had been crying for half an hour and I was worried the neighbours might finally hear her. Her cheeks were flushed and she was drooling. She was teething and I had nothing to ease her discomfort. I never take analgesics and have none of the usual paraphernalia in my bathroom cupboard: no aspirins, no paracetamol and no codeine. If I feel pain I treat it with contempt until it goes away. For a while I was at a loss what to do. Little Alice needed something to chew on. Then I had an idea.

I went into the garden with a sharp pair of secateurs. A brook runs through the rear gardens of the cottages and a young willow grows there. I cut three whip-like branches where I had pollarded the tree a couple of years ago. One branch was considerably thicker than the other two. I cut these into short lengths – around nine inches each – and headed back into the house. As I walked I heard a scream and a dull thump. We are forever plagued by foxes mating and knocking over rubbish bins and I thought no more of it at the time.

Willow bark contains the source of salicin, the natural analgesic used in aspirin. I held three cuttings out to Alice. She grasped the thickest one, rammed it into her mouth and started chewing. It was too big for her to swallow and in a few minutes she had relaxed. I went to bed and slept soundly.

At three in the morning I was suddenly awake, convinced that I had been stupidly reckless and that Alice had choked on her twig. I found her fast asleep with the willow cutting beside her. I had been worried over nothing. Just to be sure I removed it from her reach and returned to bed. It took me forever to get off to sleep.

3

When I awoke I gave Alice a second willow twig and ran the shower. It takes a couple of minutes for the water to warm up. In that time I boiled the kettle and opened a fresh jar of baby food. While I was feeding Alice I heard a police siren approach. For a second my heart jumped but the siren passed. I relaxed. Nobody knew I had Alice and I intended to keep it that way.

I showered, dressed and then changed Alice's nappy. By now I had got the hang of doing it in under a minute. I gave her some warm milk and left her to her own devices as I went down to the corner shop. It's supposed to open at eight, but as it sells papers and the Indian owner, Bas, has to be there to receive delivery, he's often open before 7.30.

There were more people hanging around in the street than usual for that time of day. They were in groups of two or three, all deep in gossip. I was not a member of their cliques and seldom spoke to any of them. As I passed one trio a woman whom I only knew by sight turned to me and asked, loudly, 'Have you heard?' Before I could answer, her male companion had hauled her back. 'She'll have heard about it soon enough,' he grunted, and all three turned away from me.

I carried on to the corner shop. Beyond it, as the village

high street ran out and just before the cattle grid, I saw a police car parked on the verge, its blue light flashing, and another car and a police van parked up on the other side of the road. I entered the shop, collected more milk, organic carrots, onions, four courgettes and a copy of *The Times* and went over to the till. A man buying milk and newspapers had paid and gone out, leaving me alone with Bas.

'What's going on?' I asked.

Bas is particular about those to whom he speaks. Some he can't wait to see leave his shop, others he likes to joke with, recount anecdotes, or discuss politics. I am among the latter. He seems to appreciate me because we both have degrees. Mine, in Greats, is from Oxford, and I also have a Masters and a PhD in Economics from Cambridge. Bas is Gujarati and his degrees are in Pharmacology and Mathematics. Unfortunately for him they are from an Indian university and count for nothing in the UK, which is why he has to stand behind his counter all day long, even when he's eating, hoping to earn enough to keep his two children at university at Cambridge and Bristol.

He came out from behind his counter and locked the door before approaching me with a whisper.

'Someone found a body in the road this morning. A car accident they think.' He corrected himself. 'They *thought*. Now they're not so sure.'

'Is it someone from the village?'

'Mrs Price. A bit racist, but a prompt payer. Not like people who demand credit all the time.'

My heart was racing, but I gave nothing away. 'When was this?'

'Sometime late in the night. Milkman found her, phoned the police.'

'So what happened to her, exactly?' I managed to keep my voice even.

'Someone tried to make it look like a hit-and-run, but they say the fingernails on her right hand were torn out. The whole house is a mess, a disaster. She was rich, so maybe she kept money or jewellery there.'

Or maybe Igor and Fashion-Plate went too far.

'How dreadful.'

I was rooted to the spot, a rictus smile freezing the muscles of my face, but my instincts were to get out of the village fast.

When I got home I strapped Alice into the back seat of the car. I felt a great sense of gratitude that she had come pre-wrapped in the baby seat, which was now fully dry. I had fed and watered her and changed her nappy one more time – what is it about children that they have to soil their nappies the moment you've changed them? I had also packed a small case of things she might need, such as fresh nappies and wipes. I had given her another feed of warm milk which got her off to sleep. Before I slid into the front seat I gently draped a square Hermès scarf to hide her and rammed a heavy-duty bin liner filled with bubble-wrap and crumpled newspapers between her and the dashboard. She still had plenty of air. If anyone saw me, they would think I was heading off to the rubbish dump. If they reported me for fly-tipping, so what. I put on a pair of rubber wellington boots. They would make driving a little difficult, but I would need them soon enough.

I drove out west, took the bypass and headed onto the A road travelling north before turning east. I had briefly considered going through the woods, but I could imagine someone waiting there in the lay-by, faking a breakdown and waiting for a little old lady with a baby to drive past. Why make it easy for them?

I removed the scarf from Alice without waking her and checked the rear-view mirror as often as I could, but there appeared to be nobody following. As I approached Forest Row I took a sharp right which led me through Ashdown Forest. Two miles later I took another sharp right and this led me onto what was no more than a track. It stopped dead at a shallow stream. I reversed, turned the car around and drove back the way I had come for about ten yards. Then I reversed into the stream and turned the wheel, backing into the water so that I ended up facing upstream.

I drove along the stream's gravel bed for fifty feet or so and stopped. I put on the hand brake, got out and waded back to where the car had left the track. I scrubbed out the tyre marks with my heel and redistributed the gravel. Anyone following me would conclude that I had come to a dead end at the stream, turned around and retraced my journey.

As I strode back to the car water splashed up into my boots. I had no time to empty them. I got in and drove on another twenty yards to where the bank consisted of impacted gravel and led to another track. I turned onto it gently, so that I would leave few marks, then continued along my way, joining a B road a few hundred yards further on. Fifteen minutes later I turned off the road and carried on along a driveway, well concealed by overgrown laurels, and stopped outside an early Victorian vicarage.

As I got out of the car the front door opened and Ambrose Flynn came out to greet me. He still had that awkward boyish way of walking, leaning forward with his hands clasped behind his back, even now in his late seventies.

'Felicity, my dear.' (This was the name by which he had known me all through our professional lives together.) 'I had a feeling I was due a visit. It's been far too long.'

'Can't stop, Ambrose, I'm on a mission.'

'A mission? Intriguing.' He scratched his nose. 'I thought you retired a year after I did.'

I gave him a look. 'Come off it, Ambrose. They may have retired me, but they still call on you whenever they're in a fix.'

Ambrose deftly changed the subject. 'What may I offer you? Amontillado?'

'I need your help.'

'I don't know that I'm much good at helping anybody these days.'

'How are your parenting skills?'

'Non-existent.'

'Well, you'll have to do.' I unbuckled Alice and handed her, still strapped in her carrier, over to him.

'What am I supposed to do with this?'

'Feed her regularly and change her nappies whenever she needs it.' We were now inside the house. I shut the door behind us.

'I have never changed a nappy in my life.'

'Then it's about time you learnt.' I unbuckled Alice, who gurgled happily. I laid her out on his desk and pushed aside Ambrose's papers.

'Careful, some of that is highly… highly…'

'Yes, I'm sure it is. Now undo the nappy and give her a wipe. It's easy. I taught myself yesterday and it barely took five minutes.'

Ambrose hesitated a moment, shifted his feet sheepishly then leant forward and pulled open the nappy.

'Oh dear,' he groaned. 'It's a long time since I've seen a young lady in the altogether, and she was a great deal more grown-up than this one.'

'You'll get used to it. I'll be back this evening. You'll find instructions on her care in here,' and I thrust an envelope into his hands and left the small case I had packed for Alice.

'I look forward to getting acquainted with the young lady,' he sighed. 'Am I permitted to know whose she is?'

'All will be revealed,' I said and walked back to the car.

I got back onto the A22, briefly joined the M25 and turned off towards Epsom. I joined the A3 and eventually took a right turn past Roehampton to Putney, passing the tree where Marc Bolan crashed the night he died. A bit of a deviation, admittedly, but the slower road past Barnes Common made it easier to spot a pursuer. There wasn't one.

Humming those bits of T-Rex's greatest hits that I could still remember, I made it to Westminster in twenty-five minutes flat and drove up to the Ministry of Defence parking lot. There was a uniformed guard on the gate.

'I'm sorry, madam, this parking's not for members of the public.'

I held up the high-level security pass I had removed from Ambrose's desk while he had been busy changing Alice's nappy.

'Ah, I'm sorry, ma'am,' the man said. He pressed a button, the barrier rose and I drove down into the bowels of the building.

Once I'd found a space to park I headed for the lift and held Ambrose's pass to the lift scanner. The door opened, I stepped inside and pressed the button for the third floor. When it opened I knew exactly where to go. I turned right and marched down the corridor until I reached the door marked Permanent Secretary. I knocked once, entered and found myself in an outer office manned by a startled young woman seated behind a desk.

'Can I help you?'

'I'm here to see the Permanent Under Secretary of State for Defence.'

'I'm afraid he's busy at the moment.' She had reached under her desk. For a gun? More likely an alarm to summon help to deal with this mad woman in muddy wellington boots.

'I want to see him now,' I said, firmly. I stepped around her desk. She stood to block me.

'He does not see anyone without an appointment.'

I pushed straight past her.

'He'll bloody well see me. I'm his fucking mother.'

4

'Well, that was fun,' Bernard said in that supercilious, sarcastic way of his which meant that it was anything but fun, for him at least. It was the tone he favoured at Christmas – when we usually met for less than half an hour. He always had family or matters of state to attend to.

He had calmed the situation and sent away the two armed Ministry of Defence policemen and the three naval officers who had swooped in to arrest me. 'Next time you want to get yourself shot, let me know in advance and I'll happily do it myself.' He shuffled through some papers on his desk, as if putting the whole episode to bed. 'Would you like tea? I can only give you a few minutes. I have an appointment with the PM in half an hour.'

'Then I shall speak fast, so listen and take notes, though you probably won't need them.' Bernard, like me, had an excellent memory and even as a child would recite entire school debates from memory. No surprise that he had few friends.

I told him about finding Alice, the two strangers – Igor and Fashion-Plate – and the murder of Phyllis Price. It all came out as one long, rushed sentence and he stayed silent, his elbows on his desk, his fingers pressed together, until I finished, a little breathless.

'I shall have to get back to you on this,' he said. Then, realising he was talking to me, his mother, and not some MP or journalist, added, 'I shall make enquiries, starting with Scotland Yard.'

'If somebody is out there murdering old ladies I should have thought speed was of the essence.'

Bernard stifled a sigh and picked up his phone. 'Mary, get me Sir Harold Ellice, will you please? Yes, I'll hold.'

Harold Ellice had been Chief Police Commissioner for the past two years. A government appointee, he and Bernard were not on the best of terms following a recent police cock-up relating to the early release of terrorists. I was impressed Bernard had obliged me by calling the Commissioner and even more so when his call was answered.

'Harold? Bernard here. I wonder if you know anything about the death of an old lady in—' he turned to me. I was not thrilled by the idea of telling him where I was living, not that he would ever bother to visit.

'West Sussex,' I said, and gave him the name of our village.

He repeated the name and waited a moment. 'Today I believe, that's right, isn't it?' These last words were addressed to me.

'Around two in the morning,' I answered, 'the local police are investigating.' I was fidgeting. The water in my wellingtons was making my toes itch.

Bernard repeated the information and waited. 'I see, thank you.' He replaced the handset and glanced up at me. 'A simple case of hit-and-run.'

'That's not what I believe.'

'The Sussex police have investigated all leads and there will, of course, be a coroner's inquiry. Open to all.' He gave me a tight smile. 'Now I really must go. I have a white paper revision to present.'

'To the Prime Minister?' He had already told me so, but it gave him a chance to preen.

He straightened up, unable to conceal his self-importance. 'Yes, the Prime Minister.' Then, to get rid of me, 'Must get on.'

'I'm sure you must.' I cannot resist having the last word.

He showed me to the door, where the two Ministry of Defence policemen were waiting.

'Please escort my mother out.'

They marched either side of me all the way to the lift and followed me inside. One of them pressed a button for the ground floor. I pressed the button for the garage.

'How did you get in the car park, love?' he asked.

'Gate was unattended,' I answered with a shrug. They looked at each other, not believing me for a moment, but decided not to take the matter further.

5

I DROVE BACK THE WAY I had come – such a nuisance that Hammersmith Bridge was still closed – and headed back to Forest Row. The sun was high in the sky and the light bounced off the fresh blossoms of wild apple and hawthorn. Ponds and lakes flashed their brightness through the trees to raise my spirits. I might have felt that all was well with the world, but I knew it was not. Something bothered me: not the nearly drowned child, nor the murder of the old lady, but something else. Thirty years ago I might have found the answer immediately. But now, pushing into my mid seventies, it was a different matter. My senses were jaded, dulled by lack of use. It was time to sharpen up.

It was only 3 o'clock when I got back, but Ambrose was already at his wits' end. Alice had not stopped crying since her lunch, which he had taken it upon himself to give her at 11 o'clock in the hope of quietening her down. He had fed her again at 1 o'clock and then again at 2.15, which was more often than instructed. Alice had eaten everything he had given her, and had drunk her warmed milk, which he had prepared at exact body temperature, 37 degrees Celsius, as per my orders. She had then projectile vomited the lot straight into his face. By the time I arrived he had cleaned up the worst of the mess and was sitting in a chair facing the child with a look of despair on his face.

'Never again, I'm never doing this again, you understand?'

I glanced over at his hob. It was covered in dried puddles of congealed milk. I wondered how many times he had let the milk boil over while trying to get the temperature exact. Typical Ambrose, taking everything literally. The encrusted milk would be hard to shift.

'Of course, Ambrose. Goes without saying.' I picked up Alice who stopped crying immediately and began gurgling happily in my arms. 'Have you got any milk left?'

'Here,' snapped Ambrose, holding out the bottle at arm's length. 'And I'll have my security pass back, if you've finished with it.'

'You don't miss a thing, do you?'

'I should hope not. Did it get you what you wanted?'

'I got to see Bernard, if that's what you mean. He was no help.'

Ambrose softened. 'Do you want to tell me what this is all about?'

I went over what I knew so far and Ambrose listened with his eyes closed and his fingertips touching, much as Bernard had done. He asked two questions. Were there any other witnesses to Phyllis Price's death? He meant apart from my hearing the late-night scream and the dull thump. It was perfectly possible, he pointed out, for someone to be dragged along the road in a hit-and-run and to get their nails ripped out as they tried to save themselves. And was I sure Bernard had been speaking to Sir Harold?

'Are you suggesting that Bernard was lying to me?' I asked.

'Sons lie to their mothers all the time. That's what sons do. Why should Bernard be any different?'

I had no answer for that. Bernard had always excelled at deception and manipulation, which I supposed was what had earned him his position. But a child is the product of its parents, and I couldn't blame him if his genetically inherited abilities came to the fore.

Ambrose was right to plant the question in my head. True, I hadn't heard the voice at the other end of the phone, but I did believe Bernard had been speaking to Sir Harold: I had caught him in plenty of lies as a child and, unless I'd lost my skills completely, I was certain that on this occasion he was telling me the truth. What convinced me was the stiffness he had adopted during the call. As I said before, he and Harold Ellice disliked each other profoundly. Even Bernard would not have been able to conceal his loathing completely.

'I can help you, of course.' Ambrose still had a stain of curdled milk on his shirt, but this was not the moment to point it out. 'But I shall need more. I suggest you go home and furnish me with whatever further information you can glean. If you get into trouble, let me know, any time of day or night. You could be in danger.' Then, as an afterthought, 'I rather suspect you're enjoying this. My advice is: play safe.'

He was glad to see the back of us. He waved through the window as we left, but he did not come to the door. It was basic operational practice. If I had been followed he would have been foolish to allow himself to be seen.

6

I took a simpler route back home. To be prudent, I approached the village after 5.30, when the tea rooms and bric-a-brac shops would be closed. I laid the silk scarf over Alice, skirted round the village and took the lane running along the back of the houses. There is a World War Two concrete pillbox that stands near the edge of the paddock. It was built for a machine gun and a couple of snipers to repel German invaders in the war, but never saw use. It was erected by public subscription. Even back then the locals considered their homes to be exceptionally desirable.

As I passed the pillbox I caught a glimpse of movement and slowed down. I saw nothing more, but I was on edge. I put the car out of gear, cruised to a silent stop and turned off the engine. I waited a while and finally a head peered out from behind the pillbox. The head belonged to Jamie Cullen, a fifteen-year-old who had built himself a reputation as a bit of a tearaway. He had been brought up on the small council estate at the far end of the village. When he was younger I used to give him a few pounds for mowing the lawn and doing odd jobs around the garden. Then one day I caught him stealing from my purse. I came up behind him and put him in a half-nelson lock, forcing his arm up hard and painfully behind his back.

'Take whatever you want,' I told him. 'Go on. There's more than a hundred pounds in there. Take it all. But if you do, don't ever come back here again.'

'You're hurting me!' he bleated.

'Or you can put it all back except twenty pounds. That's ten pounds for the work you've done today and ten on account. You can come back next week and earn your money honestly. It's the same to me either way. I won't tell anybody. You'll only have your own conscience to consider.'

He tried to struggle free but he couldn't break my grip.

'Well, which is it to be?'

He let go of the money, scattering notes over my kitchen tiles.

'You can keep your money! I'm out of here, you old bag!' He made another attempt to escape, but I held him tight: something I had learnt to do at boarding school, and which had proved more useful in my later career.

'I'm letting you go now. Stand there, don't move.' I relaxed my grip and as I took a step back he shrugged me off angrily, his pride hurt. I watched him carefully. He was large enough to do me an injury if he wished.

'Why don't you go and sit in the garden and I'll bring you a beer. You like beer, don't you?'

He looked at me in surprise. I don't suppose any employer had ever offered the poor lad a beer before.

'Any preference?'

He hesitated a moment, struggling to name a brand. 'Nah.'

'Go on, you've worked hard. You deserve it.'

He gathered up the bank notes, placed them back on the table and, unsure whether I really meant what I said, stepped out into my garden. I brought him out a Carlsberg I had cooling in the fridge. I offered him a glass, but he popped the tab and drank from the can.

'I think I'll join you.' I went back into the house and emerged with another can which I also popped open and drank from the top.

'Hits the spot,' I said. Jamie nodded in agreement. We sat there in silence. Neither of us looked the other in the eye. He needed a few minutes to calm his injured pride.

At last Jamie downed the remains of his lager and stood up. 'You mean what you said? I can take ten pounds on account for next week?'

'The ten pounds I owe you and ten pounds for next week.'

He went back into the house and returned carrying my purse. 'I've taken the twenty pounds like you said. You can check.'

'No need. I'll see you next week, Jamie.'

He left my purse on the garden table and sloped off. Since then we've had an understanding, as if we have a shared secret between us, which, in a way, we have.

*

A moment after I saw Jamie's head peer around the concrete pillbox another head appeared. It belonged to Beth Langdon, the daughter of the local landowner. Things seemed to be looking up for Jamie. Beth dropped a lit cigarette on the dry grass and ground it under her heel. Jamie, realising they had been spotted, stepped out and gave me a wave. I nodded back and drove on, parking up on the gravel stand. I waited until the youngsters had headed back into the village before unbuckling Alice and taking her into the house.

I had just fed her in the kitchen when there was a knock on the back door. I moved round to the window to see who it was. At the same time the person moved to the window and peered in, their shadow darkening the room. My heart leapt. Alice was on the kitchen table in full view. But it was only Jamie. He gave me a shy smile. I opened the door to him, my body blocking his view of Alice.

'Jamie, how can I help you?'

He shuffled a bit, and dropped his head shyly. 'Well, it's like... you saw me with Beth, right?'

'Beth Langdon? Is that who it was?' I replied. I knew very well it was her.

Jamie shuffled his feet. 'You see, her dad doesn't like her seeing me, since he's... who he is, and I'm... well, you know where I come from...' He flushed. 'I was hoping you wouldn't tell him, that's all.'

'I don't even know Robert Langdon, and your business is your business as far as I'm concerned.' Alice let out a loud gurgle and Jamie peered around me.

'You got a baby! Can I see?' He stepped past me and stood over Alice, chucking her under the chin and gurgling back at her.

'Reminds me of my little sister. Our Sally was just as cute at that age.' A grin spread over his big-boned face. 'Look at that little button nose.' The change in his demeanour, usually sullen at best, was illuminating.

'I didn't know you had a sister,' I said, hoping to get him out of the house.

'Sis was lucky. She went to live with Mum. I had to stay with Dad.'

'Jamie,' I said, 'I have a favour to ask you.'

'Huh?'

'You asked me not to mention your relationship with Beth. I assure you that I wouldn't anyway. But this little girl is the daughter of my niece Rachel who has left her abusive partner and is in fear of her life. That's why I've taken little Alice in. But if her partner, Richard, gets to hear where she is, he may try to take her away. He's a violent man.'

Jamie's father was also a violent man. I had seen the welts on Jamie's back when his T-shirt had rucked up while he clipped my hedge. Jamie turned to me and, with utmost seriousness, swore that he would never, ever, cross his heart and hope to die, reveal the whereabouts or even existence of baby Alice, and I should believe him because… well, because he had a good reason for telling me the truth. So I thanked him and watched as he headed off across the paddock, which was part of my land, past the pillbox, and off to the woods where, I presumed, Beth Langdon was waiting for him.

7

Three days went by before I felt I could relax. It was a long while since I had been so tense. In that time nobody had reported a missing baby. I realised I was becoming very fond of Alice. Her sunny disposition cheered me like an early summer's dawn. I knew I had to do something about finding her parents, neither of whom could possibly have been Igor – there was not the slightest genetic similarity – but I found myself in no hurry. Every day I thought, I'll put it off until tomorrow. Just give me one more day with her. Then something happened that made me wish I had tried harder.

I was busy in the back garden, which has the benefit of high old brick walls on all sides. It can be a fine heat trap, extending the ripening period for fruit and vegetables by two or three weeks. The cottages have large kitchen gardens. Presumably their Georgian tenants would have provided the big house (the one now owned by Robert Langdon) with their produce as a contribution to their rent. I had taken the risk of carrying Alice out into the garden and she was happily playing in the dark earth when I went back into the kitchen to get some drinks for us both.

While I was warming her bottle there was a ring at the door. I thought it must be the postman, who had been delivering letters later and later every day. I opened the door and there stood Fashion-Plate, his well-fed frame clad in a marvellous tweed suit which glistered with a golden sheen. It competed with the lustrous sparkle of his heavy watch chain which hung down to the lower left of four pockets of his double-breasted waistcoat. He wore an Eton silk scarf, raffishly tied in a broad foulard, and his silk shirt, from Turnbull & Asser I guessed, sported diamond cufflinks which sparkled in the sunlight.

'Mrs Jardine?' That was the name I was known by in the village, so I nodded in agreement. 'The name's Best-Worthington.' He handed me a visiting card. It read 'Sir Gerald Best-Worthington, Bart' and gave an address in Rutland Gate, Knightsbridge. He allowed me a few seconds to study it and absorb the fact that he was a person of some importance.

'How may I help you?' I asked.

'The fact is, Mrs Jardine, that this is the house where I was born and spent my early childhood years… and I wonder if… I know it's a lot to ask… if you would consider letting me take a look around, just for old times' sake.'

He was around fifty years of age, at most. The fat around his cheeks and chin and the absence of wrinkles around his eyes and brow made him appear a little younger, though this was just as likely to be the result of a couple of well-judged applications of Botox. I had only lived in the cottage for fifteen years but I had retained the old deeds and knew there was no possibility that he had ever lived here as a child.

'I'm sorry but you've caught me on my way out. It's half day closing at the post office and I need to pick up my pension.' It was a well-rehearsed line and I delivered it briskly and confidently. A lie tends to be delivered more slowly and I was sure he would have been trained to pick up any hesitation.

But he was not to be deterred. As I tried to close the door he blocked it with his right brogue. I noticed a whiff of annoyance as the rough wood scuffed the tan polish of the toe.

'Just a moment,' he said, holding the door open with his hefty shoulder while trying to extricate his shoe. 'I've been caught short. I wonder if I could use your loo. Just a pee. It won't take a moment.' And with that he barged past me and into my house.

'Where is it?' he demanded.

'First on your right, under the stairs.' He ignored me and cantered upstairs like a horse that had been stabled too long. I was glad that I had taken the precaution of storing anything that might have given away Alice's presence, including the baby seat, in my cellar. I had locked the door and hidden the key.

I heard doors opening and slamming, then he came clattering back down, breathing heavily. I held open the lavatory door. 'This is what you're looking for.' He strode in, took one glance into the small room and stepped out again. 'I thought you were in desperate need.'

'Fuck that. Where's the child?'

'I have no idea what you're talking about. There's no child here.' I backed towards the front door, hoping to draw him with me. I picked up the telephone. 'Now leave my house before I call the police.'

He turned, scanning the small sitting room and the kitchen. Then his eyes moved to the kitchen door and he saw that it was open. He hurried out into the garden and I was certain he would return a moment later with Alice screaming in his arms. But when he returned his arms were empty. He strode right up to me and peered into my eyes, as if hoping to catch me in a lie. I stared back, unflinching.

'I believe I owe you an apology, madam.' He left, fumbling as he closed the front door behind him. It swung open a moment later and I saw him cross the street to join Igor. They exchanged a few words and then Fashion-Plate, or Best-Worthington as I should call him, departed. Igor turned his dark mean eyes towards me. I quickly shut the door, locked and bolted it.

I hurried out into the garden. There was no sign of Alice. I searched the corner where I had left her playing, I looked behind the rows of runner beans that I had planted and checked inside the shed. Nothing.

Then I noticed the back door in the garden wall. It had an old lock and a useless deadbolt which barely reached the lock plate. It was ajar. Could Igor have slipped into the garden and taken Alice? I opened the door and peered out onto my gravel stand where my car was parked. 'Jamie?' I called softly.

Jamie stood up from behind my car where he had been hiding. Alice was cradled in his arms. 'I saw that man ringing your doorbell, so I came round the back to see if you needed help. Is he your niece's husband?'

'No, he's not,' I replied. That much was true. 'But he works for him,' I lied. Jamie relaxed now that he knew he had done the right thing. I took Alice from him and noticed that my hands were trembling. 'Come in and have a cup of tea.'

'I'd rather have a beer if you've got one.'

'A beer it is.' We went inside.

Alice squirmed in my arms so I released her onto the kitchen floor, where she scrabbled happily with some empty egg cartons. Hidden in the cellar were a couple of toys I had picked up from a shop in town. Alice had not shown any enthusiasm for them. But the egg cartons – that was a different matter. They were light, easily stackable and, though non-toxic, not appealing either as food or as a teething device.

I led Jamie into the sitting room. He sat stiffly, a little awkward at being invited into my inner sanctum.

'Jamie,' I said, 'I have a job for you.' He cocked his head, and an intelligent light which I had seldom seen before came into his eyes. 'I'm going away for a while. It might be just a day or two, it might be more. I want you to keep a watch on the house. You can pretend you're doing the gardening, but it's the house I want you to watch.'

Jamie agreed but he was worried. 'What if something goes missing?'

'I trust you.' He flushed, proud but confused by his new self-worth.

I gave him further instructions. He was to hide the kitchen key somewhere in the garden. Not under a stone or the doormat, but somewhere original. He understood. I already had a set of keys hidden where nobody would ever find them, but they were for me, not Jamie.

I got Alice changed and ready then drove out through the back route I had taken a week earlier. This time, as I reached East Dean, I pulled up opposite the Gnarly Tree garage and searched the underside of my car with a mirror on an extendable stick. It had come in useful to check for car bombs in Beirut half a lifetime ago. Now it served to ensure that nobody was using a tracking device to follow my route.

I had travelled along small country lanes up until then and was certain nobody had followed me. I checked under the hood and in the trunk of the car, got back in and carried on driving. I took the road south, heading towards the coast and then joined the A27 heading east. At the A259 roundabout outside Eastbourne I took the turn to Norman's Bay. Sluice

Lane, scarcely wide enough for two cars to pass, ran through wetlands and low fields studded with small herds of cows.

Once this reclaimed land had been under the sea. Now a complex of drainage ditches, bursting with reed-mace and arundinaria, it provided cover for marsh birds. As I took a sharp bend a flutter of sparrows erupted from a bramble hedge. A sparrowhawk stooped before me, the flapping of his wings concealed by the sound of my motor. He skimmed inches above the tarmac, powering ahead, suddenly twisting as he pursued a dunnock into the hedge and caught it in his claws. I thought of Fashion-Plate. Was he the hawk, swooping to tear me apart? Could I turn tables and become the hawk to his sparrow?

I halted at the rail crossing point where a line of cars waited to cross. The crossing lights flashed on and off for five minutes before a train of just two carriages whizzed past, heading west towards Brighton. I glanced in my rear-view mirror. I was certain I had not been followed but if I was wrong a pursuer would have had to pull up short behind me, and I would have seen him. But my car remained the last in line. A minute went by. Another train pulled slowly into Norman's Bay station. A few passengers got off and made their way over the far side of the raised road hump, heading for home. The gate arms rose. Our line waited for the cars facing us to cross. It was only wide enough for one line of cars at a time.

Four cars passed, then our line moved forward and over the hump. Most cars headed right towards Pevensey Bay. I turned left, slowing for the speed bumps as I followed the passengers walking home. I recognised one figure dropping back from the others. He wore a beanie hat and an old fawn raincoat that had become too big for him. A long scarf trailed loosely from his scraggy neck. Once so handsome and charming, there seemed little remaining of the young man who had been my close friend all those years ago. He favoured his right leg, dragging his left. I pulled up alongside, keeping pace with him. I rolled down the passenger side window.

'Care for a lift?'

Patrick did not turn, nor even indicate he had recognised me, but he spoke.

'You'll be staying for lunch? You can park up in my garage.' He limped on, giving me no other sign of acknowledgement. I drove onward, slowing at a puddle so as not to splash him. I glanced back in the mirror at the worn-out shell that was Patrick. It was hard to recognise the dashing young devil I had become so fond of in Bonn some forty-three years ago.

8

Bonn, West Germany, September 1976

I HAD FLOWN INTO COLOGNE Bonn airport on a Lufthansa flight from Vienna in the third week of the month. It had been decided that, in order to maintain my cover as a native German speaker, I was to arrive using the Austrian passport issued to me back in London.

I was met by a handsome man in his early thirties who took my bag, brushed back the lock of blond hair that flopped over his eyes – blue as my father's – and said, 'You must be the new girl.'

'*Bitte*?'

'Ah, very good, can't catch you out. Fräulein Felicie Gartner?'

It was strange to hear my first name pronounced the way my father used to. I nodded.

'If you want to have a conversation in English,' I replied in formal German, 'I must warn you that although I have a facility I am not completely fluent in that language.'

'I'm convinced,' he replied in *Hochdeutsch*, 'and impressed. My name's Dallaway. Patrick Dallaway.'

Patrick's German was perfect, as was mine. I had been given an intensive three-week refresher course in the language, the main point of which was to update me on modern colloquialisms and the sort of slang commonly used by a young woman of my age. It was certainly more relaxed than the formal version I had learnt at school, but it didn't take long to pick up. On my last night of training in London I was encouraged to visit a discotheque with three Austrian au pairs employed in the homes of British Government ministers who had, naturally enough, been thoroughly vetted. Two of them were determined to pick up wealthy young boyfriends from good families while I, in the ensuing cattle market, picked up enough vulgar Austrian expressions in one night to pass for a native. I could also mimic their rural accents, though I would be sticking to classical German in my future job.

'We've fixed you up as a replacement for a girl in the West German Chancellery. She got herself pregnant and didn't want either her employers or her family to know, so we're helping her out. You are to report there on Monday morning.' As an afterthought he threw in, 'By the way, I was sent by Chancery.'

These two similar sounding names can cause confusion. The Chancellery was the part of the West German Government which served the executive office of the West German Chancellor and was where I would be working in the typing pool. Chancery, on the other hand, was the office of the British Embassy in charge of all administration, including intelligence. Instructions issuing from Chancery were usually, but not always, issued with the full knowledge of the Ambassador. Chancery was where Patrick was stationed. That meant that he, like I, was a spy.

Patrick and I shook hands formally and he pointed to his car, a Volkswagen Beetle, parked across the road. 'The official limousine,' he continued in German. 'After you, but mind how you cross.'

As I stepped off the pavement I made the mistake of glancing to my right to check for traffic.

'Aha, got you! We're in Germany now. Where they drive on the wrong side of the road.' He was gloating. 'I knew I'd catch you out eventually. Just didn't think it'd be so soon.' He took my case and stepped off the pavement without looking either way and I had to haul him back fast as an airport bus narrowly missed him.

'That's the second mistake I've made in two minutes,' I said. 'I should have let it squash you.'

'Then you'd have missed the biggest adventure of your life. Hop in.'

The ice broken, Patrick stowed my case on the back seat and set off at speed.

'You should take a tour round the city, get your bearings over the weekend before you turn up for work.' Patrick had lapsed into English. I followed suit for as long as we were in the car.

'How did you manage to get me a position so quickly?' My work was to be in the secretarial department of the German Chancellery. Brushing up my typing skills had been tougher than remembering my German. Getting used to the layout of a German typewriter had been even worse. The Y and the Z are transposed. There are not many words with a Y in German, but every technical document contains a zillion Zs. After three weeks pounding the keys and trying to remember that the vowels with umlauts were on the far right of the keyboard, I finally got the hang of it.

'Ever since the Guillaume affair broke, the West German Government has been running round like headless chickens. They are terrified of finding another East German spy in their midst. So, rather than employing personnel from Bonn, Munich or Berlin, they have decided, in their wisdom, to hire people from the provinces, people with no possible connections in the government.'

'People who can't possibly have been planted by the Stasi or the KGB.'

'You got it.'

The Guillaume scandal centred around the former West German Chancellor, Willy Brandt, and his friend and Chief Secretary, Günter Guillaume. Guillaume and his wife Christel had been exposed as Stasi agents spying for Communist East Germany (the German Democratic Republic, or GDR). They had been infiltrated into West Germany in the 1950s to penetrate and spy on the West German Government (the Federal Republic of Germany, or FRG), which they had accomplished with consummate ease and efficiency. Guillaume had become Brandt's closest aide and confidant, with a major influence on West German policy.

When informed by the head of his intelligence agency that Guillaume had been reporting directly to Markus Wolf, East Germany's chief spymaster, Brandt almost had a stroke. The poor man had been obliged to continue working with his betrayer for weeks, even taking a holiday with Guillaume and his wife, while his people built the case against the two of them. Whatever his skills as a politician, Brandt's performance as an actor should have won him an Oscar.

'We thought that when Brandt resigned and Helmut Schmidt became Chancellor, things would quieten down,' continued Patrick. 'Not a bit. It's been more than two years and, if anything, the leaks to East Germany are getting worse. That's where you come in.'

I had been sent to infiltrate the West German Government as a 'friendly', in a reverse operation to Guillaume's, and to identify and plug those leaks.

We pulled up outside a small hotel and reverted to speaking German. Patrick collected the keys from the middle-aged woman who owned it, charming her with his easy manner and flashing eyes, and carried my case up to my room.

'Remember,' he said, before leaving. 'Your whole mission is absolutely top secret, and this may be the last time anyone will see us together.'

In the event, that proved not to be the case, but I understood the need for secrecy. The West Germans were in total ignorance about my mission and Patrick was anxious to keep it that way.

9

West Sussex, May 2019

I drove on another two hundred yards from the railway crossing, past the caravan park, until I saw the sign for Patrick's house and turned right up a short gravel drive towards the sea. The dwelling consisted of two buildings: a small cottage along the shoreline with an adjoining garage and, on its western side, a turreted lookout which had been a gun emplacement during World War Two. The lookout commanded a panoramic view of the sea and any potential enemy. Like the sniper's pillbox in my paddock, it was unlikely it would have been much use in stopping the Germans but, had it been there a thousand years earlier, it might have provided a temporary inconvenience to the Norman invasion.

As I approached the garage the shuttered door rose up. I drove inside and parked. The shutter came down behind me. As Patrick was still limping far behind me, I presumed that he had opened it with an app on his phone. He always loved gadgets.

Patrick Dallaway's garage was his workshop. It was painted in an old 1950's shade of green, of the type one did not find anymore. Workbenches lined the walls and above them he had arranged a variety of tools, some as old-fashioned as the workshop itself, others decidedly modern. A small door led into the house. As I disengaged the baby seat I heard Patrick enter the house and unbolt the garage door. Carrying Alice, I stepped inside.

The cottage had not been touched in forty years, except for the floors, which had been lined with pre-fabricated parquet – the type you buy from any DIY store and install yourself. Patrick took a look at baby Alice but said nothing. He stepped into his kitchen.

'Settle down in the sitting room while I put the kettle on. Or would you prefer something stronger?'

I caught the familiar whiff of TCP. Many of my elderly neighbours favoured a dab of antiseptic over cologne or aftershaves.

'I usually prefer something stronger, but as I'm driving, I'll settle for a pot of tea.'

'I have a large piece of haddock, and some Jersey royal potatoes. I usually prepare a *sauce vierge*, but perhaps your little one wouldn't enjoy it. I didn't know you had a grandchild.'

'This isn't a grandchild. And you're right about the *sauce vierge*.'

I set about changing Alice while Patrick made us tea, put the haddock in the oven, boiled the potatoes and made his *sauce vierge* anyway. The room was littered with books. Shelves of them lined the walls. Stacks of them covered the chairs and both sofas. The only clear surface was his desk. I pushed aside some notes he'd been making and used the desk as a changing table.

Patrick entered as I was finishing up, and I sensed more than saw him flinch as he watched me. 'I'll put the tray there when you've finished.' I bundled the nappy into a plastic bag.

'I'll take that,' he said. 'I've an incinerator next door.' I handed the bag over and perched on the arm of a sofa as he poured the tea and passed me a cup.

When he returned a couple of minutes later he let his gaze pan around the room. He had positioned various small objects and bibelots on top of the books scattered about the room. It was an old spy's trick to catch anyone who might snoop through his books and jottings. Once I might have moved a few of them just to irritate him, but today I had touched nothing. I needed him on my side.

'I did not expect us to meet again,' he said, his voice steady despite the emotion he must have felt, 'but now you're here, I'm intrigued.' Like criminals out on licence, association with old comrades is frowned upon, if not proscribed. 'I, of course, have had no communication with the office since my retirement, except for the pension cheques. Well, of course they are not cheques anymore. The money simply turns up in my account. So much simpler.'

'Simpler at a surface level, maybe,' I replied. 'One of the few things that is these days. But nothing else is simpler. I don't know if we would have managed Bonn with the current state of technology.'

'It would have been impossible. Mobile phones that can track their owners, listen in on their conversations and take their photographs without them being aware of it. Ugh!' He shivered, unnecessarily I thought. Patrick had been a proselytising enthusiast for new technology back in the old days. It seemed unlikely that he would have lost that enthusiasm, even with the passage of time.

'So, since you haven't come to reminisce about the good old days, do you want to tell me what your visit is all about?'

I talked for forty minutes, leaving nothing out. How I found the baby, my suspicions that Igor and Fashion-Plate had murdered my neighbour Phyllis Price and how Fashion-Plate had forced his way into my home and very nearly discovered Alice.

'And he's not the father? Not an anxious relative?'

'He's not. I'm convinced of it. These are not paternal feelings. He only has malice in mind.'

'Malice towards you.'

'I have no doubt about that. And perhaps the baby too.'

'What do the police say about the old lady's death?'

'A simple hit-and-run. But they won't do anything now that the trail has gone cold.'

'They can't really believe that.' He thought a moment. 'Unless they've been leant on.'

'Leant on? By whom?' The notion was ridiculous.

'Police incompetence I can believe and understand, but failing to follow up what seem to be obvious leads amounts to dereliction of duty.'

I considered this a moment. Patrick could see things from afar which I might fail to recognise.

'But these two characters,' he said, 'they are so... so obvious. No British agency would have sent them.'

'And only a British agency would have the influence to hold the police back? You're probably right there. I think I may be steering you along the wrong path.'

'Or opening my mind up to other possibilities.'

For no particular reason Alice began to wail.

'What you need to do is get rid of the child.' Off my appalled expression Patrick corrected himself. 'I mean, of course, that you should find it a safe place, where it will be well cared for. Do you have such a place?'

I picked Alice up and rocked her in my arms.

'I can't leave her with the lad, Jamie. He wouldn't stand a chance against those thugs.'

'I was thinking of someone more appropriate. Someone you could trust. Someone more… well, more *motherly*.'

I considered this while Alice's wails turned to contented gurgles. I laughed. 'I can think of one person. Well, two really. But *motherly*? That's not the first word that comes to mind.'

What did come to mind, for just a moment, was an image of my parents, and the too brief happiness we had once enjoyed.

10

My father, a fervent opponent of Hitler, left Germany in 1933. He was not Jewish, as far as I knew, but many of his friends were. After the laws limiting Jewish children in schools was enacted that year on 25 April (my birthday, incidentally – though that came many years later) he moved to Vienna where he took up the position of Professor of Economics at Hochschule für Welthandel, the university specialising in business administration, economics and law. Several of his Jewish colleagues followed him there and found jobs in education. In the spring of 1938 my father was invited to give a talk at Exeter College, Oxford and afterwards, over a good dinner, was sounded out about whether he would care to join the faculty, teaching Politics, Philosophy and Economics. This was despite his cracking one of his favourite jokes: 'Politics *is* economics and, when the economy crashes… well, you just have to be philosophical about it.'

On his return to Vienna he submitted his six months' notice and arrived in Oxford just weeks before the infamous events of Kristallnacht. Once again he was able to welcome some of his old Jewish friends fleeing Germany and help them find lodgings and employment. He had three of them living in his cramped rooms when, cycling to a lecture, he managed to run into, literally, the woman who was to become his wife and my mother.

Lady Mary Becket was the only child of Earl Melbury, an impoverished aristocrat whose dalliances with his footman had forced him, at short notice, to take a small plane from Croydon airport to Paris with the remains of what had once been the family fortune. In all likelihood he was not my grandfather, as my grandmother had taken a series of lovers during her marriage. These included several peers of the realm, one duke, an improbable marquess (rumoured to have been another of my grandfather's lovers) and even the estate gamekeeper. My mother went up to Somerville College, Oxford, to read Modern History. Her inability to ascertain whether she was the daughter of a duke or of a gamekeeper imbued her with the moral compunction to treat everybody as an equal, regardless of race or creed, no matter their family or background.

When my father ran over my mother in Queen's Lane, she was carrying a book: Adam Smith's *The Wealth of Nations*. Believing Mary to be an economics student, he had helped her up off the road (ever the gentleman, he would have helped her up even if she had not been an economist), checked she was not seriously injured (she had cracked a rib but was not going to let that interfere with her fortuitous encounter with the youthful German professor possessing the most intense blue eyes she had ever seen), and invited her for a stiff drink in the Red Lion pub. Mother had been returning the book to the Queen's College library on behalf of a friend, so was somewhat nonplussed by my father's opening romantic gambit of discussing the revolutionary economic theories of John Maynard Keynes.

Despite his tetchy complaint, 'Well, if you are not familiar with Keynes' *The General Theory of Employment, Interest and Money*, what kind of economist are you?' they were married within three months at Exeter College and their first home became a point of passage for many Germans escaping the Hitler regime. I was born sometime after the war ended. That's all I am going to say about that.

In the 1950s my father was invited back to Austria, this time to help rebuild the economics department at the University of Innsbruck. A prominent economist, he was hopeless with his own money, so the invitation was something of a financial lifeline.

I was enrolled in the Hauptschule, in Saggen, where I quickly picked up German and was taught French, Italian and, somewhat unnecessarily, English. My father was an enthusiastic skier and spent much of his spare time on the ski slopes. My mother loathed skiing, swearing that she would rather step into a freezer and pay two burly men to hit her with sticks for a couple of hours, as this would produce exactly the same effect as two hours on the slopes.

One afternoon the police came to inform my mother that there had been an accident. My father had come across an injured skier. An intoxicated ski instructor had taken a party of novices down a black run 'to give them a thrill'. The man my father found had hit a concealed rock, broken his leg and was dangling on the edge of a precipice. My father managed to haul him away from danger just as a second novice hurtled around the corner. He struck my father, sending him over the precipice and into a crevasse. My father had tried to claw his way out but had slipped further into the crevasse until he was wedged at the bottom and froze to death. They did not tell my mother the details. I had to discover them for myself later.

After my father's death there was nothing to keep us in Innsbruck. We returned to England and my mother found a job in London. She never spoke about it, even when I asked her about it directly. The only thing she would say was that she was now a civil servant. Shortly after that I found myself on a train to my new school in the Berkshire countryside. It was a well-respected 'public' school, by which I mean it was not public at all, but exclusively private, horribly expensive and run by Catholic nuns with a fervent zeal for corporal punishment.

I was a gangly child, taller than others my age, which meant I was often chosen for team games such as netball, hockey and lacrosse where other girls, considerably older and tougher than myself, would take pleasure in slashing at my face with their hockey pucks and lacrosse sticks. That is, until one particularly brutal girl rushed headlong at me. She expected to disable me and score an easy goal. More by instinct than intention I thrust out my hand in a fist to defend myself. The girl's chin struck my fist with all the momentum in her body, her legs shot out from under her, she bit her tongue so badly that it required stitches, and she dropped to the ground, wailing.

I received six strokes of the cane for 'aggressive behaviour' and was confined to school premises for two weeks, which did not bother me. Neither did the other girls, who gave me a wide berth from then on. Revelling in my new-found fame for self-defence, I enlisted in the school boxing team (a short-lived aberration by the sports mistress) and, though I never won a serious bout, learnt how to land a punch when it was needed.

My mother was less impressed. 'Not very ladylike,' was all she said about the matter when I saw her at the Easter holidays. She had never remarried and spent extraordinarily long hours at work, sometimes disappearing for days on end. I had to fend and cook for myself in our small flat in South Kensington. It gave me the desire and ability to be entirely self-sufficient, though I encountered problems when she forgot to leave me enough money for food or electricity.

The first time she left me alone was one cold winter a week before Christmas. I had just returned from a corner shop by the tube station with two pork pies and a sausage roll – I was more concerned with cheap than healthy eating in those days – when the power went off. I presumed that there had been a power cut, so I put on two sweaters and climbed into bed shivering. Two hours later Mother arrived home.

'What on earth are you doing in bed at this hour?'

'The electricity's off.'

'Well why didn't you put some money in the meter?'

That was when I first learnt about meters and how to budget.

I don't mean to say she was a bad mother. She seemed to be preoccupied with more important matters which, it turned out, she was. But I didn't learn about this until I got into Oxford myself.

It was halfway through my first Michaelmas term, around mid-November in my first year, that I was approached by my tutor who, over a large glass of sherry, asked me how far I would be willing to go. His stutter interrupted his flow and left me confused about his exact meaning. After an embarrassing few minutes it became clear that what I had misunderstood as a clumsy attempt to seduce me was, in fact, an equally clumsy attempt to recruit me to the Domestic Security Service or, as it is generally known, MI5. I turned him down gently.

I also turned down his subsequent personal proposition: I had not been wrong about that, after all.

That Christmas I was obliged to spend up at Oxford for reasons my mother did not even attempt to explain. I attended the carol service at Christchurch College and had a gloomy lunch of dry turkey and charred boiled potatoes masquerading as roast with two dons and two Chinese students who, like me, were alone over the festive season.

On Boxing Day, in a wallow of loneliness, I took the train to London and by the time I made it home it was dark. I went straight to my bedroom, without turning on the lights, threw myself on the bed and was shocked to discover a naked man asleep in it. If he had been in mother's bed I would have been delighted. After father, as far as I knew, she never found a man she cared for enough to share her life.

The man screamed louder than I did. As I leapt from the bed my mother entered and switched on the light. The man stood naked and shivering. This was not from the cold as the flat had been recently plumbed for central heating. He was terrified.

'This is Mr Bulgarov. Formerly of the KGB. We are treating this flat as a safe house. I trust you will keep it so. Supper will be ready in twenty minutes.' And that was all she said on the subject, though I was pleased that she trusted me to keep my mouth shut.

That evening the three of us dined on the remains of their Christmas dinner. Everything was of the best quality – I noticed a hamper labelled *Harrods* – and was beautifully cooked, quite unlike my college 'feast' the day before. I had not seen my mother cook anything but the most perfunctory meal since my father had died but here she was, showing off skills I never knew she possessed.

Bulgarov, recovered from his fright, enjoyed his food and his drink even more than I did. He favoured a particular brand of vodka which Mother had taken the tube to a little shop in Soho to source. She conversed with him in Russian and while I could not say they ignored me all evening – Bulgarov included me in several drunken toasts to 'Eengland and her gracioous Queen' – I was definitely not the centre of attention. When it was time to retire mother made a bed up for me on the floor of her bedroom from cushions, pillows and a spare eiderdown. We lived like that for two days and on the third I came home from a walk in Kensington Gardens to find our guest gone.

'Where's Mr Bulgarov?'

'Who on earth do you mean?' Mother gave me a blank stare and we never mentioned him again. A few days later I saw his photograph in the paper. He had defected from the Russian Embassy and had gone missing for three days while the Russians had been going mad around London trying to get him back. On the fourth day he had mysteriously turned up in New York and was escorted to the United Nations building where he addressed the Security Council, denouncing the Soviet State and exposing embarrassing details of the USSR's foreign policy. His real name turned out to be Sidorov. I was disappointed to learn that mother had not trusted me entirely. Still, it was a useful lesson in caution which I took to heart.

I heard that Sidorov went on to make a career for himself in Hollywood, where he advised film producers on the authenticity of their spy films. On this matter, I can only say that he failed abysmally. Two years later he was assassinated on Hollywood Boulevard with a ricin pellet propelled into his leg using a technique that was later repeated in the case of Bulgarian dissident Georgi Markov in London in 1978.

I returned to Oxford before New Year and this time managed to join in with the festivities, snogged a couple of boys, lost my virginity in a not entirely unpleasant manner and, before Hilary term began, received an approach to join the SIS – known popularly as MI6 – the 'rival' to MI5. After my experience with Bulgarov/Sidorov, I was open to persuasion. The opportunity for foreign travel had its appeal.

Some weeks later I met again with my tutor, a don from another college and a man from London who asked me questions: what did I think of the communists, what did I think of the far right, did I have any communist friends, and what were my personal politics? I answered carefully: 'the communists were our allies during the war, but we don't want them to take over the world,' 'the far right is a dangerous mob out to destabilise the government,' and 'I have no communist friends to the best of my knowledge.' This elicited raised eyebrows.

'You spent Christmas dining with two communists.'

For an awful moment I thought they were referring to Mother and Mister Bulgarov/Siderov. Then I thought again.

'You mean the young Chinese students? We hardly exchanged a word. Their English was limited.'

They did not mean the Chinese. They meant the two dons. What had they said over lunch?

'They asked me a few questions. Much the same as the ones you have.'

The three of them huddled together and whispered. I heard the man from London mention the word 'mother' and that clinched it for them.

I was inducted the following weekend.

11

Sussex, May 2019

I CHANGED ALICE ONE MORE time while Patrick disposed of the waste. He did not explain why he had an incinerator on the premises. I would make it my business to find out the next time I saw him, which I warned him would be soon. He seemed to like that idea and asked me to keep him informed of my progress.

Patrick checked the narrow lane to ensure I was not being watched before I drove away, heading west along the coast road towards Pevensey Bay. There I turned inland at the Bay Hotel, onto the A259 and skirted round the Roman and Norman ruins of Pevensey Castle. I took the A27 towards Polegate, where I joined the A22 up to London. I was no longer concerned that I might be followed, so I stayed on the dual carriageway all the way up to the M25. I had turned off my phone, which Patrick reminded me could be used to track my movements. It seemed a wise precaution.

I came off at the A217, my preferred route into London, and drove carefully up to the Fulham Road. I found and paid for parking on 'The Beach', as that part of the road is popularly known, so I could pop into Luigi's delicatessen for a kilo of San Daniele prosciutto and five hundred grams of *finocchiona* salami. Generous, I know, but I needed a big favour. I held Alice on my hip and the Italian staff made a big fuss of her, which she loved. Armed with a bottle of Pinot Grigio I got back in the car and negotiated the one-way system into Tregunter Road, where I parked again and paid another horrendous parking fee. I had to switch my phone back on to use the parking app, but took the precaution of walking into The Boltons round the corner to do this. I turned the phone off before returning to the car.

Carrying Alice I pushed open the low metal gate, entered the wide front garden and walked up the five steps to the front door. There were three bells, one for each of the flats carved out of this once-grand villa. I rang the lowest bell: the one for the ground and garden maisonette. After a few moments the inner door was opened by a tall, handsome young woman with short dark hair: Silvana, my daughter's wife.

'Peggy,' she exclaimed as she let me in. (Peggy is the name my children know me by – it's a long story.) '*Ma che bella sorpresa*!' She ushered me into their maisonette and broke into perfect English. 'And you have a baby! Eva didn't say.'

'She doesn't know.' I followed Silvana into the kitchen overlooking the rear garden. Eva, my daughter, wearing grubby yellow dungarees, was striding out of the potting shed with a spade and fork.

'Sit down. I'll make you a coffee. Eva's in a foul mood. Problems at work.'

I obeyed and sat, placing Alice's carrier on the chair beside mine.

'*Un piccolo regalo*,' I said, arranging my gifts on the table.

'*Ma grazie, non ce ne sarebbe stato bisogno*. You really shouldn't have.' Silvana picked up the prosciutto, pulled off a sliver to taste and inhaled its aroma. '*Che profumo buono.*

It reminds me of home.' She put my gifts away in the fridge and winked. '*Per dopo.*'

Silvana stepped around the table to pinch Alice's plump cheek. '*Ma che bella bambina!*' She moved away with reluctance and went to work on the commercial-grade Fracino coffee machine, grinding the roasted beans, topping up the machine and making a big show of steaming the milk while the black syrupy coffee gushed into the two cups under it. I prefer an espresso myself, but Eva likes a cappuccino so that's what I was going to get. Like any true Italian, Silvana would never touch a cappuccino after midday, so she made herself an espresso macchiato.

Her performance over, she hauled up the sash window and called out, '*È pronto il caffè!*' I saw Eva haul a thick shrub out of a black plastic pot and drop it into the hole she had been digging. She removed her leather gauntlets, revealing latex gloves which she wore to protect her soft hands. She stripped these off. Her fingernails were immaculate, polished a particular red mixed for her by a theatrical make-up artist. She would have preferred to get her hands grubby, but that wouldn't look right when she read the television news.

'*Guarda chi c'è,*' Silvana added, in warning.

Eva glanced up and caught sight of me. For a moment she hesitated. Then she forced a smile and waved.

'Ma, we weren't expecting you. I'll be up in a minute.' She ran her fingers through her tousled hair, setting it into the shape viewers were used to seeing, inadvertently streaking her forehead with soil. She marched into the house and her garden boots thumped up the wooden stairs.

'No muddy boots in the house!' yelled Silvana. The thumping stopped. A moment later we heard the boots landing heavily at the foot of the stairs. Eva stepped into the room, her feet in a thick pair of men's grey socks, a fixed smile on her face.

'Ma, what brings you up to London?'

'You mean what ill wind blew in the Wicked Witch of the West?'

'Ha ha!' That was enough sparring for the moment. 'Where's that coffee?'

Silvana handed her a cup. Eva sipped it, caught sight of the baby and choked. Coffee shot up the back of her throat and spewed out of her nostrils. She bent over the kitchen sink and coughed repeatedly. She tore a sheet off the kitchen towel roll, wiped her face and blew her nose before turning around.

'Where the hell did *that* come from?'

'You mean Alice?' I only had one ace to play, but I played it well. 'Why don't you ask your brother?'

Eva and Bernard were consumed by sibling rivalry. That was how my mother had controlled them when they were little: playing one off against another. They got on well enough when apart, but the slightest spark could set them off. Just the idea of asking Bernard for information or, worse still, approval, would shut Eva up and deflect her from further enquiry.

I forced a broad smile. 'I thought you and Silvana would enjoy looking after her for a week, take her off my hands while I'm in France.'

'Was this Bernard's idea?

'He has no idea I'm asking you.'

Eva relaxed a little.

'You're going to France?'

'That's what I just said.'

'Well we're not having a child in this house.' I could see

her resolve weakening. 'I'm far too busy for that. We both are.'

'Silvana said she's on holiday,' I said. She hadn't of course, but Silvana worked from home most of the week and as far as I could see, was mistress of her own time sheet.

Silvana took up the reins. 'I am due a vacation, and it would be no trouble. No trouble at all.'

'Well, we couldn't do a worse job of looking after a child than you did.' I knew Eva. She was softening.

'Why don't you take a look at what Eva's done in the garden?' said Silvana. '*È una meraviglia.*'

'I've got to get changed for work,' grunted Eva, and headed into the bedroom.

Silvana picked up Alice, cradling her gently in her arms, and was rewarded with a happy gurgle. She headed down the cast-iron fire escape and beckoned me. I took the hint and followed her down into the garden.

Silvana was telling the truth. What Eva had done was remarkable.

'When we bought the flat three years ago the garden was an overgrown wilderness,' Silvana said. 'I think that, for Eva, this was its greatest attraction.'

I had always found Silvana easy to talk to, a relaxing influence, while my daughter was quite the opposite. Whatever Silvana saw in Eva, I had no idea.

'The first thing Eva did was employ a designer. He won gold at the Chelsea Flower Show two years running. Eva took one look at his plans – all hard surfaces and spiky plants – and decided to create her own design. *Tentavi ed errori.*'

'Trial and error.'

'Exactly.'

'Our first year I helped her clear out the weeds and then

I let her get on with it. Our second summer she dug out the pond and we went to buy some plants to soften the outlines. She chose everything, of course. I know nothing about plants. That's what growing up in an apartment in Genova does to you.'

By this, the third year, everything had expanded outwards and left the beholder with a sense that this garden, a haven of calm and tranquillity, had been here for all time.

'*Mi scusi un momento.*' Silvana slipped back into the house, effortlessly bumping Alice on her hip as if it was second nature to her. I was left to contemplate the garden.

The one feature that lent a contemporary element was the fountain, which erupted from the centre of the pond. The components had been a gift from Dennis when Eva and Silvana had entered into a civil partnership and bought the flat together. I had received a grudging letter from Eva, thanking me for the length of piping. I had no idea what she was going on about. Dennis had sent it without telling me, and signed the gift card from us both. Eva had kept it in storage for years and had only recently had 'the piping' installed.

The fountain consisted of a single pillar of water, topped by a blue and yellow flame. Silvana relished the fact that admirers were dumbfounded when they first set eyes on it. Mingling fire and water simply did not compute. But the mechanics were pretty simple and when Dennis had first described his design I had understood instantly how it worked: two pipes submerged in the pond curved upwards so they broke the surface together. One held gas, which had to be lit first. Then the tap was turned on and the jet of water sent the lit gas five feet high, where it remained, flaming miraculously day and night.

I was contemplating the flame, flickering atop of the bubbling fountain and bending with the breeze, when Silvana came back out to join me.

'*Tutto fatto,*' she exclaimed. 'It's all arranged. We shall keep baby Alice while you are away, and if you want to stay in France a few days longer, then that is no problem. In fact, I would love it. *We* would love it.'

I marvelled that she had not questioned how I had come by Alice. I supposed that, to an Italian, an older woman carting a baby around was normal, as was the idea of entrusting it to another for a few days. I hurried out before Eva could change her mind, got back in my car and sped off. That is, if you call travelling at 20 mph speeding. I wasn't about to break any rules. I was not about to risk unwanted attention.

For a moment I felt a pang of something I did not at first recognise, a sort of melancholy. Apart from that second day, when I had left Alice with Ambrose, she had been with me all this time. Suddenly I missed her. It was foolish, I knew. She was safe, with people I trusted, and yet I felt the wrench as if she was my own.

12

Bonn, September–October 1976

The Monday after my arrival in Bonn I took a tram to the wrong stop – Patrick had been unhelpfully vague in providing directions. This was not entirely his fault. Bonn's public transport system had been updated and some redundant lines abandoned. When I got off the tram and asked for directions I discovered I had a brisk walk of a kilometre or so to get to work on time.

At 8.30 precisely I presented myself (Fräulein Felicie Gartner) at the front desk of the Federal Chancellery Building, a sprawling concrete block which could have been mistaken for a municipal car park. Chancellor Helmut Schmidt himself admitted it had 'all the charm of a Rhineland savings bank'.

There were three of us newcomers that day. We were met by Frau Müller, herself an Austrian whose frosty demeanour I softened by presenting her with a cake box filled with *topfenstrudel*, thoughtfully provided by Patrick who had done his research into her indulgences. I believe Patrick had made it himself, cleverly enhancing the sweetened quark cheese filling with apricots and sultanas. It created an excellent impression right from the start, and for the first few weeks I was Frau Müller's favourite. That was not to last.

The other new secretaries were Heidi Baumann, a pretty young woman, and Elsa Schopenhauer who could not possibly have been descended from the intellectual philosopher of the same name. Elsa was the slow, plodding, but efficient type which the state preferred to employ. Her eyes popped open when she saw the *topfenstrudel*, and I knew it would not be long before she and I became firm friends.

Frau Müller was tall, thin and of a severe disposition. She wore her grey woollen suit like a suit of armour. It consisted of a Nehru jacket over a starched white blouse and a pleated skirt which fell below the knees. She must have had several of these made for her. In all the time I worked there I saw her wear nothing else. Her black leather lace-up shoes had soft rubber soles, so she could move among her pool of typists silently and catch them slacking. She kept her hair in a bun so tight it was impossible to guess its length. It was held in place by a steel knitting needle, which we imagined her using as a weapon to defend her honour. Though none of us could imagine any man wanting to take it.

'Your duties will commence in the filing department,' she announced. 'Follow me and I shall show you.'

We trooped down to the basement of the massive building. It was constructed with three floors above ground and two below. The filing rooms were on the first of the two basement levels.

'You will find the work here a little tedious, perhaps. But, *if* you prove hard, efficient workers, you will soon graduate to better positions.'

Frau Müller pointed out three massive stacks of files that needed to be put away. This was the product of the whole of the last two weeks' scrutiny by the legal department. Two filing clerks had been off sick, and one (the pregnant one I was covering for) had taken a long leave to 'care for her mother'. Müller marched off, presumably to enjoy my *topfenstrudel*, and we were left to deal with the files. I took charge.

'We can do this if we are organised. You, Heidi, will sort the files into categories, I shall collect and sort the loose papers (of which there were hundreds) and you, Elsa, will put the files away in their relevant shelves. Do you agree?'

Heidi was up for this, as her job would be the least taxing. Elsa took a few moments to think it over, like a Tyrolean cow chewing its cud, then nodded in agreement.

We started at nine and worked for three and a half hours. It could have been stultifying work, but I made full use of my time to skim through any documents that came to hand to see if I could learn anything that might interest Patrick and his superiors in the British Embassy. The three of us worked in the central open section of the filing system, with long rows of shelves stretching away on either side of us. At one end was a large walk-in vault, which remained locked. It contained classified files which we were not yet authorised to handle. If I wanted to gain access to it, I would have to earn Frau Müller's trust.

At 12.30 on the dot we went for lunch. We could either go to one of the local restaurants or eat in the subsidised canteen. Elsa was reluctant to splash out, so Heidi and I joined her in the canteen and we took a table together.

In the first few minutes I learnt almost as much about Heidi as I could normally wheedle out of someone in a week. It was hard to stop her, she was so open. She was Bavarian, from the skiing resort of Garmisch-Partenkirchen. She had been recommended for the job by her local Catholic priest, though in all the time I knew her she never attended church, not even on Sunday mornings. She had one simple ambition:

to marry a politician and travel the world. A cousin had managed to do exactly that and Heidi was pretty enough to do equally well for herself, though judging by the way she went through men, single or married, during our time in the Chancellery, I doubted that any future marriage of hers would endure for long.

Elsa was an entirely different kettle of soused herrings, which turned out to be her choice of lunch. She came from the tiny island of Neuwerk (population twenty-eight) about eight miles north of the fishing port of Cuxhaven, on the North Sea, where her father was the lighthouse keeper. Up until recently the furthest Elsa had travelled had been to Cuxhaven for stores and her education. She was dumpy, provincial and sullen.

That was the first impression one got, until Heidi and I discovered that the sullenness was a cover for shyness and that, once coaxed out of her oyster-like shell, Elsa lived in an imaginary fairy-tale world, in which a handsome prince would one day rescue her from her tower (the lighthouse) and save her from the evil baron (her abusive father). As she shovelled up her herrings I thought she was the perfect candidate for a job in the Chancellery: a dedicated and blinkered fantasist. Both young women were happy to talk about themselves for as long as I would listen, so I had no need to share my own 'legend', or cover story, which I had prepared and rehearsed at length.

After lunch we moved like a well-oiled machine. Heidi, confident that neither of us posed any threat to her ambition of snaring a politician, worked fast, knowing that efficiency would get her promoted. I scanned the documents that came my way as fast as I could, though I found nothing but mind-numbing lists of costs and accounting, while

Elsa, between herring burps, did her best to keep up with us.

At four o'clock we marched back up the stairs to Frau Müller and informed her that we had completed the task. She frowned.

'Three girls usually take two full weeks to complete the job.' She marched us back down again to check our claim. Her scepticism changed to pleasure and she let us leave work early, while promising that the following day she would assign us more challenging tasks.

Heidi, who knew her way around town, led us to a smart bar nicknamed, somewhat unimaginatively, Die Kneipe, where, she told us, senior government employees hung out after work. It appeared that here alcohol, like the food in our canteen, was subsidised and even Elsa, despite her natural stinginess, eventually dug into her purse and bought us all a round of drinks.

The following day we were separated and assigned new tasks, but we still met regularly for lunch and within a couple of weeks were rewarded with desks of our own. They were situated in the large open-plan office one floor above street level, where we undertook general secretarial work. My duties consisted of typing up dictated letters and contracts but, as my security clearance was low, I found little that would interest Patrick or our masters in Whitehall: certainly no evidence of who might be leaking secrets.

After a month our security clearance was raised – probably because during that first month we had managed not to divulge the contents of Frau Müller's lunchtime *butterbrot* to any foreign power. Despite the Guillaume scandal, security was hopelessly lax and from then on we were treated like any other member of the secretarial pool, at the disposal of any civil servant or politician who needed us. In those first weeks I uncovered no scandal or leak, but quickly identified the character flaws of various cabinet members and how they might be manipulated. I felt a warm glow when Patrick complimented me on my progress.

To my surprise it was not Heidi, but Elsa who was the first of us to snag an admirer. That's not to say that Heidi's charms had lessened in any way. Frau Müller kept a strict eye on her and was often obliged to disperse the numerous young men hovering around Heidi's desk.

I noticed a change in Elsa's demeanour about six weeks after our arrival. Her usual sullen manner had brightened, and she had taken to bringing in small posies of flowers which she kept in a jar of water. My favourites were her white freesias, whose peppery scent would waft over to my desk. When I told her, she made a point of bringing them in more frequently, though she would sometimes alternate them with the odd red rose or carnation.

Over lunch Heidi and I would try to wheedle information out of Elsa, but for several days she held fast. About a week later she confided to me that he was a British businessman. More than that she would not say. However I noticed that she had started to make frequent visits to the filing department downstairs.

I mentioned this to Patrick. We met far away from the overcrowded British Embassy on Friedrich Ebert Allee, often in a park or a café where we would not be overheard. I had become an expert on avoiding surveillance back in London, where I had been assigned to trail KGB agents for my first eighteen months of service. It had been tedious work, driving around the capital late at night, but I soon got to know the city and its quirks better than any taxi driver. In all my time in Bonn I was certain that I was never observed or followed. Except that last time, of course.

Patrick and I decided that I should check out Elsa's British admirer. It should not take me long to identify him. Bonn was swarming with Brits angling for government contracts and they usually registered with the British Embassy, though that was not compulsory.

'You'll have to get close to her,' Patrick insisted.

'I couldn't get any closer than I already am without sharing her underwear. If she has a weakness for educated Englishmen, perhaps that's more in your line.'

Patrick glanced at Elsa's staff photograph. He studied her sullen frown and double chin. 'Ugh,' he shivered. 'Definitely not my type.'

The next day found Elsa in an exceptionally joyful mood. After work I followed her to Die Kneipe, the bar we visited that first evening. She entered at exactly six o'clock and I gave her a minute to settle in before going in after her. After depositing her coat Elsa went straight to the bar where she found a drink waiting for her. It was thick and yellow, some sort of sickly eggnog. She looked around, then greedily downed her drink. A tall man broke away from a group of businessmen, stepped up behind her and slipped his large hands over her eyes. She turned around, her eyes glistening with delight. He was facing away from me, so I could not make out his features. If I got any closer Elsa might notice me and call me over to meet her paramour, and then I would lose my advantage.

Elsa wanted him to join her in another drink, but he was keen to move on. With a wave to the group he swept her out of the room, up the steps and onto the street where there was a taxi waiting. I hurried out after them. Patrick was waiting for me. I hopped into his car and we followed Elsa and her beau at a discreet distance.

There was never much traffic on the road after rush hour. Bonn had grown in the last couple of decades but its population never reached more than 250,000. With nothing to do in the evenings, other than the odd diplomatic party, most people went straight home to their families. There was a local joke which went:

Visitor: 'Is there any night life?'

Resident: 'Yes, but she's visiting a punter in Cologne tonight.'

The taxi drove to Bad Godesberg, five kilometres south east of Bonn, and pulled up outside the Maternus restaurant. Elsa's escort got out. At last I caught a good look at him under the lamplight as he opened her door. He was an impressively good-looking man, broad-shouldered, narrow-hipped and with a noble nose and neatly trimmed beard that gave him an almost regal air. He offered Elsa his arm and they disappeared inside the restaurant.

'Shit,' said Patrick. 'We've lost them.'

'We can go in.'

'Not this place. It's where the top politicians take their mistresses.'

I slipped a silk scarf over my head and perched a pair of sunglasses on top.

'What are you doing?' Patrick was curious, but excited.

I dug into my handbag, found a bright red lipstick, and applied it to my lips. 'We are going in and you are going to find us a table.'

'Have you any idea of the prices they charge? I have to justify every Deutschmark to accounts.'

'Get us a table near theirs, but not too close.' I straightened

Patrick's tie for him, turned up the collar of his raincoat and shoved an unlit cigarette in his mouth.

'You know I don't smoke.'

'It's just dressing, distracts from your face. We don't want him recognising you next time.'

'What "next time"?'

'He's working her, I'm sure of it.'

'Because?'

'He's too bloody good looking. He could have any woman he wants.'

Patrick got out of the car, entered the restaurant and two minutes later emerged to beckon me inside.

13

West Sussex, May 2019

When you don't know your enemy, you should either proceed with the utmost caution, or do the exact opposite: parade yourself in plain sight. With luck you may draw him out. Then you can identify him. With the caveat that if you fail in this, you've given your enemy an easy target. Take your pick.

With that in mind, I drove home to Sussex. As I passed the county border I switched my mobile phone back on. I knew that by now they would have secured my phone records and be tracking me. That was exactly what I wanted.

I parked in the lane at the back of the house and let myself in through the garden door. Immediately I sensed that they had gained access. Nothing seemed out of place, but the unmistakable scent of testosterone and stale sweat pervaded the house.

I checked my bedroom. Both chests of drawers had been opened and closed again carefully and any fingerprints, if they had been careless enough to leave any, had been wiped away. A short length of dark thread I had placed on the lip of one drawer had been replaced, though not exactly as I had left it.

In the other bedroom I found a piece of white lint caught in a chest drawer where the wood had splintered over time.

So they had been wearing white cotton gloves, which would account for the lack of fingerprints. Over this chest I had laid a slab of glass, under which I had placed a number of slightly faded colour photographs of two boys and an older man. I had found these in an album dated 1958 that had been thrown into a skip. I had no connection whatsoever with this man or these boys, but if the people who had searched my house wanted to waste their time discovering who they were, that was their lookout. The important thing was that they would not be able to threaten me by doing them harm. Their dates of births and death had been written in black ink in the album under each portrait. So I knew I was not risking their lives. I had erased any evidence of Eva and Silvana, not that I had much of that anyway. Eva had long ago destroyed most of the few photographs taken of us together, on the odd school or university visit. In almost all of them she had cut out my image and destroyed it. I could hardly blame her. But it was with some relief that I knew there was little if anything linking me to Eva, and certainly nothing connecting me or her to Alice.

I had placed one of my thumbprints very clearly on the glass. This my invaders had managed to smudge. I was pleased they had made mistakes. They were not infallible. That told me they could be beaten.

I returned downstairs and checked the small pantry that led off the kitchen. I had placed a small fingerprint there too, less visible than my thumbprint upstairs. It was as I had left it.

Below the house was a cellar of an unusual design. In some ways it resembled a lift shaft built entirely of concrete, not dissimilar to the construction of the pillbox in my paddock. Both had probably been built around the same time. I suspected my cellar had been designated to store supplies in the form of military ordnance: machine-gun ammunition, grenades and the like. The steps descended between two walls of concrete, impervious as the lining of the cellar itself. The rear wall was faced in brick, as if a previous owner had tried to make it feel more homely before giving up on the idea.

Beside the pantry concrete steps led down to the cellar which was blocked, halfway down, by a solid oak door whose lintel was just below the level of the ground floor. Three heavy locks had been set into the door. Beyond it the steps descended another few feet before reaching the floor, also of concrete which, though cold, remained dry in all weathers. Someone must have installed a very effective damp course at the time of its construction.

My intruders had not managed to pass through the door. To do that, they would have needed to find all three keys, each of which I had concealed about the house. There were signs of scratching around each keyhole, evidence that there had been a desultory attempt to employ some sort of skeleton key. But these were old-fashioned deadlocks of an antiquated design and almost impossible to open without their original keys.

Perhaps inspired by Eva's garden, but mostly to work off the anger I felt at having my home invaded, I set about hacking down the weeds. It had rained frequently during the last month and much of the garden, both front and back, was overgrown. I worked up a healthy sweat as I cut down the undergrowth and reduced many of the bushes by as much as half. I made myself very evident in the front garden, where my early roses had lost their blooms. I took a perverse pleasure in attacking these with bare hands, enjoying the pricks of the thorns as I dead-headed them, imagining each head to be that of one of my intruders.

By late afternoon I had filled four heavy duty waste bags provided by the council. These I dumped along my front path, so the postman would have something to grumble about and the village gossips could complain among themselves that I should have had the decency to wait until the fortnightly collection before putting out my garden waste. The point is, I wanted to be noticed. By as many people as possible.

Before I went upstairs and showered I checked the whole house for hidden cameras. It was not the first time I wished I had installed some myself. After my shower I dressed smartly in a knitted twinset and my mother's pearls, as if off to attend some drinks party. I got back in my car and drove to the nearest market town.

I found a slot in the main car park – paying a modest sum for just an hour's parking – and made my way to the library where they kept a public telephone. If they were as professional as they appeared to be, they would in all probability have tapped my house phone, and most likely my mobile phone too. If they were following me now I would have a clear view of anyone entering. But nobody did. Nobody came into libraries these days, which is why this one was about to close down and become a coffee shop.

I dialled the number Ambrose had given me and replaced the receiver immediately. A moment later the phone rang and I picked it up.

'What number do you require?'

I squinted at the note I had made. 'Nine, three, seven.'

'Putting you through.'

A moment later a man's voice answered. 'I can be with you at ten tomorrow morning.'

'You'll need my address,' I replied, somewhat smugly.

'I already have it.' The line went dead.

I borrowed a couple of books without paying much attention to their titles – I have a library card that works for every library in a twenty-five mile radius.

'By the time you return them, this place will be closed down.' The library assistant seemed remarkably sanguine about the situation.

'Then what am I supposed to do with the books?'

'You can keep them as far as I'm concerned. I've worked here thirty years and they're chucking me out.'

'So what will you do?'

'Go on income support. I think they call it universal credit these days.'

'Perhaps you could write a book. "Thirty years a librarian".'

'Oh no, I've seen enough bloody books to last me a lifetime.'

I carried the books in full sight so nobody would be in any doubt of what I'd been doing. I drove home and double-locked every door and window behind me. Then I realised I hadn't taken out the rubbish, so I had to open the front door again. As I put the rubbish in the wheelie bin and hauled it out for early morning collection, I thought I saw a flicker of movement from the corner of my eye. But when I looked again, whatever had been there was gone.

14

Bonn, November 1976

Patrick had been lucky in securing us a table in a corner banquette, some distance from Elsa and her beau. We sat at right angles to each other, so we only had to turn our heads a little to observe the whole room. A waiter brought us menus. Patrick scanned his with a growing expression of dismay.

'Just choose something inexpensive,' he hissed in French.

'My menu doesn't show the prices.' We continued speaking in French. It helped maintain our cover.

'Shit, I'll choose.' He scanned the menu, took out a small black book and made some notes in it. He left the book by his side plate. 'With any luck they'll think I'm a food critic and scrap the bill.'

'Then you'll be drawing attention. Let's keep things simple. Order a starter and the pudding, and we can share them. Ask for a spare plate.'

We sat with our backs to the warm wood panelling. The restaurant was busy and, as Patrick had explained, many tables were occupied by members of the Bundestag and wives, some of them even their own. Ria Maternus, the eponymous owner, petite and with her hair permed in a rigid helmet, flitted between tables, greeting the rich and powerful celebrities dining at her establishment. As foreign tourists, we did not merit her attention. That suited us fine.

Patrick had been concerned that Elsa might glance over and recognise me, but her eyes were fixed on her handsome escort and never once strayed in our direction. Patrick studied my disguise with something bordering admiration. 'Grace Kelly meets Jackie Onassis. Twenty-six million dollars. We could stretch to a couple of main courses with that.' The details of Jackie O's settlement from Greek shipowner Aristotle Onassis had recently been made public.

I nodded towards Elsa's table. 'Have you ever seen him before?'

Patrick made a show of looking round for a waiter, which gave him time to study Elsa's companion. 'Funnily enough, I feel I have. I just can't for the life of me think where.' The waiter, taking his cue, approached and Patrick made a hurried choice from the menu. The waiter returned to the kitchen.

'You've just ordered soup. Hard to share on a plate.'

Flustered, Patrick attempted to summon the waiter back. 'Leave it.'

We made small talk and kept a close watch on our subjects. Elsa fluttered her eyes at her beau as he talked. She hardly touched her food. She would be hungry in the morning. The waiter reappeared and placed a soup bowl in front of Patrick. '*Et pour Madame*?' he asked in poorly accented French.

'*La regime*,' I answered, patting my slim belly, as if I were following some strict diet. The waiter collected a second soup bowl from a sideboard and placed it in front of me along with a soup spoon and a cheerful wink. Watching his performance, I almost missed the moment Elsa's companion slipped a small velvet box across the table to her. Her squeal of delight when she opened it was enough to snap me back to attention.

Elsa reached into the box and eased out a small diamond ring. Her hands shaking, she dropped the ring on the table. Her man picked it up, took her left hand and slipped the ring on. At least, he tried to. Her finger was far too fat.

Patrick, sipping water, stifled his laugh. He spluttered and coughed, red faced, as the water went down his windpipe.

'You're making an exhibition of yourself,' I snarled, turning my face away the moment Elsa glanced up at us. She had gone pink with embarrassment. Her man removed the ring and slipped it onto her little finger, where it nestled tightly. He leant forward, raised her pudgy hand to his lips and kissed it. In any other place this might have elicited a polite round of applause from the nearest tables, but it had all been done so surreptitiously that it went unnoticed by anyone but Patrick and me.

The waiter reappeared with a tureen of soup, from which he filled our bowls to the halfway mark. In a moment of generosity he added one more small ladle to each. I had to shift my seat to watch the couple at the other table.

Elsa clasped her hand to her bosom, shaking her head in disbelief. Her companion leaned forward and spoke to her intently for nearly a minute. Her beam of delight turned to one of dismay. She shook her head vigorously. If this scene had been enacted a century earlier, it would have been a classic portrayal of Elsa defending her virginity from an older roué. But I sensed that, in this case, her man was asking her to sacrifice something else entirely. The mood on their table changed and Elsa stood up and tugged at her ring, as if she were about to hurl it back at him. The ring would not come off. She stumbled away to reclaim her coat, while he called the waiter over and, producing a wad of bills from his trouser pocket, counted out several large banknotes. He went to join Elsa, but she was already leaving the restaurant. He grabbed his coat, threw a tip to the cloakroom attendant and hurried out into the street. I stood up.

'Pay the bill, darling,' I said in French, 'I'm going for a fag.' I did not, as a rule, smoke and in those days it was perfectly acceptable to light up in a restaurant and puff smoke all over your fellow diners, but I took my coat, draped over the back of my chair for a fast escape, and followed Elsa and her man out.

In the street Elsa was trying to get into a taxi while her companion was trying equally hard to prevent her leaving. He towered over her. I lit my cigarette and got a better view of him as he pleaded. I caught a few words on the breeze: 'I wouldn't ask you to do it if it didn't mean everything to me.' His German was good, but I caught a strong trace of an accent.

'You told me *I* meant everything to you,' threw back Elsa.

'You do, but without this deal I may be recalled to England, and I can't lose you, Elsa.'

This seemed to appease her. She calmed down. 'You are asking a lot of me.'

'I know, but if it means our long-term happiness, it's not too much to ask.'

'Let me see what I can do.' Elsa shook herself free of his grip. She got in the taxi and it drove away. He waited a few moments, perhaps to see if she would change her mind and come back to him, but when she didn't he waved down another taxi.

Patrick came out of the restaurant.

'I got them to cancel the pudding. But that was a bloody expensive bowl of soup.'

We reached Patrick's car just as our man's taxi drove away. Patrick started his car and followed from a safe distance.

As we left Bad Godesberg and headed back towards the centre of Bonn the taxi turned sharp left. Bonn, though an ancient Roman town, had been kicked into the twentieth century by the construction of more than one hundred and fifty post-war embassies. With Berlin divided between East and West, it had made no sense for the FDR to try to govern from there. So Bonn had been chosen, possibly because its position was equally inconvenient for everybody, and that included members of the cabinet.

The taxi passed through this suburban estate of embassies and stopped in an area which, had Bonn possessed a slum, might have been classed as such. Patrick slowed down in anticipation before the taxi did. The man got out, paid his fare, and disappeared into the first of five concrete apartment blocks surrounded by a scrub of earth and weeds.

'This is where they house the cleaners, the maids, the cooks and gardeners for the embassies. This doesn't look right.' He thought about it a moment longer. 'I'll put a team on surveillance.'

15

West Sussex, May 2019

At exactly 10.00 the next morning the doorbell rang. I opened the door to a man equipped with a ladder and two large boxes of tools.

'I've come to fix the bathroom,' he announced with a Caribbean lilt, for the benefit of whoever might have overheard. 'All right if I bring my stuff in? The name's Aaron, by the way.'

I watched him bring in the two boxes then head to his van, from which he carried a large trunk with a combination lock.

'Don't like to leave my tools in the van, they might get nicked.'

'Very sensible,' I replied. 'I'd like that leak fixed today if possible.'

'Shouldn't be a problem.'

He lugged the trunk inside and nudged the door shut behind him. He undid the lock with a six-digit combination and opened the trunk. The contents glistened under the hall lights: a score of miniature CCTV cameras, movement sensitive devices, control panels, a couple of table lamps and other pieces I could not identify.

'This should cover the main rooms. What you got? Two rooms and a kitchen down here, two or three bedrooms and a bathroom upstairs?'

'Yes. There's also a lavatory on this floor under the stairs, and I have a pantry off the kitchen and a cellar which might be of interest.'

He shot me a look of the kind I hadn't seen since I had left the service and began to unpack his toolboxes. 'Do you have an attic?'

'Just a box room under the eaves. You can access it via a ladder.'

'Then I'll start there.'

'Do you want anything? Cup of tea, biscuits?'

'When I've finished in the attic I'll come down for a glass of water. In about an hour.'

I let him get on with it. I could hear drilling and hammering above, but I concentrated on writing down what I knew of my situation so far. I did it by hand. I can use a computer. I've been using them since 1984, when I first learnt word processing, and now I possessed the latest model of MacBook Pro, but since I could not guarantee somebody could not hack into it, what was the point? I'd be arming my enemies, whoever they were.

This is what I knew so far: a baby had been lost in the river. Several people had been dispatched to find or kill it. They were desperate enough to murder for it, as Phyllis Price had learned to her cost. They had broken into my house and searched it. They had found nothing useful. Of this I was sure.

I scratched out the 'kill it'. This was surmise. If I was going to surmise, I should make a second list. That they had found nothing useful was fact, not guesswork. I kept nothing in the house that told them anything more than they would have discovered from general enquiries in the village. I kept to myself, attended church only at Christmas (for appearances' sake), attended the odd bring-and-buy sale when I had nothing else to occupy myself, but avoided all meetings in the village hall and had never put myself up for the council or the civic society. I was a face the village knew, but not a familiar one. I had no friends, few acquaintances, and generally kept myself to myself. Nobody bothered me.

The doorbell rang. It was one of those two-tone electronic bells which I had been meaning to change ever since it had been installed. Ironic, I thought: one moment I was convinced nobody would bother me and the next somebody did exactly that. It might have been the postman. He was getting later and later every day, and sometimes asked me to take in parcels for the neighbours. It could also have been my intruders, back for a second go. Fashion-Plate or Igor? I wasn't too worried, as I was not alone in the house. I was on the point of answering the door when Aaron called down with a description. 'Gentleman in tweeds, pocket watch and a hat.' Well, that sounded like Best-Worthington, my old friend 'Fashion-Plate', but it could also describe four or five gentlemen 'worthies' from the village. I took a deep breath and opened the door.

The man who stood in my porch was familiar. Percy Bishop had earned himself a reputation which stretched across half the county. Aged around seventy, he still considered himself a ladies' man. He was fit and trim, with a full head of salt-and-pepper hair, a well-trimmed moustache and bright hazel eyes that crinkled when he smiled, which was most of the time. The only thing that stopped him seducing every widow in West Sussex was his lack of height (he stood around five foot eight inches in his shoes) but that didn't stop him trying. I had been warned of his professed ambition to live off wealthy widows until their funds dried up, but so far he hadn't bothered with me. I was definitely not his sort: the over-made-up women who spent their money on hair and nail salons, trips up to London during the social season and an expensive wardrobe and jewellery from Bond Street.

He removed his hat and smiled. 'So sorry to bother you, Mrs...?' I didn't supply my name. He could discover the one I was using easily enough just by asking around.

'We've never actually been introduced,' he continued, 'in all the time we've lived here. My name is Percy Bishop and I live in the old manor house.'

The 'old manor house' was simply the vicarage which some owner, possibly Bishop himself, had glorified. The name now featured on an aged oak board attached to the wrought-iron gates that led up its wide path.

'I don't know you,' I replied. I was curt. I didn't want him hanging around while Aaron was making the cottage secure.

'It's just that I was passing about an hour ago,' he continued, 'and I saw a man entering your house. I wondered if you were all right.'

'Why shouldn't I be all right?' I demanded. 'Because he's black?'

For a moment he was taken aback. Nobody likes to be accused of racism. I thought that would send him packing.

'Black? Is he? I didn't notice.' Percy made a good recovery but he was certainly on his back foot. 'As I'm sure you know,' he continued, 'there's been a recent murder in the village and the police seem to have no clues, so a group of us are ramping up the neighbourhood watch, checking on any single women in the area and watching out for anything suspicious.'

'I'm having a leak fixed in my attic. There's been a lot of heavy rain and I need the work done before the situation gets any worse. I don't think there's anything suspicious about that.' I stepped back to close the door on him but this proved a mistake, as he took it as an invitation to step inside. He placed his hat on the hall table, as if that gave him squatting rights.

'What a charming home you have,' he exclaimed, stepping further inside before I could block him, 'Queen Anne beams, I believe.'

'Nineteen-fifties fakes,' I replied brusquely. 'The oldest thing in this house is me.'

'Ah, but you're the genuine article,' he replied, quick off the bat. He gave a deep warm laugh, even though what he'd said was not particularly funny, and I could see how he could win over a lonely soul. Charm, warmth and persistence will always win out.

'I have to check on the builder,' I said.

'Quite right.'

I stood there, looking at him, waiting for him to take the hint and go. But he had no desire to move.

'I'll wait here, just in case.'

I grunted impatiently, but he had me trapped. If I went upstairs I'd be leaving him alone on this floor. Perhaps he was working with Best-Worthington. I could not take the risk. I called up. 'How much longer, do you think?'

'Just finishing now,' Aaron called back. There were a few sharp knocks with a hammer, which I suspected were simply for show. 'I'll be down in a minute.'

I turned back to Percy. He beamed another of his smiles.

'I can see you would like me to leave, but I shall only do so on one condition.'

'What condition would that be?'

'That you join me at the tea rooms at four o'clock this afternoon and let me get to know you better. I'm not budging until you agree.'

I should have simply bundled him out of the house and be done with it, but that might have aroused suspicions. Besides, I felt an element of curiosity about my notorious visitor. What did he really want?

'Very well, I shall see you at the tea rooms at four, but don't expect much. You'll have to take me as you find me.' The tea rooms were a public place, busy most afternoons. I would be safe there.

'I so look forward to it, dear lady,' and, before I could snatch it away, he had taken my hand and kissed it. He picked up his hat, bowed and walked backwards out of the house. I sighed. What had I got myself into?

16

Once he had finished setting up his system, Aaron took me down to the cellar where he had placed a monitor and recorder fed by the cameras he had hidden around the house. They gave me good views out into the street and into the rear garden. I also had several angles of each of the main rooms. Nobody could hide in any dark corner without my being able to see them. Further coverage was given by cameras concealed in the two lamps, one in the bedroom, one in the sitting room, and in various knick-knacks that Aaron had placed on shelves, mantelpieces and cupboard tops. They were the sort of things I loathed. Unnecessary frippery, but they would be overlooked by an intruder.

'You can access all this on your computer anytime, and also your phone, if you'll let me download the app.'

I opened my phone, he brought up the app and, moments later, I was able to see each room in turn on its screen. 'There's a way you can see them all at once, but the images would be too small to be much use, so I'd leave it on that setting if I was you, yeah?' he said. 'The cameras are very hard to spot, but if you was really looking for them, you'd find them. But wherever you are in the world, you can check your phone and you'll see these screens. There's an alert too if anything larger than a housefly enters. You got no cat, yeah?'

'No cat,' I replied. 'I'm very happy with it all.'
'Just don't get your phone nicked, yeah?'
'I shan't. What do I owe you?'
'Nothing. I'm doing this as a favour for Ambrose. He sent me a text he'll pick up the tab on the equipment, but it won't cost much. I get so many of these cameras wholesale, they cost nothing really.'

He packed up his equipment and left the house. As he got in the van he called out, 'That repair should hold for ten years. If it doesn't, call me and I'll fix it free of charge.' If he wasn't careful, he'd have half the village signing up for his services.

I glanced across the road and there was Percy Bishop, watching. When he realised he had been spotted he grinned with all the eagerness of a bullfrog eyeing a mayfly. He raised his hat and blew me a kiss. 'À *bientôt, madame*!' His words, thankfully, were drowned out by the roar of Aaron's van as it pulled away.

I whiled away the rest of the day by playing with my new toy. Carrying my phone around the garden I checked each room in turn. It gave me a sense of security. I was not afraid for myself, of course, but I hoped I would spend more time with little Alice, and that she would be safe.

It was only when I saw the images of the garden that I was startled. There was a scruffy old tramp wandering around the rose bed. That was my immediate impression until I realised that the 'tramp' was, in fact, me. It is always a shock to see yourself as others see you.

I spent the early part of the afternoon soaking myself in the bath. I scraped the dirt out from under my nails, gave them a neutral varnish, and did what I could to shape my unruly hair. If I was going to sponge tea off the local Lothario, I might as well make an effort.

17

Bonn, November 1976

At work the following day Elsa looked troubled. I found a reason to go over and have a chat. Her little finger looked red raw and she was no longer wearing her admirer's ring. It must have taken some effort to remove it.

'Are you all right, Elsa?' I asked. She nodded without looking up and concentrated on her typing, but I could see a big tear trickle down her chin and drop onto her page. 'If you want to talk about it, I'll be taking my break by the coffee machine.' She nodded silently and I went back to my work.

At eleven we were allowed fifteen minutes. As I stood up to go to the coffee machine Elsa hurried after me. She must have been waiting all morning to offload what was bothering her.

'I have a boyfriend,' she blurted without preamble.

'That's wonderful.' I pretended surprise and delight.

'And last night he asked me to be his bride.'

'I hope I'll get to meet and congratulate him.'

'No, no, that is impossible, you have to keep it a secret.'

'A secret?' I asked.

'He is getting divorced and he doesn't want his wife to know about us.' She fiddled with the coffee machine. 'Not until the divorce is finalised.'

'Divorces can be difficult,' I said, in my most understanding tone. 'If you want a friendly chat over a drink tonight, let me know.'

'Oh no, not tonight. He and I are meeting tonight.' That was interesting. 'But perhaps tomorrow night.'

'I would love to.'

Elsa nodded and turned away. During our conversation she had never once looked me in the eye.

The rest of the day I kept my mind on my work, occasionally glancing over at Elsa. At some point in the late afternoon I noticed she was no longer at her desk.

I approached Frau Müller. 'I need to ask Elsa about this paperwork,' I said (I was often asked to translate documents into French, English or even Italian – my weakest language), 'do you know where she is?'

'She went down to check some files, so that is where she will be,' Müller replied.

I went downstairs. The three women who did the filing had taken their break and gone to the canteen. They still took as long to file one day's work as we had taken for two weeks' output. The place appeared to be empty.

Then I heard the stifled sobs. I edged forward, concealing myself behind the high rows of shelves, until I was level with Elsa. Through a small gap I saw she was standing at the open steel door of the walk-in vault. She had her head bowed and was weeping over an open box file. She held a document up to the light, checking its contents, folded it twice and stuffed it into her bra. She replaced the other papers, shut the box file and placed it back in the vault, which she shut and locked. How had she acquired a key to open it?

I crept back to the foot of the stairs then called out, 'Elsa? Are you down here?' I saw her start and move quickly away from the vault.

'Just coming.' She waddled back towards me, snatched up a file at random and put it down further along the row for my benefit. She forced a smile. 'What do you want?'

'Just to say... well, don't forget you have friends who care about you.'

Her lip quivered and she gave me a tight little smile. We returned to our desks under Frau Müller's watchful eye and said nothing more.

Elsa kept glancing at the office clock until it was time to leave and the night staff came on duty. Sometimes we stayed on a little if we hadn't finished a particular document, but Elsa was straight out of the door at the stroke of five.

Two hours later I met up with Patrick in the small piece of scrub and hard clay that masqueraded as a public park. We sat on a bench some distance from the street lighting. We both wore parkas with fur-lined hoods, which did a good job of masking our faces. If anyone saw us, they would have presumed we were a courting couple.

'Elsa is not the sole object of your man's affection.' Patrick produced photographs of her 'fiancé' with three different women.

'At eleven he went for coffee with Hannelore Yildirim, German wife of the Turkish Ambassador. After lunch he spent two hours with an unidentified young woman in a room at the Maritim Hotel. This evening he met with Elsa Schopenhauer. She passed a document to him. After he checked it he kissed her and they parted. It's not looking good for your friend.'

'Elsa's a colleague, not a friend.' This wasn't entirely true. I was fond of Elsa and her lumpish ways and was sad that she had let herself make such a desperate mistake.

'Well now she's a traitor and she's in big trouble.'

'Do we know who her lover is?'

'He has a passport in the name of Michael Callan which says he's British.'

'Interesting.'

'We also found a second British passport with his photograph in the name of John Macallister. It's possible he may have other passports if he's carrying them on him. I've asked London to go through the records. See if either is genuine.'

The following week Patrick introduced me to his number two at the embassy, Giles Airdry, who, though younger than either of us, dressed in fusty tweeds and spoke in a slow, modulated and pedantic tone – a classic young fogey. Once Patrick and I had identified Callan as Elsa's admirer, Giles had mounted surveillance on Callan, or Macallister, or whatever his real name was. He informed us that Callan (as we called him from then on) had enjoyed assignations with yet another young woman in the typing pool.

I knew the woman. Marianna Schultz was thin, nervous and, like the others, from the provinces. The German government's policy of hiring provincials for their innocence and loyalty to the state was backfiring. Relocating these women to Bonn, where they knew nobody and had no friends, left them lonely and vulnerable to predators. And predators like Callan could be working for any foreign government. A classic case of the German state shooting itself in *den fuss*.

Patrick, Giles and I had to come up with a plan.

*

Since our adventure at the Maternus restaurant Patrick and I had drawn close. A frisson of danger while working in the field can have this effect on anyone, and we were no exception. But I was taken aback when Patrick invited me to accompany him to a concert at the Beethovenhalle. He was thrilled: the world-famous Herbert von Karajan would be conducting the Bonn Beethoven Orchestra in a performance of Beethoven's Ninth Symphony. The concert was in aid of a children's charity and the ticket holders were exclusively members of the international diplomatic corps. Not surprisingly, von Karajan's fee almost matched the sum the charity event raised.

I was reluctant to expose our professional relationship. Up until then, Patrick had kept me as far removed from the British Embassy as possible.

'Just because you're working for the FDR doesn't mean you're not expected to have a social life,' he reassured me. 'Several unmarried diplomats will be dating girls from the German Chancellery, you'll see.'

He was right, as it turned out. It had become something of a competition between the South American missions to be seen with the most beautiful blonde German women on their arms. I recognised one or two from the Chancellery, though none of them worked in the typing pool. Patrick made a point of approaching the British Ambassador, Oliver Wright, and introducing me as his date. I simply smiled and said nothing, but I noticed that Wright gave Patrick a nod of approval for his good taste.

I also noticed that many of the embassy wives wore long black evening dresses and carried musical scores. Patrick enlightened me: the choir that evening was to be made up of a professional core, supplemented by a choir drawn from the various embassies.

As we took our seats Patrick found himself sitting next

to a particularly beautiful young woman whose escort, an overweight Argentine, fell asleep at the beginning of the first movement. Once he started snoring the mortified woman glanced across at Patrick for help.

He leant across and tapped the Argentine sharply on the nose with his programme. The snorer woke with a start, his jowls wobbling. The young woman stifled a laugh, which set Patrick off giggling. He managed to do it silently, but I had to stamp on his foot to make him stop.

Karajan was a masterful showman, throwing himself about in a frenzy of wild energy. He had such confidence in his musicians that he conducted with his eyes closed, as if he were blind. I was drawn to make the comparison with Beethoven himself, who attempted to conduct his symphony when so completely deaf that his colleague Michael Umlauf did the actual conducting. Beethoven, facing the audience, as conductors did those days, was unaware that Umlauf and his orchestra had finished his masterpiece several bars ahead of him.

It was about eight minutes into the first movement that, at the big downbeat that repeats the opening theme, Karajan suddenly stiffened, his face wracked with pain. He managed to complete the first movement and make it through the second, but I could see he was in trouble.

At the intermission we headed to the bar and Patrick again found himself next to the beautiful woman, who introduced herself as Helga. She was trying to extricate herself from the unwelcome embrace of her amorous Argentine. As Patrick gallantly interposed himself between the two, Helga and I started up a conversation. At that moment an announcement was made over the public address system that von Karajan had been taken ill (his exertions had put his back out) and that the rest of that evening's programme was cancelled. The Argentine pounced, offering to take Helga home. She responded that she had already accepted a lift home from us. I caught the pleading look in her eyes. The three of us marched out of the hall before the Argentine could recover.

We drove Helga back to her apartment which, she told us, she shared with two other girls, both of whom were away attending a seminar. Setting her sights very pointedly at Patrick, she invited us up for a nightcap. The look in her eyes showed she hoped I would not accept. Patrick hesitated, saying he'd promised to see me home safely. I bundled him out of the car after her and told them I was happy to make my way home alone. At that time Bonn was probably the safest town in the world. Police cars and diplomatic security squads patrolled half the night, ensuring that drunken diplomats could make it back to their well-guarded embassies and residences without hindrance or scandal.

Once Patrick and Helga had disappeared inside, I lingered a while until I saw the lights go on in the top-floor apartment. Congratulating myself on my matchmaking, I crossed the street and had only gone fifty yards or so when the front door to Helga's building opened and Patrick bowled out. He looked ruffled. I stepped into the shadows.

Patrick hurried off down the street, leaving his car where he had parked it. Helga opened her top-floor window and leant out. She watched Patrick go. She shook her head in frustration and slammed the window shut.

Intrigued, I followed Patrick. He walked swiftly, with purpose, never once looking back. After about half a kilometre he stopped at the entrance to an alley. He looked around to check he was not observed – I made sure he did not see me – and disappeared through a dark doorway which led down into some basement nightclub.

I did not have long to wait. A couple of minutes later Patrick emerged again. This time he was accompanied by a young man in black leather jacket and trousers. In the dim light I could barely make out a fumbled embrace. They broke apart. Patrick strode briskly back towards his car. The young man waited a few seconds then followed. Patrick got into his car, started the engine and threw open the passenger door. By the light of the street lamp I recognised Giles Airdry slipping in beside him. Patrick gunned the accelerator and his car moved off at speed.

Homosexuality had been decriminalised between consenting male adults in Britain in 1967 and in West Germany by 1969. But a loving relationship with Giles still left Patrick vulnerable to blackmail. That was why he had been so keen to parade me in front of Ambassador Wright. I resolved to do my utmost to protect Patrick and keep his secret safe.

18

West Sussex, May 2019

'… so one lunchtime in a Soho pub this actor – I can't tell you his name, that would get me into trouble – he starts chatting to this beautiful blonde. They have a few drinks together and, as things warm up and they get friendly, he informs her that there's this wonderful play that she simply has to see and he sends his assistant round to pick up a pair of complimentary tickets.'

Percy was proving more entertaining than I had expected, reeling off a wealth of stories about London and theatreland where, he claimed, he had been an 'angel' for more than thirty years, backing a variety of plays, both on and off the West End.

'Well, one thing leads to another and he takes her back to The Savoy, where he retains a rather swish suite. A few hours later they wake up, a little tired and still thoroughly sozzled. He finds the theatre tickets tucked in his breast pocket and rushes her off to the show. They take their seats in the centre of the second row, the curtain comes up and the play commences. Then, about ten minutes into the drama, a thought occurs to him. He suddenly stands up, still reeking of alcohol, loudly exclaims, 'Oh bugger, I'm in this!' and runs backstage to get into wardrobe.'

I found myself laughing and, as I looked up, I noticed

half the tea room watching me. As my eyes met theirs, the ladies of West Sussex quickly looked away, ripping into their scones and teacakes with their manicured nails, sipping their tea with their little fingers pointed outwards, in a way they probably imagined the Queen Mother did. She didn't, I can assure you, and I had tea with Queen Elizabeth and her mother on more than one occasion. It's what they do when they are giving you an award the government doesn't want the world to know about. You know, special services rendered, and all that.

I had made some effort with my appearance as a special concession to my rendezvous with Percy, but that was as far as I went with social etiquette. I glanced around the room and saw more eyes lowered. They were either jealous, I realised, or curious. Some were probably Percy's old flames, ditched when they'd run short of funds: the funds he'd 'invested' in theatre productions. Others were probably on his list for future conquest, and all of them were probably wondering, 'why her?' or 'what's he see in that old bat?'

I had asked myself the same question a couple of times before we met up at the Chestnut Tree Tea Rooms. There's no chestnut tree anymore, by the way. The council panicked about conkers dropping and hitting people – which they have done without serious consequences for at least three hundred years – and decided to chop it down. There were protests of course, but then the council, made up of several local worthies, pointed out that we were living in a world of litigation and that should someone suffer from 'conker drop', real or imaginary, the council would be sued and would most likely lose. That would probably lead to the doubling of the council tax. At which point the protestors backed down. It seems that green idealists lose their ideals pretty quickly when it affects their wallets. Mind you, I hadn't contributed to the debate myself. As I said, I keep a low profile and putting my name to petitions would have raised mine. So I really didn't know what I was doing having tea with Percy.

Our tea arrived. It was the 'full Monty': a pot of tea each – mine Assam, his Lapsang Souchong – four large scones with separate bowls for clotted cream and strawberry jam, two chocolate éclairs and eight finger sandwiches on a two-tier display stand.

'Absolutely super-stantial!' exclaimed Percy. 'Shall I be mother?'

He stirred the tea in my pot briskly, waited for the maelstrom to slow and then, using a strainer, poured the tea into my cup. 'I know many people put the milk in first, but if you don't know the strength of the tea, well, that can be a disaster. And there's nothing worse than weak tea.'

'I'd say Phyllis Price might have preferred weak tea to her own cold-blooded murder,' I replied, helping myself to a chocolate éclair and taking a large bite. Whipped cream shot out the far end and I just managed to stop it flying onto Percy's waistcoat.

'Well, yes, I suppose you have a point there,' he agreed, somewhat deflated. Then he straightened up. 'Still, we can't let gloomy thoughts spoil our afternoon together, can we?'

He poured a cup for himself, sipped it, then reached for a scone.

'Cornish or Devonshire?'

'What?' I said, my mouth full of the remains of the éclair. I knew exactly what he was talking about but I let him continue.

'You know, jam first or cream first? One's supposed to be the Cornish way. I think that's with the jam on before the cream. Makes sense. The jam clings to the scone. The other way you can't get the jam to stay.'

He spread the jam on thickly and added a good dollop of cream. He looked at it a moment, and then glanced up so his eyes met mine. He quickly looked away, as if he had been waiting for the right moment for him to get something off his chest, and had decided that this was not the time.

'I can see you enjoyed that éclair,' he said. 'Why don't you have the other one?' It wasn't what I'd expected. I had been hoping to get the business element out of the way. Now it was my turn.

'When are you going to tell me what this is all about?'

He had just taken a huge bite out of his scone and he chewed and swallowed it before he spoke.

'Just a matter of getting to know you, dear lady. You've been living here quite a few years. And the village knows as little about you as they would a total newcomer.'

He took another mouthful and I could see him enjoying the sensation of the cream and jam slide past his taste buds and for a moment it took me back to my childhood home. I remembered my mother, on her knees in the kitchen of the big house in Oxford, scrubbing the linoleum floors so they shone. She and my father had had to sell up, but she wasn't going to let the new purchasers, a brash and gaudy couple from London, think she couldn't keep a clean house. I knew she was dying inside, obliged to let go of the home where she and her little family had been happy, but she refused to show it.

Then there had been a ring on the doorbell. 'It's them,' Mother had exclaimed, in a shaky voice I had never heard before. But it wasn't them. It was a delivery man with a package, which I opened. Inside was a pot of thick Devon cream and a jar of honey. Attached to the cream was a note saying sorry for the delay and offering the honey as an apology. And suddenly I remembered. The summer before I had been sent to visit distant cousins in Cornwall. We had stopped at a small farm shop and I had placed an order for clotted cream to be sent to my parents. Somehow the note had fallen behind a shelf in the shop and had just been discovered earlier that week. The shopkeeper had despatched a fresh order as soon as it had come in. We unpacked our box of spoons and Mum, Dad and I tucked into cream and honey, and suddenly Mum burst into tears. Dad went to comfort her, and I could see that he was holding back his own tears. I wrapped my arms tight around them. It was the last time I could remember us three being so close.

'There's nothing interesting about me,' I said. I accepted the second éclair and bit into it. I hadn't eaten éclairs for years.

'Oh, I think there is. You're the woman of mystery, and every man sees a mystery as a challenge.'

'You want to worm information out of me?'

'Something like that. I think prising snippets out of you could become an enjoyable occupation.'

I finished the éclair and placed a cucumber sandwich on my plate. 'I wouldn't count on it. Here's my life story: I left university with a 2.2, got a job as a minor civil servant, retired at sixty – it was just okay then to retire at that age, nowadays women are forced to carry on until sixty-six – and collected my index-linked pension. That's it.' All nonsense, of course.

'Marriages, children?'

'None.'

'Well, I can't say I'm much the wiser. I notice you've adopted somebody.'

I almost choked again, but controlled myself and did my best to adopt an air of lack of concern. After all, it had been part of my training. I finished my sandwich.

'Adopted somebody? Whoever can you mean?' My heart was pounding just that little bit faster, but I knew how to calm it.

'Jamie Cullen.'

My heart returned to its normal pace, slow with just the occasional mis-beat.

'He has a somewhat unsavoury reputation in the village,' Percy continued. 'Pilfering, burglary, making a general nuisance of himself.'

'He comes from a broken home.'

'Perhaps I'm being a bit unfair without evidential proof, but you're doing yourself no favours.'

'Should I be?' I took a fair swig of my tea. I did not want it getting cold.

'Well, let me tell you my reason for inviting you here – apart from the very great pleasure of your company.'

At last, I thought, and waited for it. What did he know?

'It's to invite you to join our civic society.'

The tea that was halfway down my throat rocketed forward into my mouth, half of it going up my nose and dribbling out, in an echo of Eva's reaction to seeing little Alice. I coughed and went puce in the face as I struggled not to choke. I grabbed my napkin, dabbing at my nose while reaching for my canvas tote bag that passed as a handbag. I found a couple of discarded tissues and blew my nose furiously. Tea-stained snot quickly coloured them an unpleasant shade of beige.

'Did I say something funny?' asked Percy. He was mildly amused by the situation. 'Can I get you a glass of water?'

I shook my head; held up my hand to stop him saying any more.

'I'll… I'll be all right in a minute,' I gasped. I was just about back in control when I noticed her: a middle-aged woman I had never seen before. She had entered the tea room by its far entrance – the Chestnut Tree Tea Rooms had once been two cottages that had been knocked together – and she had been hovering by the door. She was staring at me with a look of pure hatred of the kind I had only ever seen in the field of action. She plunged her hand into her handbag and strode towards me.

I tensed, grabbed my fork and held it ready to stab her before she could produce a weapon. My other hand reached for the knife. If I got my timing right I could put her out of action before she struck. It would lead to questions, but it would keep me alive.

Her hand came out of her handbag. It didn't hold a gun, as I had feared, but a handful of letters, bound together with pink ribbon. She stopped beside Percy and, with all the bitterness of a woman scorned, she hurled them onto his plate.

'Here,' she croaked, her voice cracking, 'take back your letters, you… you absolute shit!' She reached across the table, lifted the bowl of clotted cream and dumped it over Percy's head. She turned on her heels and there was a smattering of applause before she slammed out of the tea room.

Percy glanced across at me, and his look had an element of apology about it. He wiped the cream dripping from his hair.

'I may be a shit,' he admitted, 'but not an absolute one.'

19

I SNATCHED UP A COUPLE of sandwiches, shamelessly stuffed them in my tote bag and left Percy to pick up the bill. What with one thing and another, I had enjoyed my outing and reflected that, should he ever be inclined to ask me out again, I would accept his invitation. He was guaranteed to provide entertainment, either with his anecdotes or with some form of humiliation piled on him by any of his former admirers.

As I thanked him and stepped out into the street I turned and saw two smartly dressed women, better coiffed than most, hurry over to Percy and attend to his hair. They wore expensive gold bangles and Cartier tank watches on their wrists and their nails were beautifully manicured. In those brief moments I could not decide if they were rivals for his favours or both hoping to share them simultaneously. Lucky old Percy – a ménage à trois – possibly involving a large bowl of cream.

I walked the few hundred yards home, unlocked the door and went straight down to the cellar and checked my video. Aaron had set it to record any movement, so there were only about twenty minutes of footage, which I was able to watch at four times the speed without the risk of missing anything. I saw nothing out of the ordinary, but I did notice the two blonde women whom I had just seen comforting Percy. Was it my imagination or did they slow down as they passed my house? I rewound and played the recording again. They *did* slow down, but it seemed that they did so only because one of them needed to touch up her lipstick in the street – a vulgar faux pas that jarred. I replayed it again. The woman applying the lipstick seemed clumsy at best. She dropped the stick and bent to pick it up. She was out of sight for only a moment, but that moment seemed longer than it needed to be. She straightened up, put something in her handbag and the two of them kept walking. I wound on the recording, watched a couple of other passers-by – neighbours I knew by sight but to whom I had never spoken – and the last person I saw onscreen was myself, returning home.

I waited till dark before going outside and checking the low flint wall which separated my property from the pavement. Using the torch app on my iPhone I scanned the wall carefully. An old lady on her hands and knees in a street at night is liable to attract attention – all too many people will be telephoning for an ambulance or trying to lift me off the pavement before I knew it – but I had my answer ready. If anyone were to ask me what I was doing, I would say that I had seen an injured hedgehog and was trying to rescue it. Hedgehog rescue is a priority and a laissez-passer in the British countryside.

In the event, nobody bothered me. There's a quiet period every evening when the oldies are trying to watch their favourite shows on the streamers, the middle-aged couples are out wife swapping or whatever it is they do to amuse themselves, the young are about to get drunk or high on drugs, and the very young are occupied teaching the oldies how to operate the remote controls on their Apple TVs without accidentally logging out.

At first I could see nothing out of the ordinary. The wall, like that of my house, was made up of napped flint cobbles set in brickwork. But there were a couple of places where the old mortar had dropped out and I had not got round to having it replaced. One of these gaps was now occupied by a shiny new flint. At least, that was what it looked like at first sight. Closer inspection revealed this to be a camera lens, disguised to fit in with the flints. So the two women had done their reconnaissance, photographed the wall, designed a camera to fit, camouflaged it and then managed to slip it into position. A highly professional job. But why? The camera, with its fish-eye lens, took in the whole street. What it failed to do was point at my house or show what I was doing. Short of seeing when I was leaving the house or, indeed, returning to it, which anyone in the village could do for free, it did not serve to spy on me. Ergo, it was there to spy on others. So was it there to protect me? Perhaps. I left it in position. Anyone monitoring it could not miss the fact that I had discovered it. So I gave whoever was watching a 'thumbs-up' and went back inside. I slept a little more easily that night, though I did have a recurring dream of Percy being immersed in clotted cream and I woke up wondering if he had lured me out of the house precisely so that the camera could be installed. It was not out of the question. I drifted off again.

The next morning I called London early. Eva answered.

'Mummy, how are you?' were her first words on hearing my voice. She hadn't called me 'Mummy' in years. Usually it was 'Ma', or else I'd be acknowledged with a grudging grunt.

'How are you managing with Alice?' I asked.

'Silvana's in love, and I think I'm heading that way too.'

'I thought you didn't like children.'

'I have no interest in bearing children; that's a different matter altogether.'

'So she's not giving you any trouble? I can come up and fetch her if—'

'No trouble at all,' she interrupted. 'There's no rush for you to pick her up.'

'Really? You're sure?'

'Really, Mummy. Don't worry, she's happy with us.'

'That makes me feel much better, thank you.' I almost added 'darling', but thought better of it and simply ended the call with 'goodbye'.

I am not sentimental. It's never been part of my character. So I have no idea why I replayed the previous night's ten o'clock news on 'BBC catch-up'. Eva had sounded more relaxed than I had heard her in years. I suddenly had the urge to watch her on television and see if her new happier mood had revealed itself onscreen. I sat down and pressed *play*.

Well, all I can say is that Eva looked just as cold and frosty as she always does. But that's why they pay her all that money. She is supposed to remain completely impartial and she makes sure that she looks it.

As the news moved on to another item and an on-location reporter, I let the programme run on. They would return to Eva in a minute or two. I stepped closer to the screen to spot if any flicker of emotion revealed itself in her beautifully made-up eyes.

It was then that I saw him. The news reporter was standing outside the Russian Embassy in Kensington Palace Gardens, summing up what we already knew of Russia's total denial of yet another poisoning of one of its own dissidents, when I caught sight of a familiar figure attempting to avoid being photographed. He had his head turned away from the camera as he walked past, but there was no mistaking that shapeless head, that weirdly undefined face. As the reporter moved away from the embassy gate, the camera swung around to follow him. In the background I saw Igor dart away and disappear from view.

20

Bonn, November 1976

I made my way to Die Kneipe, the bar Heidi, Elsa and I had gone to on our first evening together and where, only a week or so before, I had watched Elsa meeting Callan. Patrick and I had decided that it was the best place to engineer an encounter. I had visited Die Kneipe three evenings running but Callan had yet to make an approach.

On this fourth evening I sat alone at the bar and ordered a Martini. I wore very little make-up. Frau Müller discouraged it, for a start. In any case it was my preference: minimal make-up and just a little lip salve. Even before my Martini appeared Callan had slipped in beside me. He was preceded by a light whiff of aftershave which I could not identify. It was a blend of Dunhill for Men and something undefinable. I later discovered this to be distilled male pheromones, concocted in a lab in Moscow.

'I'll have one of those,' he said, in his accented German, 'and put them both on my tab.'

'I'm quite capable of buying my own drinks.'

'Please don't deprive me of the pleasure of your company. It's taken me five minutes just to pluck up the courage to speak to you.'

I turned to look at him. His eyes dropped to the counter, as if embarrassed by his own forwardness.

'I'm waiting for a friend,' I replied.

'Well then I don't suppose your friend will mind if I sit here and behave myself.' He stuck out his hand. 'My name's Michael, Michael Callan.'

It is today, I thought. He would stick to that name in Die Kneipe. But what would his name be tomorrow, in another place? I took his hand. It was warm, reassuring. 'Where are you from?'

'I'm English, in Bonn on business.'

'You speak very good German,' I replied in accented English.

'And you speak very good English.'

'We were taught English at school in Austria, but the English I was taught was rather... how do you say? Formal.' I put a little stiffness into my delivery. 'I do not have a facility with colloquialisms.'

'I'd agree with you there.' He laughed. The waiter placed our Martinis before us. '*Prost.*'

'*Prost.*' We each took a sip.

'Have you been in Bonn long?' I asked.

'I come and go. Some contracts take longer to negotiate than others. Looks like I'm stuck here for the time being. I don't suppose you'd care to show a lonely guy around the sights some day this week?' As an opening gambit it was as good as any.

'I work every day. I am not free.' A bit of resistance, a challenge.

'What about the weekend? I could pick you up on Saturday afternoon.'

'Then I shall have no time for my weekly shopping.'

'Sunday then. You're free Sunday.'

'I have church.' I hadn't been inside a church since I had

left convent school, aside from weddings and funerals, but it created the right impression.

'Fine, after church. Then we can have lunch together.'

I looked him up and down, as if only now taking him seriously. He was tall and broad shouldered and held himself erect. He had a fine head of chestnut brown hair, bright green eyes with amber flecks and high cheekbones. His sideburns were long, as was the fashion, sweeping down towards a chin covered by a neatly trimmed beard of chestnut lightly flecked with grey. I could understand why women were drawn to him. If he had been a breeding bull in a cattle market, he would have fetched top dollar.

'You can pick me up outside here at eleven thirty.' I did not want him to know where I lived, not yet, at any rate. I was still staying in the little hotel, to separate myself from the other girls in the typing pool, many of whom were housed in state owned dormitories. I finished my Martini. 'Until Sunday.' I shook his hand formally, turned on my heel and walked to the door where I stopped a moment and turned back to look at him, as if I couldn't believe my luck. He was still looking at me, as if he had expected this, and raised his glass. Any of his conquests might have blushed at that moment. After a lifetime of concealing my emotions, blushing did not come naturally to me, so I simply smiled back at him and left.

Patrick was delighted with my success. He told me he had reported to Chancery and the decision had been taken not to expose Elsa until we had a clear line of evidence.

'How long do they want to wait?' I asked. 'She could pass him the contents of the entire vault.'

'We're playing the long game. Let's see what other worms wriggle out of the woodwork.'

Although this decision risked the loss of more confidential documents, I was, in a way, relieved that poor Elsa could carry on her romance a while longer. For a mad moment I even thought of warning her off Michael Callan, but I could not see how I could manage this without the risk of tipping off the man himself. My job was to uncover where the documents were going. That would expose his handler and perhaps a complex network of spies. Unless I could manage that, my whole mission was pointless.

*

I duly attended 11 o'clock mass at Saint Elizabeth's church on Sunday. I had no idea of the correct responses for the service. My father had been a lapsed Catholic and my mother a lapsed atheist (lapsed in the sense that she never expressed her atheism out loud). She had sent me to a school where we found amusement in making up our own responses to familiar prayers. The Lord's Prayer became the London bus driver's prayer: 'Our father, who art in Hendon, Harrow Road by Rye Lane, Thy Kingston come, Thy Wimbledon, etc. etc.' The only reason I now attended church was in case Callan already had me under observation. If he had, his people would most likely already know where I lived. That didn't matter. What was important was that my character, the 'legend' I had created for myself, was kept intact.

He picked me up outside the church at 11.30 on the dot in a Mercedes car with a driver. 'I've got him all day if I want him. It's a good deal, as long as he can go home for lunch after he drops us off.' He had ignored our arrangement to meet outside Die Kneipe. I did not feel it prudent to point this out.

We took a drive along the Rhine and, like a diligent tour guide, I explained to him that Bonn was originally named Castra Bonnensis when the Romans established a fort station in the first century. I did not add that it was now more famous for the gummy bears made by Haribo in Kessenich. I suggested visiting the Academic Art Museum, but Callan showed no interest in history or art. 'What about restaurants? Where's a good place for lunch?'

'The most popular, where many politicians go from Der Bundeskanzler, is the Maternus.'

'You work in the Chancellery? That must be interesting.' He said it so innocently.

'Not as a rule, but sometimes we get to hear a piece of gossip before the rest of the world does.'

Callan ordered his driver to head to Maternus.

'We will never get a table on a Sunday.' I suggested another, reliably cheaper, restaurant.

'Let's take a chance. I'm feeling lucky. And as for the expense, well hang that. My contract is as good as signed and I don't think I'm taking too much of a risk opening a bottle or two of champagne today.'

We pulled up outside Maternus. Callan asked me to wait in the car while he checked if he could get us a table. I shook my head, in a show of 'first date' concern that I was causing him unnecessary expense. While he was inside, my eyes met those of the driver. They were cold, hard and dark as shards of jet. I averted my face. A moment later Callan bounded back to the car. 'All fixed, we're in.' He held the door open for me and escorted me into the restaurant.

'How did you manage this?' I asked, as the waiter helped shift my chair forward.

'A few sponduliks to the maître d'.'

'Sponduliks?'
'Slang for cash.'
'Sponduliks,' I repeated. 'I shall remember that.'

Callan had got us the best table in the house. This could not have been a lucky chance. My guess was that he had the table permanently reserved – he could always cancel at the last moment, as the restaurant was always popular on the weekend. That was why he had asked me to wait. It made him look spontaneous and successful.

Any apprehension that I might be recognised from my visit with Patrick was quickly allayed. The weekend staff were not the same as the weekday evening staff, so I relaxed and let Callan spoil me. We started with champagne, as he had promised, then he made a big thing of examining the menu as if he had never seen it before. I chose simply and avoided the soup.

If I had expected a full-blown seduction I was in for a surprise. It came subtly, bit by bit and by insinuation. As we drank the champagne he told me about the contract he was expecting to be signed off any day soon.

'You see, I represent a firm in London that holds a licence to build Bailey bridges.'

'Really?' I feigned interest.

'These bridges are put up in a matter of days and they can span almost any river.'

'Remarkable.' I was struggling here.

'We sell a lot in South America, especially to Colombia. We've got the FARC guerrillas to thank for that. The moment we put one up, they blow it to pieces, so we get another contract for another bridge.'

'It sounds a good business.'

'They're just as popular in Europe. Many of the old bridges

that survived the war are crumbling and need replacing. So what we do is construct a new Bailey bridge alongside the old bridge and then engineers divert the road. That gives local contractors the chance to repair or replace the old bridge with something more substantial. Everybody wins.'

'Fascinating.'

I was beginning to wonder how this crashing bore could have wheedled himself into the hearts of so many young women. That was when he reached into his pocket. 'Let me show you the love of my life.' He produced a photograph and laid it flat on the table before us.

The most exquisite sailing yacht I had ever seen lay in clear blue waters a few yards off a sandy beach dotted with coconut palms. It was the stuff that dreams – and commercial advertisements – are made of.

'It's beautiful.' This time I was not putting on an act.

'I keep her in Barbados, where we have our head office. I spend as much time with her as I can.' He put the photograph away. 'But what's the point of a boat like that if you don't have someone to share it with? I'll put her up for sale next time I'm out there, and perhaps you'll come with me for one last cruise around the island.'

It was at this point, I expected, that most young ladies, imagining themselves on a Caribbean island with this rock-solid hunk, would grab his muscular arm and beg him not to sell his beautiful boat. But I had no intention of making things so easy for him.

'I get seasick,' I said. 'Even with the slightest swell.'

'Try sleeping on deck for just one night and you'll be cured.'

I knew his method worked. I had done exactly the same thing two years earlier when I sailed in a small boat to

Cyprus to help Archbishop Makarios escape an assassination attempt. His presidential palace had been shelled by his own Cypriot National Guard under orders from the Greek military junta. I, and three others, had got him out the back door and up into the Troodos mountains, and from there to the British base at Akrotiri from where the RAF flew us to Malta. After that Makarios had flown on to New York and my services were no longer required.

'She does look pretty.' The water was so clear the boat seemed suspended in mid-air. 'How often do you get out there?'

'As often as I can, especially in winter.' He beckoned the waiter to pour more champagne. 'But what's the point in going alone?' He took hold of my cold hand in his warm one. 'Think about it. Once I've got this deal signed, I'll be free. And you could be too.'

Callan's assault on my defences carried on in much the same vein. He produced two more photographs, one of a small 'plantation house' with a veranda set in a grove of mango trees.

'All Alphonso mangoes. The best. They fall right off the tree into your hand when they're ripe.' This was the house he claimed he owned. Outside it stood a young black man, smiling a welcome. This was his 'friend and servant', Delroy. The other photograph was of a larger house, more stately, white with tall columns and a classical pediment, which he planned to buy from the proceeds of his bridge deal. 'But what's the point of a big house if you don't have someone to share it with? Someone with whom to share the best things in life?'

His cards now on the table, Callan leaned forward, took my hand in his and apologised. 'I'm so very sorry. You've let me do all the talking and I've let my mouth run away with me. You must think me the most awful bore. You see, I've never met anyone who fascinates me as much as you do. It's making me quite nervous. I'm so frightened of losing you now, when we've only just met. Stupid really, but I can't help myself.' He let his voice choke up, as if he was overcome with emotion, and his last words were hardly more than soft whispers. 'What I really want to say is… well, I just want to get to know you. So please, tell me about yourself. Tell me everything.'

Then he demonstrated what made him a successful seducer: he shut up and listened. It was the oldest of all seduction techniques: listening with interest. His technique was to ask simple, innocent questions that led the speaker to open up to him. Sooner or later she would reveal her most precious dreams, her greatest weaknesses, her hidden secrets, and then she would be his. It must have worked every time. But not with me.

My problem was that I had been trained to give nothing away. But I knew I had to give him something to work with. So I took a deep breath and recounted my well-rehearsed 'legend' which, for simplicity's sake, was a reversed version of the truth: that I had been born in Austria, grown up in Innsbruck and had been schooled for a short time in England. But as for my hopes and dreams, well, now I had to make some up. And as for my weaknesses… well, whoever likes admitting those?

So I told him what he wanted to hear: I had always dreamt of a place in the sun – anywhere far from the sullen Rhine mist of Bonn. I did not have to fake this. Who doesn't prefer bright sun and blue skies to dark grey clouds? As for weaknesses: I had to invent some. It wasn't hard. Hanging around the coffee machine waiting for the water to boil in the presence of frustrated young women in the typing pool provided plenty of material.

He sat there, all the time watching me with such warmth and compassion in his eyes that he almost had me believing that the guff spewing from my mouth had him transfixed. It was a trick I have often used myself. Let a man explain to you in detail why he is important and simply nod back, misty eyed, in agreement at everything he says, and he will consider you the greatest conversationalist of all time. I kept talking as long as I could.

'I never seem to get my work done fast enough, and yet I am more accurate in my translations than anybody. Frau Müller is a real Tartar and she is impossible to satisfy.'

'So you work in the translation department?' I knew he must know that, but played along.

'Typing and translation. Both.'

'Sounds a thankless task.' That was all we spoke on the subject, because at that moment our lunch arrived. We had decided against starters. I had ordered a wiener schnitzel (how original) and he had ordered the same, but Holstein style, with anchovies and capers, topped by a fried egg with creamed spätzle on the side. I imagined he would need it and more if he had to service all the women in his address book.

Lunch drew to a close without us discussing anything deeper than our parents – he claimed that his were deceased, buried in Northumberland, and that he had spent his teenage years trying to get rid of his Geordie accent. But when I asked him to 'do a Geordie accent' he declined, saying it brought up too many painful memories. So I had already spotted the flaw in his legend. He was no Geordie.

After lunch we parted. He offered to have his driver take me back home, but I said I would prefer to walk, despite the cold. He had hoped to discover my address. He would learn it soon enough, but now was not the time. I had provided him with a crack and a lever. All he had to do was push.

21

London, May 2019

The following morning at around 9.15 I parked alongside Rassells Garden Nursery in Pembroke Square, paid the blasted parking fee, and made my way east along Kensington High Street then turned up into Kensington Church Street. Once I reached York House Place I turned right and headed down the alley, or 'shit creek' as we called it when I lived in South Kensington, on account of the dog walkers encouraging their pets to defecate in this shady spot. I strode past the sign that forbad me taking any photographs, and then into Kensington Palace Gardens, the gloriously wide avenue lined with London plane trees which backed onto Kensington Palace. My reason for entering this way was that guard posts are situated at the north and south ends of the avenue, above and below the alley, positioned primarily to prevent unauthorised vehicular access. The guards are less concerned with dog walkers and joggers heading for the park. Both the guard posts and the mansions have cameras, of course, some obvious and, I presume, some expertly concealed (perhaps installed by Aaron), but I knew nobody would pay much attention to a harmless-looking old lady.

I dug into my tote bag, a freebie from Daunt Books in Holland Park, and extracted my iPad. I opened the photos app, and then selected the photograph I had downloaded from the internet. I shifted to camera mode, set it to video and pressed 'record'. I then hauled out my iPhone and opened QuickVoice Pro. I set this to record and held the phone in front of me as if I were dictating or making a long, involved WhatsApp call. Holding the iPad to my chest and with its lens pointing to my left I set off north, up the slope towards Notting Hill Gate.

As I walked I described each house I passed. This was to give me a cover story should I need one: I was a Kensington resident interested in furthering my architectural education. I commented aloud on the style of architecture – at the southern sloping end, Palace Green, they are mostly in Queen Anne style with red brick dressed with Portland stone. Those mansions further north as the ground flattens are of Italianate style, though the architectural details vary. Some are clearly embassies, as their flags proclaim. Others are residences, leased from the Crown. As I walked I identified those that I could – though one flag had me puzzled. Many of the houses at the Palace Green end were clearly private, featuring burly security guards standing behind their tall gates. Several of the embassies had workmen polishing brass plates and repainting repaired cornices. One even had two men climbing a balcony with ropes. Either the French Ambassador was taking abseiling lessons or he was having a bit of fancy paint work done to his balcony repairs.

I eventually reached my target: the Russian quarter. Before the revolutionary events of 1989 this had been the Soviet quarter, but with the collapse of the Soviet Union most of the buildings had been annexed by the Russian state. I had familiarised myself with the area during my early twenties and thirties, when I was on stakeout duties, as they are now called. We used a different word for them in those days. The first building that attracted my attention was the Russian Ambassador's residence, or Harrington House, as it was formerly known.

Harrington House is, in my opinion, the ugliest Gothic building ever designed by Decimus Burton. He should have known better but suffered from the disadvantage that he was obliged to work from the designs of his patron, the Earl of Harrington.

I continued to walk northbound. As I got closer to the Russian Embassy, where two armed police officers were stationed, I crossed over to the west side of the avenue towards the Czech Embassy. My real interest was in the Russian Chancery building at numbers 6–7. For me to get there without attracting attention I would have to cross over to the east side, executing a wide U-turn past the north guard post, then follow the avenue back down. I was hoping to slip past the guards without them noticing me. For this I needed a vehicle to enter from the north gate of Kensington Palace Gardens, situated by the North Lodge, to distract them. So I hovered around the Czech Embassy at the north-west corner, as if captivated by its award-winning brutalist design. In the meantime, I saved my recording, gave it a nondescript name, and emailed it to myself at an address I had set up specifically for this purpose. In all probability I would not need this recording. It was the next section of the street that interested me. I also saved my phone recording, sending it to myself via WhatsApp. A few seconds elapsed before it loaded up. Then I set the iPad camera back to 'record'. My purpose was simple: to get the lay of the land and, if possible, see if I could identify Igor's master.

While I was thus occupied a car entered through the north gate and stopped at the barrier. A set of bollards rise from the ground to prevent people driving in with trucks full of explosives. I took advantage of the distraction to cross over to the east – the Russian – side of the road. At the same moment a car horn sounded loudly behind me and I froze. A near-silent electric car had approached from the south at speed and braked hard bare inches from me. I cursed myself for not being more cautious, more alert. A security guard, most likely a former Gurka, stepped out of his booth towards me.

'Can I help you?' he asked, in that tone adopted by people who have no intention of helping you at all.

'Yes, you can,' I replied. I opened my photo app on my iPad. 'I'm looking for my great aunt's house.' I showed him the photograph I had ready. This was my alternative cover story. It helps to have more than one.

The guard hesitated. He was suddenly less certain that I had no right to be there. He glanced over at the booth. The second guard, his superior, stepped out. He forced a smile. 'Let's take a look.'

I showed him the photograph. 'Number twelve, it says in the photograph,' I said, 'but I heard that they renumbered the houses some years ago, so I'm a little confused.'

He studied the photograph. 'No, that's number twelve all right. It's a few houses down on the left-hand side,' he said, pointing downhill. 'Mind you, they've probably made a few alterations since that was taken.'

'That must be why I didn't recognise it. I haven't been there in years.' In the photograph there were many shrubs and trees growing around the house. Now almost all of the mansions had had their shrubs trimmed back, to afford no hiding places to protestors or terrorists. 'I would love a photograph, but it says photography is forbidden.'

'No photography, sorry. That's the rules.'
'Even if you turn a blind eye?'
'No photographs.'

While we had been talking I had kept my iPad lens trained on the Chancery. I also ensured that I remained partially screened by the two guards at all times. Any cameras trained onto the street would not be able to identify me. The two armed police guarding the Russian embassy strolled over.

'Very well then, I shan't. I don't want to go causing you any trouble.'

I shuffled off, and the policemen followed me for a few paces, helpfully providing a screen between me and the Chancery building. I had no intention of letting Igor know I had traced him back here. Not yet, anyway.

I returned the way I came, walked back to Rassells Nursery and resisted the idea of browsing for salvias for my garden. I got back in my car and drove up Kensington Church Street to Pembridge Square where I paid for parking on the Kensington side (cheaper than the east side, which is in Westminster) and walked through Ossington Street to Notting Hill Gate. I headed to the Café Diana, dedicated to the memory of Princess Diana. In her lifetime it had been a tribute, its walls lined with photographs of her at charitable events and magazine covers. After her death it had become a shrine. I knew it well.

I strode past the red banquettes and was lucky enough to find the small round window table vacant. From where I sat I had an excellent view of the north gate to Kensington Palace Gardens. There was no chance that the security guards would spot me. The facade of cream plastered brick that divided the 'in' and 'out' gates concealed the guard post. While I had no clear view of the guards, they had no view of me either.

A young Arab woman brought me the menu and without thinking I ordered the first item: the full English breakfast with a cappuccino. As she went off to fetch it, I made a mental note of my dining companions: two Lebanese couples who were sharing dishes of kofte and moutabal. I thought of changing my order, but then the waitress would have remembered me. There were at least three other people who looked like writers sitting alone at tables, pounding the keys of their laptops and then staring into space for long intervals, carefully considering their next *mot juste*.

I kept my eyes fixed on the gate. As my coffee was brought to me I noticed one set of guards replaced by another. The guards who had stopped me thirty minutes earlier strolled off towards the Euro Car Park nearby. They gave no sign of having seen me. I was certain they had not.

My breakfast, when it arrived, was adequate. The great British sausage is like the Holy Grail: many are convinced of its existence, but it remains elusive, its resting place unknown. I had been up since half past five in the morning and hunger overruled my taste buds.

I ate slowly and kept my gaze on the activities across the road. Several cars with diplomatic number plates came and left, as did a few delivery vans – Amazon Prime being the most popular – while pedestrians and cyclists were allowed through without question.

A large white truck pulled up outside the café and blocked my view. The passenger dashed out, disappeared into a shop, returned a couple of minutes later, got back into the cab and, putting his feet up on the dashboard, proceeded to roll up a cigarette. I presumed his only haste had been to have a pee. I shifted my seat to get a better view of the exit gate.

Around seven minutes later the passenger and driver of

the white truck got out, went round to the back and unloaded two boxes of fruit which they carried into the shop. A minute or two later they left the premises, each carrying a styrofoam cup of coffee. The driver, cup in one hand, mobile phone in the other, started up the truck and drove off slowly.

At that very moment a maroon Rolls-Royce Phantom with smoked glass windows and diplomatic number plates eased out through the exit gate. As it pulled onto Bayswater Road and turned east, pointing towards Marble Arch, I could make out a tall figure in the back, silhouetted by a beam of sunlight. I could see nothing more. Then fortune favoured me. The white truck that had been blocking my view stalled, and the Phantom was forced to stop. The front passenger window rolled down and a hand tipped the ash from a cigarette. The window rolled back up again, but in that instant I had recognised the man inside. Riding shotgun beside the chauffeur was Igor.

22

'A DIPLOMATIC NUMBER PLATE IS harder to trace, for obvious reasons.' This was Ambrose, speaking to me on a secure line.

'You don't want to help me?'

'Not so much don't want to, my dear, it's really a matter of going through the right channels.'

'It comes down to the same thing. You won't help.'

'I didn't say that. But we don't want to go stirring up unwanted attention.'

I took a deep breath. 'I think the murder of an elderly woman in a quiet Sussex village has already garnered attention, unwanted or not.'

'I meant unwanted attention for *you*. No point stirring up a wasp's nest. We all would end up none the wiser.'

'Whom do you mean by "We all"?'

'Just a figure of speech. Why don't you leave the matter with me and let's see what happens?' The line went dead.

Leaving the matter with Ambrose bothered me. I have a need to take charge, to manage every aspect of what I can control in life. It comes from having had so little control during my past missions. Knowing I might have to wait days for an answer made me tense and my throat dry up.

Then I realised I already had the answer. Or part of it at

least. I went down to the cellar, extracted an old file and rifled through it for my old surveillance notes. Of course I should not have been holding any of this material. It wasn't top secret, and most of it was not even classified, but everything should have been returned to the service on the day of my retirement.

I found the document. It was a list of country codes on diplomatic vehicle registration plates in London. I ran my finger down it. The first three numbers of the Rolls-Royce's registration had been 251. Numbers 248–252 were listed as Russian (somewhat confusingly placed 'alphabetically' between South Africa and Spain, with the explanation that these numbers had been allocated, originally, to the Soviet Union). That, at least, made things clear. Igor was working with the Russians. Did that make him a Russian agent? Almost certainly. But whereas in my day this would have been a foregone conclusion, in recent years the KGB (or FBS as it was now called) was known to freelance itself to any number of oligarchs who were associated with the Kremlin but who kept themselves at arm's length, in order to avoid the sanctions endured by members of the Russian Federation.

This was all guesswork. Intelligent guesswork, if you will. My list, of course, was out of date and it occurred to me that perhaps the car had belonged to an old satellite state of the Soviet Union – Belarus, perhaps, or Estonia. Suddenly the possibilities seemed too much, too challenging. I felt myself slump. If Ambrose was not willing to help, which he clearly was not, then who? Well, dear old Patrick Dallaway of course. Maybe not as well-connected as he had been in the days when we worked together, but he still had useful contacts, or so he claimed. I phoned him, told him what I wanted and he promised that he would get back to me. 'Via

WhatsApp, if that's all right with you? Encrypted, at least for the foreseeable future.'

I resisted the temptation to get into bed for just a few minutes – I knew I might fall asleep and lose precious hours – and instead went out the front of the house, locked the door and took a brisk walk round the village to clear my head and think.

Ours is a delightful village, and the two streets running parallel either side of the high street are made up of traditional cottages. We won the 'best kept village in Sussex' award three years in a row. Until, that is, one particular resident neglected her window boxes, once rich in pelargoniums and nasturtiums, and left them to rot. Well, I was away for a year on forced secondment, so I was not entirely to blame.

As I set off west I heard the honking of geese. Overhead a flock flew in V formation. They moved daily from ponds in the south to the lake on a private estate to the north and back again at night.

I studied the homes nearest mine. Six weeks earlier the first cottage had been draped with panicles of purple wisteria. Now young leaves robed the red-brick walls, threatening to block the light through the top windows. In a month or so they would have to be pruned.

The next house was topped with thick thatch, rare to find in Sussex. Sourcing the reeds is hard when there are few reed beds around. Our village, however, is famous for its thatched houses, so home owners gang together to order the reeds in bulk and import a thatcher from Norfolk. The work is expensive and usually lasts no more than thirty years before it needs replacing, which is why I am glad to have a tiled roof that will last out my days.

As I walked, I kept my eyes fixed on the roofs of the houses. It was a way to avoid neighbours and pointless conversation. The sun hit my upturned face and for a moment I was blinded as I stepped forward and slipped on a green pile of goose shit, my right foot skidding out from under me. I fell flat on my back, stunned and winded.

It took me a few moments to get my breath back and, as I did so, I heard a door slam and the clatter of running feet.

'Dear lady, dear lady!' It was Percy, who had run from one of the nearby houses. 'Can you move? God forbid you've broken anything!'

'Apart from my pride, you mean?' I touched the back of my head. I had had the presence of mind to curl my neck forward as I fell. That had prevented concussion, but I would have a big lump on my head later. I checked my legs and twisted my body, rocking it forward a couple of times. 'Nothing broken.'

'Do let me help you up.' He took my hand and hauled, and when that didn't work he came round behind me, put his hands under my armpits and lifted.

'That's the ticket. Take your time.'

I stood up, swaying slightly, and checked my hands and arms. I had given my right elbow an almighty crack and I could feel it stiffening up, but I flexed my arm, gave it a shake and turned to my rescuer.

'Keeping an eye on me, Percy?'

He didn't blink, or blush. 'The writer's weakness, I'm sorry to say. Staring out the window, hoping for inspiration. Watching the world go by.'

'Or falling on its bony arse.'

'We all do that, sooner or later.'

I could not decide if Percy was a threat or not. Was it just coincidence that he'd seen me fall, or was he keeping me under observation? Perhaps working with Fashion-Plate and Igor?

'You didn't tell me you were a writer.'

'We all have our vices. Some of us manage to hide them better than others.'

I was ready to walk on, but Percy invited me to come home with him for tea.

'I would love to, Percy, but I'm expecting visitors,' I lied. 'I don't want to keep them waiting.'

'I won't let you walk home alone. You've had a nasty knock.' He took my arm – the one I hadn't bashed – and we strolled back towards my house. His grip was tight. A little too tight for comfort.

'I know I can seem a bit… well, pushy at times,' Percy said, 'but I don't think I'd be wrong in saying that we both rather enjoyed ourselves the other day in the tea room.'

'Not just us. The whole room was entertained. Who was that woman?'

'My lips are sealed. Oh look, your guests are waiting for you.'

Standing in my porch were two men in suits. The younger one noticed me first and said something to the older man, who turned to watch us approach through the gate and up the path.

'May I help you gentlemen?'

'Felicity Jardine?' the older man asked.

'Yes.'

'Mrs Jardine, I am here following information received to arrest you on suspicion of the murder of Phyllis Price. You do not have to say anything, but it may harm your defence if you do not mention, when questioned, something which you later rely on in court.'

I turned to Percy, but he was no longer by my side. It was as if he had simply melted away.

23

Bonn, November–December 1976

I HEARD NOTHING FROM MICHAEL Callan for three days. In this time Heidi, true to her man-eating nature, had selected her rising politician and cut him off from the herd with no chance of escape. It was only a matter of time before the nuptials were announced. Meanwhile Elsa, seldom a bundle of sunshine at the best of times, had become more morose than ever. Her fiancé, as she called Callan, had, she believed, left Bonn and would not be back for two weeks. I did not disillusion her. On the third day Callan and I met up again, but only for a drink in a quiet bar at the edge of town. He told me that the details of his contract had been agreed, a few small changes made, and that it would finally be signed by the Deputy Chancellor the following Monday.

He showed me another photograph of 'his boat'. The one he had shown me before could have been taken from any beach. This new one showed him aboard the boat, with 'friend and servant' Delroy at the tiller. As proof that the yacht was truly his, it might have been more convincing if the yacht had not been moored alongside a quay. As it was tied up there would have been no need to operate the tiller. Callan and Delroy could have snuck aboard, taken a few photographs, and been gone before the true owners returned.

'I do miss sailing in it.' He had slipped up. On our previous meeting he had been careful to call his yacht 'she'. Calling such a beautiful boat 'it' revealed he was no true yachtsman.

He showed me photographs of himself in Barbados, including one of him at a bar on the beach with an empty seat beside him. 'I think of you sitting there beside me some day. Perhaps a day not so very far away.'

I wondered how he could seriously think such a rushed, unsubtle seduction could work. But I had seen how successful he had been with Elsa and knew he had several other victims lined up. If he failed with one he would most probably move on to another until he got what he wanted.

I thought of Elsa and how she might have looked when he spun her his lies: starry-eyes, cheeks flushed, mouth hanging open – perhaps a slight, unconscious drool. But I am not made that way. I glanced at my watch and picked up my handbag, as if I had a more pressing appointment. He asked me to meet him again on the Saturday afternoon, and this time I agreed.

'Are you going to sleep with him?' Patrick had a virgin's salacious interest in all matters relating to sex, though I felt confident he was no virgin.

'If I have to.'

'I don't think you'll find it too much of a sacrifice.'

I almost slapped him.

The following Saturday afternoon Callan took me to bed in the Adler hotel in Bad Godesberg, close to the Maternus restaurant. It was inevitable and I had acknowledged it as part of my mission, but as the date and time came closer I found myself quivering with nervous anticipation. I had been to bed with men before, of course, with varied results. I had, after all, come of age during the sexual revolution of the swinging sixties. For some reason – call me contrary – I found I gained greater sexual satisfaction with unattractive, somewhat boorish men. Perhaps it was in the secure knowledge that I would form no long-term attachment that I found myself truly able to let myself go. The better looking, more amiable young men held little attraction for me, animal or otherwise. However, the thought of Callan, with his superb physique and his magnetic, mesmerising eyes stirred a curiosity and desire in me that I had never experienced before.

Before leaving home I made an effort with my make-up and clothes. I wore my best dark grey skirt – I had three, all of similar slim-cut design. Above this I wore a white silk blouse and over it a dove grey cashmere cardigan. As Callan, at six foot two inches, was substantially taller than me, I splashed out on an extravagant pair of black stiletto heels before remembering that he was supposed to be seducing me, not I him. I still have the stilettos, hardly worn, in the back of my wardrobe somewhere.

When I got to the hotel I made my way, unannounced, up to the room he had booked. I knocked on the door, he opened it, I stepped forward and stupidly stumbled in those bloody stilettos. Any impression I wished to convey of myself as a sophisticated woman of the world went straight out the window, but it helped break the ice. Callan stepped forward with the easy grace of an athlete and, literally, swept me off my feet. I found myself in his strong arms as he kissed me gently on the lips. I felt an unfamiliar, exhilarating shiver run through my body.

He had a bottle of Dom Perignon on ice. We finished two glasses each before he produced a Hermès *carré* scarf, which he presented with a flourish. I was about to accept it when he whipped it away again.

'I want you to do me a favour first.'

'A favour?'

Holding opposite corners of the large square scarf he whipped it around itself so that it formed a long, thick length of silk. 'Turn around.'

I hesitated. Was he going to strangle me with it? I had told Patrick where I was going and if I was rumbled and discovered dead in a ditch, he should have enough proof to convict Callan. I obliged and turned my back to him, uncertain what to expect.

I felt Callan move closer and his warm breath on the back of my neck. As I stiffened he raised his hands over my head and brought the scarf down in front of my face.

'Shut your eyes.'

I did as I was told. He tied the scarf tight. I could see nothing. He turned me around to face him. Gently he removed my cardigan. It had eight buttons but he undid them as quickly as if it had been fastened with a zip. As he eased me out of it I concentrated on his confident touch, the raw energy emanating from his body, and inhaled his faint musky odour as it enveloped me.

My skirt dropped around my ankles. I had not even felt his hands on its buttons. He gently raised each of my feet in turn and slipped off those damned uncomfortable stilettos. He must have picked up my skirt as well, for it was no longer on the floor.

I had decided to wear a black lace suspender belt to hold up my black stockings. He picked me up in his powerful arms and laid me on freshly laundered sheets – the top sheet and coverlet had been thrown back – unclipped my stockings and slipped them off my long slim legs. He slipped his hands firmly under my body and turned me over so that I lay face down, ready for whatever he wanted to do to me.

He could have ended my life so easily there and then but, whether it was the effect of his enhanced pheromones or my own curious desire, I no longer seemed to care.

The scent of lavender wafted over me. Warm oil dripped between my shoulder blades. His practised hands had my bra undone in an instant. I arched myself up off the sheets and the bra was slipped from under me. I relaxed back, legs slightly apart, feet pointed downwards.

I felt his hands – warm and powerful – press down where the oil had dripped and then spread out left and right, rubbing the scented oil into my skin until it covered my back all the way down to my panty line. His fingers brushed up and down my sides, setting off an exhilarating shiver deep within me.

His hands returned to my shoulders, massaging, caressing, relaxing them. They moved up to my neck. It was wonderful. His hands and fingers teased my tense muscles, working the oil up into the base of my hairline, kneading out the knots and caressing my skin until I truly relaxed and gave myself over to him.

Then his hands began to travel all the way down my spine, setting off a tingle like a mild electric shock. I inhaled sharply and held my breath.

'Breathe,' he said.

I let go of my breath, exhaling deeply before taking another.

Callan raised each of my arms in turn, shook them until they went limp, then ran his fingers all the way down them, stroking my well-tuned muscles. He concentrated on my hands, rubbing in fresh oil and attending to every finger joint in turn. My arms felt completely relaxed. As for the rest of my body, it was already jangling with anticipation.

Then he started on my legs. He ran his fingers down my left thigh, following the natural lines of my muscles, stroking them with increasingly powerful movements. He took my calf, kneading it until it, too, relaxed, then he moved on down.

I detest anyone touching my feet. My soles are ticklish and sensitive. But when Callan took hold of my left foot in his tight grip and manipulated it with strong, twisting motions before moving down to my toes and teasing each one in turn, I almost cried out with pleasure.

Then he started on my other leg, nipping and pinching my thigh until the pain and joy was almost too much to bear. He caressed my leg then took me by surprise by moving fast down to my other foot and working his magic down there.

Then he stopped. Was it over? Was that it?

His hand touched my back lightly, as if to reassure me that more was to come, as he moved around the bed. He leaned over me and I felt his hot breath as he ran his tongue over my neck and licked around and inside my ears, each in turn.

He returned to my back. He rubbed more warm oil into my shoulders and over my shoulder blades. His fingers ran down my spine, isolating each vertebra in turn, easing them apart, all the way down to my sacrum. His hands slipped around my hips, raised them and then my underpants were being delicately eased off down my legs.

Callan rubbed oil into my buttocks and massaged them in turn, each sweep taking his fingers closer to my warm, wet centre. Each time he brushed the inside of my leg a small gasp of pleasure escaped me. I felt I was ready for him.

Gently he spread my legs further apart. He slipped his oiled hand down between my legs, stopping just short of where I wished him to reach.

I could not control the raging hormones rampaging through my long-neglected body. I needed him so badly. *Come on*, I begged him silently, *do it, enter me.*

Then, as if he knew the exact moment when I could bear it no longer, he slipped a hand under my hips and eased me over onto my back.

He started on my breasts, his fingers teasing my nipples into erect hardness. He stroked them a long while and then withdrew, brushed his fingers lightly over them and again withdrew, and each time I gasped with a need deeper than any I had ever experienced before.

As my breaths came shorter and faster he ran his fingers lightly down my chest, down my belly and began to massage the inside of my thighs. I moaned and raised my pelvis to focus his attention, but he took his time, edging closer and closer to my centre of pleasure with each slow and studied movement.

At last he obliged me. One hand moved onto my wet lips, stroking them gently apart. The fingers of one hand slipped inside me. The fingers on his other hand gently circled my clitoris, bringing me to the very edge of orgasm. My breaths came faster and faster and I thrust my hips upwards, against his rhythm, seeking the moment of my blessed release.

He removed his hands. I gasped. Was he going to delay my climax forever?

Just when I felt I could bear it no longer, he again inserted his strong fingers and immediately withdrew them. In my blindfolded state I could not see what he was doing, but his fingers now stroked me so gently I could scarcely feel them. The effect was of an exquisite, prolonged pleasure which I never wanted to end. It was a technique I have tried to replicate many times since, but have never managed again successfully, either alone or with partners.

I reached out for him and found that he, too, was naked. I grasped his erection, tugging it towards me with a desperate longing. My need could only be satisfied one way.

I felt his body move over me, barely weighing on me but alerting every sensitised nerve ending when it did. Then he was inside me, filling my need, moving his hips gently, then a little faster and then with powerful, bestial thrusts. At last, this was it. But he was a master of his art. By stopping and varying his strokes he managed to keep me from coming for what seemed an eternity. And suddenly I was beyond the point of no return. My belly experienced an involuntary series of spasms and a vast surge of pleasure came over me, exploding from my groin and every part of my being, as if my brain and body were dissolving together.

I screamed out, overtaken by an animalistic passion I had never experienced before or, regrettably, since. He clamped the palm of his hand over my mouth, silencing me.

'We don't want the other guests to think I'm killing you,' he whispered, which was funny, as I had half suspected that to be his intention.

He stayed where he was, deep inside me. He was still hard as a rock. After a while he started again. I felt so sensitive that I could not bear even the slightest friction in my groin. I moaned with pain, but he was careful, moving ever so subtly and then increasing the depths of his thrusts until I was responsive again.

This time he did not delay my climax for long. We both came together in an ecstasy of shuddering orgasm… and I suddenly realised that he had won. I wanted him, and I wanted him for ever.

In that moment of exultation I whipped off my blindfold, expecting to find his warm green eyes smiling. Instead his eyes were hard and dead as flint. I had caught him without the mask. In an instant it was back, the smile in place, the eyes radiant and loving. He raised himself off me.

'The shower's all yours.'

He had laid a towel on the bedside drawers. I took it and walked – no, staggered, I was still quivering with ecstasy from head to toe – to the bathroom and stepped into the shower. A minute or so later he joined me, massaging me all over with the hotel's scented liquid soap.

We parted with a remarkably chaste kiss. I kept the Hermès *carré* scarf – it's the one I used to cover baby Alice – and the concierge ordered me a taxi. As it took me home I checked my handbag. I had left its clasp partially closed. Now the clasp was firmly shut. I could find nothing missing or out of place, but I knew Callan had given it a thorough search before he joined me in the shower.

24

'I want to know all the details,' said Patrick, when I told him what had happened. 'He's got big hands and feet. What about his other extremities?'

'You can be very vulgar for someone who has enjoyed the privilege of an expensive private education.'

'*Enjoyed*,' Patrick snapped, 'is not how I remember my time in that place!'

The expense of Patrick's private education had nearly ruined his father so he was lucky, as we all were in those days, to be supported with a grant to go up to Cambridge, where, after being approached by the secret service and having accepted their offer, he got a disappointing 2.2. 'Too many distractions,' was all he would say about that.

Callan called me on the Monday evening. He was distraught. His contract had not been signed. He asked to meet me in the Baumschulwäldchen – the park where Patrick and I usually met up.

Callan kissed me warmly. He let me tease out his concerns. He put on a very good act, pretending he did not want to burden me with his bad news, then letting it all spill out in a torrent. At the very last moment a competitor had put in a lower estimate for a dozen bridges and he suspected that someone in the ministry was getting a backhander. Was there any way I could help him? If he lost this deal he would lose his boat and his house, both heavily mortgaged, and have no chance of saving them.

I played the naive innocent. How could I help? I asked. I was on a meagre government wage and had no savings to speak of.

'Darling, I wouldn't take your money even if you were loaded. I just need to know what kind of a proposal my competition has made. If it's close to ours I can go back with a counter-offer that will blow them out of the water.'

I chewed my lip, as if torn between my heart and my loyalty to the state.

'In the long run, what we are talking about is saving the state money. It's what they call a win-win situation.'

'I only have limited access to contracts, but… ' and I let myself choke on the words, 'let me see what I can do.'

In fact it was a simple matter to find some excuse to go down to the filing department and search through recent government contracts. I found what Callan wanted in a matter of minutes, took it to the Xerox machine and made a copy. I put the original contract back right under the eyes of the filing clerks, who were immersed in their own gossip, and headed back to my desk with the copy.

Elsa was weeping silently over her work. She wore headphones as she typed dictation, so did not hear me approach. I tapped her gently and she jumped, startled. She removed her headphones and her puffy eyes, partly masked by her glasses (she wore contact lenses when dating Callan) were red raw. She asked if I could meet her that evening, but I had to turn her down. I would be meeting her lover to hand over the photocopies.

Callan and I met at the Beethovenplatz end of the

Baumschulwäldchen park. We sat on the bench and I handed over the photocopies. In an appalling show of recklessness he held them up and shone a flashlight over them.

'This is wonderful. I'm so grateful.' He hugged me and kissed me passionately, and for a moment I thought he was going to make love to me there and then on that hard bench. But he jumped up and said he had to telex the pages to head office and that I had ensured our future happiness together.

*

Finding myself at a loose end, I went round to Elsa's little studio flat. She was in a state of despair. Her fiancé had not phoned in over a week and she was desperately worried that something serious had happened to him. Callan had told her he was in the oil business and had contracts to work in both Israel and Egypt, travelling on two passports so that entry and exit stamps from one country would not set alarm bells ringing in the other. It had not been long since the Yom Kippur war in which Israel had driven back the Arab coalition, led by Egypt and Syria, and the world had seen oil prices spiralling out of control. Elsa was convinced that Callan had been arrested by one side or the other and was now languishing in some filthy prison being gnawed by rats. I did my best to reassure her and let her rest her head on my shoulder while deep sobs wracked her bosom. Sometimes keeping one's own counsel can be painful.

Two days later – it was now early December – the newspapers carried an account of the bridge contract. It had been awarded to the German company which had underbid Callan's. I expected him to be sorely disappointed, so when we met again I told him that I adored him and that I would continue doing so even if he lost his boat and his house.

'Darling, darling,' he said to calm me. 'We won the contract.'

'No, that's impossible, you didn't.'

'When you showed me their bid I cabled my bosses and they contacted their competition. The two companies came to an agreement: the contract for the bridges will be a joint venture. Obviously my commission will only be half what I had hoped, but at least I can keep the boat and the house, and that's all down to you. What you have done means so much to me. I just won't be able to get the new house, not without another healthy commission. But there's a way you can help me do that too.'

'How? The bridge contract is over. There's nothing else I can do.'

'The company we are partnering with is owned by a large arms manufacturer. This is an area I have absolutely no knowledge about. Bridges are my expertise.' He hesitated a moment. 'I know this is a terrible imposition, but if you could just do one more thing for me, I will never ask you to do anything like this ever again.'

'What is "this thing"?'

He turned away, as if too embarrassed to ask. 'No, I can't ask it of you. It could get you into trouble, and if that were to happen, my dearest darling, I could not bear it.' He shook his head, dismissing the whole idea. 'No, I can't ask you. It would be unfair. And immoral.'

He took me to dinner and refused to discuss the matter any further. Afterwards, we had sex. This time his technique was quite different. He was soon thrusting away at me with powerful rhythmic strokes. There can be such a thing as too much extended foreplay. Sometimes all you need is a good hard fuck.

I marvelled at his ability to delay his ejaculation, which only came after I had orgasmed twice. I refused his offer of a lift home. He waited with me until a taxi came. As it pulled up outside I snuggled up to him, looked up into his lying green eyes and asked, softly, 'What exactly do you want me to do?'

25

West Sussex, May 2019

If you ever find yourself locked up in a police cell, you should know you are in for a long wait. It's like going to Accident and Emergency: they're in no hurry to see you. So I knew exactly what to ask for when they led me to the cell and removed my handcuffs. 'I'm not going in there without something to read.'

'What?' asked the confused young constable.

'Anything. A novel, a romance, a "how to" book. Reading matter. Something to occupy my mind through the numbing hours of boredom while you sit at your desk and play solitaire on your computer.'

'Most people want their phone call. You are allowed one.'

'All in good time. When I've thought of someone I want to call, I shall let you know.'

'What about your lawyer?'

'I do not have a lawyer at present but when I need one, as I said, I shall let you know. Now, a book, please?'

'Step inside.'

'Not until I have my book. I know you keep a small library of literary trash somewhere.'

The constable sighed and sloped off down the corridor, while my arresting officer waited. I flashed him a smile and he looked away. A few more moments passed and I sensed he felt removing my handcuffs at this stage had been a bad move.

The young constable reappeared with three books in his hands. 'I've got this one, a detective thriller—'

'I'll take it.' I grabbed the book and stepped inside the cell. I needed something to distract my mind while I considered whom best to call. If I took the decision too hastily, I might come to regret it.

The door slammed behind me. The constable peered at me through the observation hole, then shut that too. I was alone.

I was glad. I liked to be alone. It gave me time to think. Someone had set me up for the murder. But how? Had they planted false evidence in my home while I was out? I hadn't checked the video recordings since late last night. If someone had planted vital evidence it would be hard to explain it away. But whom should I call? The obvious person was Ambrose, but he would not appreciate becoming involved, and it was better to keep him up my sleeve. That decision could wait. I sat on the hard bench and started in on the thriller.

I had only got to page thirty – two murders down, both unsolved, though I thought I had already worked out who the murderer was – when the observation hole opened, the constable peered in and, having assured himself I was neither hanging from the window bars nor poised to attack him, swung open the door.

'Your solicitor,' he announced, and stepped aside for a bulky man wearing a pin-striped suit and carrying a briefcase. It took me a second to recognise him. It was the man I had nicknamed 'Fashion-Plate', the man who had tried to pass himself off as Sir Gerald Best-Worthington, Baronet, with an address in Rutland Gate, Knightsbridge. It had been easy to check out. It was as phoney as the man himself. He wore what looked like a regimental tie, though I could not immediately identify it. A blue polka dot silk handkerchief flopped from the breast pocket of his jacket and on his lapel was a small blue badge featuring a compass and set square over a pair of quills. The door slammed behind him, the observation hole shut and I could hear the constable's footsteps retreating along the corridor.

'What are you doing here? I didn't ask for you.'

'No, of course you didn't.' He eased his bulk onto the bench beside me, forcing me to bunch up against the wall.

'You are a Freemason, I see.'

He tapped the badge on his lapel. 'This? Got it from a junk shop. A guaranteed free pass into any police station.'

'So you're not my court-appointed solicitor?' I asked with as much sarcasm as I could muster.

'Never told the desk sergeant I was. But the suit and the briefcase imply it. Simply said I was here to see you and they let me in, no questions asked.'

'Have you come to get me out of here?'

'Oh no, nothing like that.'

'What then?'

'You've been seen. In Kensington Palace Gardens. And in Café Diana. We have a camera there.'

I stared at him. 'What do you want?'

'What we've always wanted. The child.'

'I don't have your child.'

'I wish I could believe that. We did believe it, in fact, until you came looking for us. Rather gave yourself away there.'

I cursed myself. How could I have been so stupid? These people were professionals. As I had been, once. Now I had blown my cover and they could plant – and perhaps already had planted – any evidence they wished to implicate me in Phyllis Price's death.

'I'm often up in town, and I meet friends in Notting Hill. Café Diana is one of our regular haunts.'

'You were quite obviously alone. And, as far as we can ascertain, you have no friends. I would go as far as to say you are quite unpopular in your village. Nobody is going to miss you one little bit.'

If this last jibe was supposed to get me talking, it was never going to work. I knew only too well that what he said was true. That was the way I liked it. I was the strange old woman without family or friends who minded her own business. The village should be grateful I was not one of those nosey people complaining every time anyone wanted to install a dormer window in their home or dig out a basement. Not that they would. Our village is in a conservation area and most of the houses had not been altered, on the outside at least, for three or four hundred years. Best-Worthington's comments were no more than water off an old duck's back.

He waited for his words to have their impact. As far as I was concerned he could wait all day and all night.

'No comment? About the child?'

'I have no idea what you are talking about.'

'The police are searching your home as we speak. They will find evidence that implicates you in a murder.'

Just as I thought. No big surprise. I would have done the same in their place.

'Then you've already done your worst. It's always a mistake to play your best card first.'

'I have another card to play.'

'I doubt it.'

A frown of irritation crossed his face. He clenched his fist. He had expected me to crumble by now.

'We have a witness who can explain the evidence away quite satisfactorily... if you comply.'

I said nothing.

'Come on, we do not have much time.'

'Oh, I think I do. I've been in worse places than this, and I think I could adapt to prison life quite well.'

There had been a time, when I was at convent school, when I had considered becoming a nun. I might have relished the monastic life. Though possibly not the kneeling. Nor the praying. But the solitude... I could have handled that.

'If you want me to stop this, I can,' he hissed.

I smiled the most beatific smile I could manage, a smile that would have made the nuns proud. I saw I was annoying him. He opened his fist, raised his arm and swung it round to slap me.

He had made the mistake of letting his guard down. Before his hand could strike I had stiffened my fingers and rammed them hard into his throat. His slap went wide and he collapsed to the floor, clawing at his throat, struggling to breathe, his eyes popping in fear as he wondered if I had somehow managed to snap his neck. I hadn't of course. I had done him no serious damage.

It was at that moment that the door opened. The young constable hesitated at the sight of Best-Worthington clawing at his throat.

'What's the matter with him?'

'I think a grape went down the wrong way.'

Best-Worthington had gone puce in the face.

'I know how to do Heimlich's manoeuvre,' the constable offered.

'I wouldn't bother. He'll calm down in a moment.'

'I'm supposed to bring you into the interview room for questioning.'

'I'll come quietly. No need for handcuffs.' I stood up and approached him.

'What about your lawyer?' He looked down at Best-Worthington, gagging on the concrete floor.

'I really don't think he's up to it. Poor dear wants to go home.'

Best-Worthington scrambled up with difficulty. He seemed unsure whether he could speak or not. He waved the constable away. 'I've got to get back… ' he croaked, 'to my office.' He swept up his briefcase and hurried out. 'I'll see myself out.'

He had forgotten where he was. He marched five paces along the corridor and found himself blocked by a steel-barred gate.

'Not before I'm ready for you, mate,' said the constable cheerfully. He led me down the corridor in the opposite direction and threw open a door. The plainclothes officer who had arrested me was sitting behind a desk. He gestured for me to sit down and turned on a machine to record our conversation. I looked up and saw a camera recording my every move.

'I am Detective Inspector Morris and I am questioning Felicity Jardine in regard to the recent death of her neighbour, Phyllis Price.'

I said nothing.

'Do you wish to have your solicitor present?'

'I have no solicitor.'

'Oh. I was informed that one had visited you in your cell.'

'He's incompetent. I've dismissed him.'

'You really should have a lawyer present, for your own good.'

'I would prefer a pen and paper.'

He handed me a pencil and paper. I wrote down a few words, stopped and looked up at him.

'What is the date and time?'

He checked his digital watch.

'May the fourteenth, and it is three thirty-five in the afternoon.'

I wrote a few more words, signed and dated the page and pushed it back towards him. He picked it up and read what I had written.

'"My name is Felicity Jardine. I was arrested today but wish to state that I am innocent of any crime and have no desire to say anything except in the presence of a lawyer chosen by myself. Up until such time I reserve my right to remain silent." And you've signed and dated it.'

I nodded and folded my arms in confirmation that I was finished.

'Do you have anything at all to say?'

'Please stop hitting me.'

He leant forward and stopped the recording.

'I wasn't hitting you.'

'No, but think how it will sound when you have to read it out in court.'

He sighed. 'I suggest you get yourself a lawyer before our next session.'

I was led back to my cell and settled down for a long wait. It turned out I didn't need to. I had only been back in the cell twenty minutes or so – I couldn't be exactly sure as they had taken my watch, so I would have no idea how long I had been incarcerated, and my shoelaces, in case I had a sudden desire to kill myself. There would have been nothing sudden about it at all. What was sudden was the arrival of the constable together with Detective Inspector Morris. The door swung open and Morris stepped inside.

'You've been bailed. You're free to go.'

26

I found Percy waiting for me at the sergeant's desk.
'Sorry it took me so long, dear lady,' he said, as he watched me collect my scant belongings from the desk sergeant. 'But persuading the Chief Constable that he has no need to hold an innocent citizen whom he has no grounds, or indeed need, to hold can take a little time. Especially when he's in the middle of executing a difficult putt on the golf course.'

Percy seemed to be taking my side in all of this, but how could I be certain? I could not afford to let my guard down.

I said nothing while the desk sergeant produced a large brown envelope containing my belongings and demanded I check them. He pointedly got me to sign the receipt in triplicate. It was a process designed to humiliate; to suggest 'you got lucky this time, but don't think we won't be keeping our eyes on you'.

It was the kind of thing the nuns used to do at school. Any mistakes in Bible class and you would be hauled brutally from your desk and forced to kneel before Mother Superior. After a half hour of kneeling before her peers the errant pupil would be dismissed. The humiliation was such that the child would be wracked with bitter sobs all through the next class, which would occasion further punishment.

All very Christian, I suppose. At least whatever life threw at us later never seemed quite so awful. I suppose this was its purpose: my mild discomfort and humiliation before Percy counted for little.

'You must at least allow me to escort you home. I've had to delay the pleasure by at least' – he checked his watch – 'four hours, and I shall brook no refusal. Now if you will just avail yourself of my arm, we may proceed.' He stuck out his arm, crooked his elbow and I took it.

He led me to his car, a well-polished Jaguar XJR in British racing green. He held open the passenger door and helped me in. I struggled a bit with the seat belt. My bruised elbow had stiffened up and was paining me.

'Permit me,' he said, reaching round me and securing the belt. I caught a faint whiff of his Dunhill fragrance for men, the same Dennis had worn when he had taken me out for a special treat – and then he shut the door with a gentle click. He got into the driver's seat and started up his car. 'I think it's best we take the extra circuitous route.' He put the car in drive and edged forward. 'I have information of a particular nature to impart.'

Percy enjoyed this arch, old-fashioned way of speaking, like some prep-school master from the 1950s – which was probably where he had picked it up. As we left town and headed out into the countryside he began. 'We are somewhat fortunate that the overwhelming percentage of our neighbours are long-term subscribers to the snoopers club.' He glanced over at me, to check I understood his meaning. 'Allow me to elucidate. Almost all of them have some form of CCTV installed in their homes, many in their doorbells. These are recorded digitally and retained on hard drives for around thirty days.'

'Go on.' We were in the middle of the countryside, fields rising to downland on either side of the road. On the south side the fields were occupied by cattle. On the north were sheep. Percy checked left and right, as if to confirm he was not surrounded by eavesdroppers. He leant in close to me. 'I prevailed upon your neighbours to download those recordings for me.'

'And?' He had my full attention.

'A brief perusal of the material would seem to indicate that you went into your house around sunset the evening prior to the murder and did not emerge until the following morning. Further scrutiny would indicate that you showed no untoward signs of stress. In fact, I believe a jury would say you looked nothing like a murderer.'

I had been trained by years of hard experience to give that impression, even when I had been obliged to kill, but I was not about to spoil his narrative. 'And what about Phyllis Price's house?'

'Aha, there we have a very sinister story. Around midnight on the night in question a noxious black fluid was sprayed onto the lenses of three doorbell cameras by an unseen hand. And at about the same time the cameras of houses with more sophisticated apparatus mysteriously stopped functioning. It seems the external wires had been cut, again by hands unseen.'

'A bit of a giveaway.'

'It's exasperating, I know, but people spend vast sums on technical equipment and seldom check that they are working. As long as there's heating in the house, food in the fridge and fuel in the car, they're happy.'

'There's one flaw in your thesis. I have a back door. I could easily have slipped out, murdered Mrs Price and been back indoors rehearsing my "nothing like a murderer" look all night.'

'The Chief Constable has accepted the evidence. Why kick sleeping dogs in the balls, if I may express myself somewhat crudely? There may be other hurdles to overcome, so let us give praise and thank our blessings. *Et alii desperant.*'

'Let others despair,' I translated.

'Very good. The benefits of a classical education.'

We drove on in silence for a while. We were reaching the outskirts of the village before Percy spoke again.

'In regard to that back door of yours.'

'What about it?'

'You may want this back.'

He reached into the breast pocket and produced a set of keys, which he dropped in my lap just as two cyclists straddling the road appeared before us. He grabbed the wheel with both hands and, giving them a wide berth, overtook the cyclists. I snatched the keys before they dropped to the floor. They looked familiar.

'My sincere apologies, most sincere, but I took it upon myself to enter your house through the back door shortly after they arrested you.'

'What on earth for?'

'Well, call me an old fool, but I rather suspected that someone might have planted evidence in your home that would be to your perpetual disadvantage.'

'You mean you searched my house?'

'Mea culpa, mea culpa, mea maxima culpa.'

'And did you find anything?'

'I confess that I did, dear lady.'

'What?'

In answer Percy pulled up onto a grassy bank where

the road widened and stepped out of the car. He waited a moment to let the cyclists he had overtaken pass him. One of them yelled out, 'Well done, old timer! Run us off the road, then stop and make us go round you. Bloody brilliant, you old fart!'

Percy bowed with a flourish, and earned himself a 'V' sign from the second cyclist. 'I have something to show you.'

I got out and followed him round to the back of the car. He popped open the trunk. Inside was a small blanket that he had folded carefully. He opened the folds to show me the bloody object they had been concealing.

'I found it at the back of a drawer in your bedroom.'

It was a car jack, misshapen by its force of use.

'I would say that, for reasons you may know but into which I shall not pry, someone has gone to considerable trouble to cause you not inconsiderable inconvenience.'

27

Bonn, December 1976

Finding the documents Callan needed proved much harder this time around. Security had been stepped up and passes had to be requested for access to the vaults. Frau Müller had shifted her favours to another translator, one who worked even longer hours than I did, and had taken to questioning my every visit to the filing room.

I did not need my PhD to understand Callan's modus operandi, which was simplicity itself. He singled out young women to work his charms on and once he had his victim hooked, he would ask for her help in some small business matter. It did not matter whether or not he was connected to the business, just as long as she believed he was. Once she had betrayed the state's trust he would escalate his requests. Soon these request became demands involving sensitive state secrets. Before she knew what was happening his victim was trapped in a spiral of treachery and deceit from which it was impossible to escape.

While the bridge contract had not been particularly sensitive to anyone outside the bridge building world, the information Callan had now asked me to provide was dangerous, both to the state and to me. The Official Secrets Act prevents me from disclosing the details, but it concerned the sale of British high-grade military weapons to West Germany. If caught, I could hardly claim diplomatic immunity. I was a foreign agent stealing papers that could compromise the security of the Federal Republic of Germany itself. The loss of trust between our two nations would be devastating, and my career would be over.

Callan had assured me that he merely wanted to ascertain what the FRG lacked in its arsenal, so he could earn an extra commission that would get him out of financial trouble. He had provided me with a key to the vault. How he had acquired it I had no idea, but he must have given a duplicate to Elsa. Perhaps she had refused to help him, or perhaps she had failed to find the documents he wanted. It seemed unbelievable that, in the face of numerous leaks, the Chancellery had not changed the vault locks and did not keep the keys under permanent guard.

It took me three attempts to reach the vault. Each time I had to ask permission from Frau Müller and my excuses were getting thin. Once down there I would have to ensure that the filing clerks were not present and that nobody from the typing pool would surprise me.

I finally made it down those stairs late on a Friday afternoon. The filing clerks were packing up for the day and Frau Müller was in a hurry. She issued me my pass and told me to be back shortly, as she had a difficult translation that needed completing before I went home.

I hurried down the stairs and headed for the vault. I turned the key in the lock, pulled the handle and nothing happened. I turned it again, keeping an eye on the time – I had less than ten minutes to find the right documents, photocopy them and return them to the vault – and this time the heavy handle budged. The door swung open.

I cursed the inefficiency of the filing clerks. Many of the

relevant documents were stacked randomly. Several had been filed incorrectly. This was probably the way they had been received, but nobody had bothered to sort or label them. It took me seven minutes to find the specific folder Callan wanted. It consisted of more than fifty pages – too many for the old Xerox machine to manage in under two or three minutes.

As I let the photocopier warm up and set it printing I heard Frau Müller call my name. I answered that I would be up in a minute. I cursed the office accountants. If only they had approved a few more Deutschmarks for updating our equipment. The new breed of photocopiers would have handled this number of pages in seconds. I rammed the originals back in their folder, stuffed the folder back in the vault and managed to shut the door just as Müller appeared. Under the rattle of the photocopying I had not heard her coming down the stairs.

'What's taking you so long? I've got the Ministry of Finance screaming for those translations by yesterday.' She strode up to the vault, glanced at the work table and turned to face me.

'Well? What's keeping you?' She had her back to the vault and, to my horror, I saw that I had left the key in the door. I averted my eyes.

'I'm just checking some of my earlier work from this morning, Frau Müller. I think I may have mistranslated some technical words and I needed to see the original files again.'

'And the photocopying?' Behind her the vault door, which I had failed to lock, slowly swung open.

'The filing clerks wanted to get off early and I said I would copy and put away the files for them while I checked my own pages.'

'We have enough work of our own without tidying up after those *schwachköpfe*.' She marched back up the stairs.

I closed the vault door, levered the handle up, locked it and pocketed the key. I slipped the photocopied pages into a folder of general correspondence and hurried up after Müller. It had been a near miss.

*

Callan expressed admiration that I had managed to gather so much information so quickly. We had met in the Baumschulwäldchen park again, and again he held up the dossier and shone his flashlight over it, which I considered extremely rash of him, but he insisted on checking each page for authenticity. In a hurry to leave, he promised to take me to dinner in a small Hungarian restaurant where the food was excellent… and cheap. All of a sudden, spoiling me was no longer a priority.

The following evening I made my way to Callan's Hungarian restaurant. It had the simplest of awnings announcing its existence and, from what I could see, was not yet open. Yet Callan had told me to meet him there at six. The door was unlocked. I pushed it open and found myself in a small foyer, separated from the restaurant by a thick velvet curtain to keep out the draft. I drew the curtain aside. A dozen or so tables were laid for dinner and shadowy figures worked in the kitchen beyond. The place was deserted except for Callan, seated alone.

'Sit down.' His manner was brusque, peremptory. I sat and waited for him to speak again.

'There were two pages missing from those documents.' As he looked at me I felt a cold shiver, even though a fire roared in the hearth. 'If it had just been one page, I might have thought it was a mistake. But the two most important pages – without which all the rest are useless – are absent. Where are they?'

'I have no idea. I took what you asked for. I didn't have time to read them.' I had, of course, realised which pages were too dangerous to pass on and omitted to copy them. They were back in their original folder in the vault.

'You will go back and find them.'

'No I won't. What I did, I did for... for love.' I stifled a sob for his benefit. 'But now you are scaring me.'

He laid a set of photographs on the table before me. He did it with all the confidence of someone who had done this many times before. One showed us at Maternus, with me exhibiting the stupid grin of infatuation that I had rehearsed in front of a mirror for thirty minutes at home. The next showed me leaving the Chancellery building. A third showed us in the throes of passionate lovemaking (nothing fake on my side there) and the others showed me handing over documents in the park on two separate occasions. I could even make out the Ministry stamp marking them *streng geheim* – top secret. No wonder he had used a flashlight. He had needed to provide enough light for his photographer, hidden somewhere in the scrubby bushes.

'If I send these to the Chancellery, you will be arrested and put on trial for spying. A traitor to your nation.'

'Not correct. I am Austrian. As I told you.' I could not bear to watch him gloat without some form of retort.

'That's worse. An enemy snake in their bosom. You will get me the two missing pages and more, and only when you have done that shall I destroy these photographs and the negatives. Do you understand?'

I nodded. He pushed over a scrap of paper. 'Read this.' He watched me closely. As I read, and understood what he wanted me to do, I felt the blood drain from my face and, despite all my training, I felt my head swimming. He withdrew the paper, set his lighter to it and used the burning twist to light his cigarette. I stood up and, weeping, staggered out of the place on wobbly legs. It was an act not entirely put on for his benefit.

28

'You were crying?' Patrick asked. 'Seriously?'

'He had betrayed me, so it was a valid and believable reaction,' I answered, somewhat peeved. 'It was exactly what he expected. Remember what we were taught? "Always fall back on the most natural reaction. It's the easiest lie to sell."'

Patrick finished reading my report and shook his head in disbelief. 'He wants a complete list of all the nuclear weapons held on German soil?'

'Correct.'

'And you're going to give it to him?'

'How do you think Chancery will react?'

'They'll go ballistic… bad pun, sorry. You can't possibly give Callan that list.'

'I have no intention of doing so,' I said. 'In any case, there may not be a complete record in the vault.'

'Oh, and suddenly someone's showing a bit of responsibility in the German Chancellery and deciding that this dossier is so fucking ultra-top secret that perhaps it should be kept under strict lock and key in the bloody Chancellor's own bloody desk?'

'Stranger things have happened.'

'Not in this town.'

The FRG had signed the Nuclear Non-Proliferation Treaty only one year ago. Despite this, the United States had provided Germany with a number of nuclear bombs under a NATO nuclear weapons sharing agreement. In the event of war, the bombs would be armed and delivered by Luftwaffe warplanes, in direct contravention of the treaty. Any enemy of the FRG would do anything to find a way to put them out of action.

'We need to know who his masters are,' I said. 'Or if he's simply selling secrets to the highest bidder.'

'Any brilliant ideas?'

'Just the one, though I'm not sure I'd call it brilliant.'

What I had to do, I reckoned, was acquire some headed Bundeskanzler writing paper, of which Frau Müller held reams under lock and key and handed out sparingly. Then I could create my own list to present to Callan. So I duly requested a few extra sheets, in case of mistakes. Müller allowed me three, with a warning not to waste them.

While listening to dull dictation supplied by the Finance Minister on the subject of his three-year budget plan, which I was supposed to type up and distribute to the press office, I typed a fictional list of nuclear sites on the German border. I also managed to type up the dictation in record time. Everyone was familiar with Fliegerhorst Büchel, the US airbase at Büchel, so including it in a list of half a dozen imaginary sites, which I invented with the help of a map of military barracks, many long disused, gave my list a ring of authenticity. I never expected it to stand up to intense scrutiny but it would suffice for my immediate purposes.

While Frau Müller was taking her lavatory break I popped down to the filing floor and found a rubber stamp with '*streng geheim*' marked on it. There was a good reason for the stamp's existence. Many dossiers contained top secret papers but occasionally ministers, or their assistants and secretaries, would forget to stamp a page. It was the job of the filing clerks to ensure that every page of a top secret document was properly identified. I stamped each page of my concocted document *streng geheim* and hurried back upstairs. I had been away from my desk for less than two minutes.

Frau Müller was waiting for me at the top of the stairs. 'You know that you must request my permission to visit the filing floor. What do you have there?'

I showed her. She studied the pages. 'These are from the Finance Minister's speech?'

'Yes.'

I had taken the precaution of concealing my 'top secret' pages with simple sleight of hand, learnt from a friend who had joined the Magic Circle. 'I thought I had left a page downstairs, but I had it in the file all along.'

'You are becoming increasingly *schusselig*, young lady. When you first came here I had great hopes for your promotion. Now I am not so sure.'

*

I told Callan that, because of their highly confidential nature, and for my safety, I would only hand over the list in a public place.

'Where?' he growled.

'Why not Maternus?' Where he had first taken me. I might as well get a decent meal out of it.

'The whole town will be watching.'

'Watching a man and his girlfriend dining together.'

'You are taking a big risk.'

'It's that or nothing.'

That Saturday evening Patrick and Giles drove me to the Maternus restaurant. Patrick parked some distance away, scraping his hub cap against the raised pavement, while still retaining a good view of the entrance. He assured me that he had two of his people in the restaurant. They would be dining at his expense.

'A shared soup only, I hope.'

'Don't try picking them out. It'll give them away.'

Patrick was edgy. I said nothing, got out of the car, crossed the road and walked to the restaurant as the clouds opened and the rain came down. In the reflection of a window I caught sight of two men sitting in a black car, watching. Were they Patrick's people?

Who they were became obvious the moment I entered. The Chancellor himself, Helmut Schmidt, sat at a table with his wife, Loki, and friends of theirs whom I did not recognise. They were being fussed over by the owner, Ria Maternus, herself. When tipsy, Ria was notorious for dancing on the tables. She seemed sober enough that evening. At a nearby table sat two men who, though they had the most delicious-looking dishes before them, never once took their eyes off the Chancellor: his bodyguards.

In the corner banquette, at the same seat he had occupied on our first date, sat Callan. Gone was the warmth and charm. His eyes were cold, like those of his chauffeur, and his mouth, so often smiling, was now twisted into a scarcely concealed scowl. He stood, took my coat and handed it to a waiter. He made a show of helping me into my seat, pushing the table out as I slid in and then, with the waiter's help, pushing it hard against my waist, trapping me. He leant in close.

'You have it?'

'All in good time.'

He sat and fiddled with the menu. 'This is a stupid place to meet. There are secret service men stationed all around. We will be in serious trouble if we are caught.'

'Do they still have a firing squad for spies?'

He looked at me with scorn. 'You find the situation amusing?'

'Not at all. But if we behave as if we are exchanging state secrets we may well attract attention, whereas if we look like we are having fun, we'll fit right in.' We gave our order – steak for him, a starter and then veal chop for me – to the waiter and, once he had disappeared into the kitchen, I produced the dossier from my bag. 'I received such a lovely letter from Aunt Toppie yesterday.'

To his consternation I laid the pages before him on the table. I picked up the top sheet. 'Look what she's written: the snow in Innsbrück is three metres high this winter!' He forced a smile as I shuffled the pages. 'There's too much to read now,' I said. 'Why don't you take it home with you and read it there?'

I thrust the pages into his hand and he stowed them into a small briefcase. 'Thank you, I so look forward to reading them.' He forced a smile.

'Shall I choose the wine?' I reached for the wine list. He grabbed my arm to stop me but I pulled away hard. I scanned the wine list. There wasn't a great selection. I wanted something really expensive. I went for their finest red.

'There's a perfectly good white there,' he said of an inexpensive Drachenburg Riesling.

'With your steak? My dear, whatever were you thinking?'

He struggled to control his fury. Like Patrick, he must have been on a limited budget and obliged to account for every *pfennig*. He forced another smile when the waiter arrived with my first course. I had chosen *Gebeizter Wildlachs und marinierte Artischocken* – cured wild salmon, or gravadlax, with marinated artichokes. Callan had declined to order anything other than a main course. He wanted to get out of there with his prize as soon as he could.

The room had gone silent. I looked up and saw that all eyes were on a pale dishevelled figure soaked by the rain. It was Elsa. She was wailing a strange, soft cry of despair which had stopped all conversation. With unsteady steps she made her way to our table. She stared at Callan, her eyes red with weeping, her upper lip trembling. She took another sudden step forward and slapped Callan's face with all her weight behind her. Though she left a red welt across his cheek, he hardly flinched. Elsa straightened up, shot me a look of pure hatred, then turned and fled the restaurant.

It was a few seconds before anybody spoke. I think it was Chancellor Schmidt who, with the skill of a diplomat, called over a waiter and sent his compliments to the chef. Ria Maternus sidled gracefully up to Callan and asked him to leave. There was no need to pay the bill, she said. Just leave, please, now.

Once I had put my coat on Callan took me roughly by the arm and hauled me outside.

'What the fuck are you playing at?'

'What do you mean?'

'Half the Chancellery present and in front of everybody you lay out what could get us both arrested.'

'And where is it now?' I asked. In his fury he had left his briefcase behind. He dashed back inside. Perhaps I was at risk of letting my own mask – that of the naive provincial – slip. But if I had nettled the professional in him that much, I was achieving exactly what I had set out to do. It was a dangerous plan, but if Patrick held his nerve it might work. My only regret was that my behaviour had wounded Elsa.

Callan emerged clutching his briefcase to his chest, gave me a filthy look and signalled to his driver to pull up alongside. Callan got in and they drove off at speed. I jumped into Patrick's car and, as soon as Callan's car had rounded the corner, we set off in pursuit.

'I've got Giles in another car tailing him.' Patrick swerved to miss a cat.

'Then there's no need to chase him, is there? We don't want him spotting us.'

Patrick slowed and a nondescript grey car overtook us. 'There's Giles,' he said.

Callan's Mercedes-Benz accelerated into the dark night.

29

West Sussex, May 2019

I poured Percy a double whisky and gave myself a triple shot, neat. Whether it was my delayed reaction to being arrested and locked up or discovering that there had been enough evidence to put me away for thirty years (a life sentence at my age) that had left me feeling the way I did, I could not tell. I had managed to hide it up to that point but as I handed Percy his glass I noticed my hand was shaking. He put his hands over mine and held them there a moment. They were warm and, I had to admit to myself, comforting. My first instinct was to pull away, but I desisted. Percy, looking into my eyes, seemed to read my thoughts.

'You've had a shock. There's no shame in showing it.' He removed his hands and raised his glass. 'To your excellent and continued health.'

'Your health,' I replied, raising my glass. I sat down more heavily than I intended. I sipped my whisky slowly. Drinking it fast would give me heartburn. Percy followed my lead and we sat silently for a few minutes, I with my thoughts, he with his.

Of course my thoughts were all about Percy. What on earth had driven him to get into my house and hide the evidence against me? How had he got in without alerting anyone? What did he know? What wasn't he telling me? He couldn't be working with Igor and Fashion-Plate, so he must be working against them. But for whom?

Percy broke the silence. 'There will be talk in the village. But then, there always is.'

'Not much I can do about that.'

'No, but I could give it a spin in the right direction, if that's what you'd like.'

'I don't care a damn, one way or the other.'

He gave me a look which said he did not fully believe me. 'As you like, but in a small place like this, you don't want daily life becoming any more difficult than it already is. We are none of us getting any younger.'

I thanked him and, when we had finished our drinks, rather than offer him a top-up I asked him to leave. He was gracious about it. Once he had gone I went down to the cellar and watched the recordings on fast replay.

I fast forwarded from the night before. Nothing untoward occurred until this morning, shortly after I had gone out for my walk and had my fall. A slight figure in dark clothes, wearing a peaked cap with its brim hiding the face and black gloves on its hands approached the house through the back garden. The figure carried a long package wrapped in a black bin bag. I could not see how he or she got in through the locked back door – I had inadvertently left my ironing board propped too close to the concealed camera – but the kitchen camera showed the figure already inside, removing their shoes and hurrying through the house with the package. A moment later the intruder was in my bedroom. By now I was certain it was a man. He checked inside the wardrobe, then opened both chests of drawers, selecting the bottom drawer of my Georgian chest, a bequest from my grandmother. The drawer held items for which I had little use: my grandmother's collection of antique lace that I should have sold off years ago, a spare blanket and Eva's christening dress.

He left the bedroom, found the airing cupboard and extracted an old towel. It had grown stiff with age and over-washing and I never used it except to clean up spills or leaks from the fridge. It was now being used to wrap the object – the bloody car jack – which the intruder carried back into my bedroom and placed in the open drawer before carefully covering it with the blanket, Granny's lace and the christening dress.

At that moment, as he bent to close the drawer, the peaked cap dropped to the floor. I caught a glimpse of a bald patch at the back of its head. It was definitely a man. Snatching up the cap, he partly turned towards me and I could make two small moles on his cheek. He was neither Igor nor Fashion-Plate, but most certainly sent by them. He rammed his cap back on tightly and made his way out of the house, stopping only to slip his shoes back on.

I scrolled down the video stream until I could see Detective Inspector Morris and his sidekick sergeant parking up outside my house and walking up the path. They pressed the doorbell, waited, then pressed the doorbell again, more insistently this time. Moments later Percy and I appeared round the corner. If I had been on my own I would have walked right past and ignored them, but Percy's presence had made escape impossible.

I watched as the police addressed me. Percy bent down, as if to tie his shoelaces, and with a couple of backward steps disappeared into the bushes. As I was handcuffed and driven away by the police, Percy reappeared. He spoke briefly into his iPhone then listened intently. He put away his phone, went to the end of the street and walked around the back of the cottages. A few moments later he reappeared through my rear gate and stepped into my back garden. Without hesitation he made straight for the brick wall running along the south side. It took him just a few seconds to find the loose brick and extract it. He reached into the hole and produced the set of house keys I had hidden in the event of losing the ones in my handbag. Percy had moved mountains to get me out of that cell, but how had he known where I kept my keys? I had made a big effort to make that loose brick blend into the rest of the wall. I had worked at night to excavate a hole in the cement large enough to contain the keys and a small packet of anything else I wished to hide from prying eyes. I had smeared it and the bricks around it with live yoghurt and within a few weeks a rich coating of algae and moss had grown over them. How could he possibly have known they were there? Not even Jamie knew about this set.

I fast forwarded and watched Percy produce a clean handkerchief and unlock the back door, ensuring he left no fingerprints. He cautiously eased himself into the kitchen and, in quick succession, checked every room on the ground floor for hiding places. It was if he knew exactly what he should be looking for.

After searching my pantry, he headed upstairs. He, like my intruder, went to my bedroom first. I suppressed my flash of regret that I hadn't tidied up before going out. I had not made the bed, and there was a large brown stain where I had spilt my morning cup of tea. I wished I had changed the sheets for fresh ones, but when you live alone, well, what's the point? Only a short while ago I hadn't thought I would care about anything ever again.

Percy checked under the bed, in the wardrobe and in my escritoire. In the top drawer was my final letter that I had left for anybody who cared enough to read. Percy studied it, as if somehow he could see right through the envelope and read its contents. He proceeded to the chest of drawers. He reached in to check through my underwear, all perfectly clean I'm glad to say, shut the drawer and gave the second drawer an equally rigorous search. In the third drawer he found the car jack, hauled it out, placed it on the floor and unwrapped it. The old towel was stained red with blood, but he showed no emotion. Somehow I felt he had seen such things many times before.

He wrapped the towel back up and proceeded, methodically, to search all other possibilities of concealment. I approved of his thoroughness. He expected to find more than that single piece of evidence and, to my surprise, he was successful in the kitchen. Tossed behind the waste bin in the corner he found a scrap of kitchen towel with blood on it. I had not seen my intruder plant it – he must have done that as he departed, throwing it away with his left hand while his right shoulder was turned to the camera – but its presence would have been proof that I had tried to clean up any traces of blood and had failed. The obvious stowing of the car jack in my drawer might have sent the police signals that I had been framed. But the scrap of bloody tissue would have been enough to convince any jury.

30

I SLEPT UNEASILY THAT NIGHT. I had that insidious feeling that my intruder might make another attempt to get in the house. I had bolted the back door and stored the ironing board so it no longer blocked my camera. It was just as likely that the police might have second thoughts about giving me my freedom and decide to keep me under observation, possibly in one of their cells. My concern was not for myself, but for Alice. If I was not free, who could find her mother, who would prevent whoever was after her from doing her harm?

I was up before dawn. I made myself a cup of tea and ate two chocolate biscuits. I went for another walk around the village, though this time I steered clear of the goose flight path. My thoughts on what I should do next, which had been so clear the day before, were now confused. How could I move safely with either the police or *they*, whoever they were, monitoring my every move?

I felt my phone vibrate. I checked my WhatsApp. It was a message wonderful in its brevity: *'Come'*. It had been sent from one of the five numbers that Patrick Dallaway had given me. None of their SIM cards were registered in his name, so if anyone got hold of my phone they would have no idea that the message was from him.

Encouraged, I went home. It was too early for me to catch a train, so I got back into bed in the hope of a short snooze and fell into a deep sleep.

At five to eight the radio came on, as it was programmed to do, gave me the weather forecast for the day – fine – and the news headlines, or 'headlice' as Eva called them, as these days TV news mostly consisted of politicians' talking heads because of budget cutbacks.

Cursing that I was late, I showered, checked my appearance, gave my hair a quick brush and, lining my eyes with what Sister Mary at convent school had always mispronounced as 'massacre', plucked a dark hair that had sprouted from my upper lip. I spotted another and dealt with that too, and then another and thought, *No, I can't spend any more time on my appearance.* I suppose this was Percy's influence, though God knows why. I had no romantic interest whatsoever in the man. I hurried out of the house – taking great care to double-lock the doors – and made it to the stop just as the county bus was pulling in.

I hung back until it was on the point of leaving. Just before the doors shut I hopped on and scanned my pensioner's bus pass. I took a seat on the back bench and held up a make-up mirror, as if I were applying lipstick, but in reality to check that there was nobody trailing me. No car suddenly pulled out or sped up after us.

There was, however, a small white car running ahead of us. Every time we pulled in to a stop it would scoot on only to be found idling round a corner as we caught up with it. Then it would accelerate away and put some distance between us again.

This continued until we reached town. I was headed for the train station but got off two stops earlier and walked through back streets, turning left and right as the mood took me, until I eventually arrived at the station entrance. I purchased a return ticket to Cooden Beach on the automatic machine. It took me two attempts, as the machine suddenly stopped halfway through the first transaction. At the second the payment went through and my tickets spat out at the bottom.

I hovered around the westbound platform for a few minutes, so that I could discreetly scan my fellow passengers. As my train pulled in on the far track I studied my ticket in some confusion and made a sudden dash for the footbridge. I was up one side and down the next in thirty seconds. I reached the train and leapt into the carriage seconds before the doors shut. The station guard blew his whistle. I turned and saw a young man, wearing trainers, jeans and a hoodie, almost reach the train and fail. He turned away before I could catch his face. As the train pulled out of the station he produced his phone and made a call.

I managed to get a seat at a table for four. The carriage was almost empty and nobody else joined me. At the next stop two families with children got on, one taking the table next to mine. At the stop after that a woman got on with a laptop and seemed on the point of joining me. I fixed her with a stare and demanded, in a loud voice, 'Do you want to be saved by Jesus?' The woman stopped dead, turned around and bolted for another carriage. The family at the next table held a whispered conference and quickly got up and followed her. That way I ensured an uninterrupted journey all the way to Cooden Beach.

My destination, of course, was Patrick's house. I took the coastal path, Herbrand Walk, which would lead me to Norman's Bay. I checked my lipstick again, ensuring that, this time, there was definitely nobody following me, and strolled nonchalantly along until I reached Sluice Lane, where I found Patrick asleep in his car.

I tapped on the windscreen. He woke with a start and unlocked the passenger door. I slipped in beside him.

'Why didn't you take your car?' he asked.

'My every move is being watched,' I explained. 'There's probably a tracker on my car and I'm getting too old to crawl around the underside and find it. Besides, they make them so small these days I probably wouldn't spot it anyway.'

'Feeling nostalgic? About the old days?'

'Not a bit of it.'

He executed what seemed like a ten-point turn – Patrick had always been a poor driver and even worse at parking – and we drove back to his house and stopped in the shadow of the gun emplacement. We went inside, where he had laid out a spread of smoked salmon, cucumber and cream cheese.

'I thought we'd have some smoked salmon sandwiches while we talked,' he said.

'Marvellous. Where's the bread?'

'Oh God, I knew I'd forget something.'

'No matter, salmon and cream cheese is fine. Any wine?'

'I've got something chilling in the fridge. Tesco's finest.'

Also typical of Patrick: the desire to boast how cheap he was. We had only met these two times in over twenty years and he was enjoying an excellent government pension, so he had no reason not to splash out on a decent bottle of Burgundy – I fancied a Puligny-Montrachet – and a loaf of freshly baked bread. At our park meetings in Bonn he would often produce sandwiches that were curling up at the edges. He seemed to prefer them that way.

Over the wine, which I confess was not as bad as I expected it to be, he talked.

'My little mission proved not as impossible as expected.' He smiled, pleased with what he considered his wit. 'The car registration plate was issued to a Russian citizen based in Belarus, its neighbour.'

'I know where Belarus is.'

'Of course, forgive me.'

'And where does this individual reside?'

'He has several residencies around the globe. Having distanced himself somewhat from the Kremlin, as well as the government of Belarus, he is not subjected to any of the sanctions pertaining to either nation.'

'Come on, a London address, please.'

He reached into his jacket and produced a small folded note.

'London and country address. I thought you might want both. The country estate is particularly fine. Perhaps you know it?'

I unfolded the note and read. Patrick was right. I knew it well.

31

Bonn, December 1976

Giles kept up radio contact. Bonn is a small town, jokingly referred to as a village. There were not many places where Callan could disappear. Once out of Bad Godesberg we followed his Mercedes-Benz west into the suburban sprawl of Surrey-style residences that housed the international diplomatic corps.

The Mercedes slowed and Patrick held back, switching off his headlights and parking up with his usual lack of care. Callan's car pulled over in the distance. Callan got out, clutching his briefcase, and stepped into a service alley that led into the next street. Giles leapt out of his grey car and hurried into a parallel alley. He carried two Pentax SLR cameras strapped around his shoulders.

Patrick got out and slipped into the alley after Giles. I followed close on his heels.

Patrick kept going until he reached the next street. He retreated suddenly and I ran straight into the back of him. He shoved me away from the glare of the street lights.

'There's another car. A limousine.' He extended a pocket telescope and peered into the street. He muttered the details of the limousine's registration and jotted them in his little notebook, a bit hastily I thought. As the limo swept past he yanked Giles, busily snapping off a succession of photographs, back into the shadows before its headlights could catch him.

It took less than thirty minutes for Giles to process the films from his cameras. One had been loaded with Ilford HP5, a fast stock, 'pushed' to extend its range. The other contained infra-red film. He emerged from a makeshift darkroom in his small apartment and showed us the prints, still wet from the fixer.

The photographs clearly showed Callan handing his briefcase to another man whose face, in most of the photographs, was turned away from camera. One single shot on the fast film and another one on infra-red had captured his face full on.

'Grigori Golubstov,' said Patrick, 'the *rezidentura*, working under official diplomatic cover at the Russian embassy.'

Giles hovered over us. 'Those were the best shots I could get, but I have some of Golubstov leaving and entering the Russian embassy, if you need them for confirmation.'

Patrick sat me down. 'I've had information from London on your friend Callan. A boy by the name of Michael Callan was born in 1943 in Leeds, Yorkshire. His mother was Finnish. After the war she and her husband separated and the mother, Olga, took her son back to Finland. He is believed to have died in 1951 in a skating accident – fell through the ice of a frozen lake. The Soviets obtained his papers and provided your "Mr Callan" with his identity. He even spent time in England as a police officer in the Metropolitan Police, would you believe, before being thrown out for corruption – caught planting evidence – more skating on thin ice. It seems that's Michael Callan's speciality. As he was a Freemason, and times being what they were, he was discharged from the police force but not prosecuted. He held down a few odd jobs in London, security, that sort of thing, then in 1968 he disappeared on a holiday in Yugoslavia. Now he's popped up here in Bonn. A Romeo spy.'

'Working for the Russians.'

'Trained in Moscow, sent as a sleeper to England in the fifties. Somehow accepted into sixth form grammar school, though it's likely he was already in his early twenties. His English can't be faulted, and his French and German are excellent.'

'Then he'll be swearing in all three languages when he realises those papers I gave him are worthless,' I said.

'What do you mean? Are you telling me they weren't genuine?'

'You said it: we can't give them what they want.'

'That wasn't what I meant. What you did was idiotic.'

I remained silent, confused.

'If they realise we are onto them,' Patrick continued, 'they will simply withdraw Callan and someone else will take his place. Someone we don't know, and we'll have to start this game all over again from the start. It's so stupid of you not to stick to orders.'

His comments stung, I can't deny it. We had discussed handing over part of the information Callan wanted, but I never thought Chancery would want me to hand him genuine secrets. It made no sense.

*

When I went to bed that night my feet were cold. I made a hot-water bottle and shoved it down the foot of my bed, but the cold I felt was of disappointment, most of all in myself. I was supposed to act the naive Austrian, not the smart agent, and I had let myself and Chancery down. How could I have been so stupid as to risk exposing my mission?

My sense of failure hung over me all the next day. On Monday Elsa did not come in to work. As she had not phoned in sick, Frau Müller sent a security officer round to her bedsit to check on her. An hour later he returned, hurried over to Frau Müller and spoke to her in whispers. She got up, went over first to Heidi and then to me and told us to follow her into the conference room, which was retained for staff meetings. She told us to sit down, as she had something important to tell us.

'It's about Elsa. I know you two are her closest friends.' Well I may have been, until the previous night, but Heidi had not so much as spoken to Elsa for at least ten days, ever since Elsa had started moping about her absent 'fiancé'. 'I'm sorry to have to tell you that Elsa is dead. She has hanged herself. I shall be informing the rest of the staff this evening, after work, but in the meantime, did either of you have any idea what Elsa has been doing?'

Elsa had, she informed us, been copying and stealing documents from under the very eyes of the filing department. In a foolish attempt to protect herself, she had hidden extra copies under her floorboards. The security team believed her suicide had been the result of her overwhelming sense of guilt over her betrayal. They were certain that these were the only copies she had made. Their report to their superiors claimed no secret documents whatsoever had been passed to alien agencies. I knew different.

So when Patrick said he had an idea how to turn Callan and expose Golubstov, I listened. I was only too eager to be the instrument of Elsa's revenge.

32

West Sussex, May 2019

The Ashendon Estate in West Sussex consists of some 5,000 acres of rolling chalk downland. Traditionally, much of the land was rented out to tenant farmers for sheep grazing. The Southdown sheep, a hornless variety, is the oldest of all British breeds. It produces good wool and has an ideal conformation for meat production. The chalk stream brook which runs through the estate is stocked with some of the largest specimens of native brown trout to be fished. The estate was created by the Hartley-Gascoigne family, treasurers to Queen Elizabeth I, and was passed down through fourteen generations before it was sold in the early 1960s to pay death duties. Since then the house has had a chequered history. It was bought in 2008 by a private foundation based in the Cayman Islands, which restored the house to its former glory. The estate has been run privately ever since. The owners have been gracious enough to open the estate, as has been long-standing tradition, on major feast days, including May Day, Midsummer and Michaelmas Day. All other days the house and gardens are closed to members of the public.

All this information I gathered from the leaflet that was handed to me as we entered the grounds. I had managed to secure the last seat on a 'May Day Butterfly Experience' excursion to Ashendon, which had been postponed for two weeks because of bad weather. The lawns backing onto the mansion, which had been rebuilt in the last year of Queen Anne's reign, had been sown with wild flowers by a previous owner, and the meadows now attracted myriad butterflies, moths and other insects. The current owner had improved the paths crisscrossing these meadows by digging them out to a depth of three or four feet, which meant that the visitor, traversing a path, would be at eye level with the flower heads and the abundant insect life. While this had been carried out purely for the current owner's pleasure and convenience, the meadows attracted as many old ladies and their partners as it did insects on that beautiful late May morning.

I suspected that throwing open the gardens to visitors three times a year was some sort of tax dodge that would benefit the owner. In this I was later to be proved right.

My fellow oldies and I plodded through the butterfly pathways with all the urgency of tortoises suffering the sedative effects of a double dose of diazepam. Couples kept pausing to examine the wildlife in detail. I was impatient, as ever, but on these narrow paths it would have looked unseemly, and out of place, to barge past and overtake.

'Oh look, darling, I haven't seen a Duke of Burgundy since I was a child, and here is one right before my eyes!' These words were uttered by an elderly man who had been unable to manage more than a slow shuffle. When he turned I saw that he was probably five years younger than I. He and his wife were inspecting what, to my untrained eye, appeared to be a small tortoiseshell. The old boy suddenly collapsed onto a tree stump and put his head in his hands.

'Is he all right?' I asked. The heady scent of sweet peas, allowed to tumble, seemed to have overcome him.

'Take no notice,' replied his wife. 'George always gets like this when he's excited.'

I skirted around them and made my way forward. I stopped and squinted as if I had just seen the most remarkable example of Lepidoptera. I was trying to fix the layout of the house in my head.

Ashendon itself, its name derived from the old Saxon *Assendun*, was made up of many parts. The original wood fort (denoted by the 'dun') had long ago been dismantled or burnt. The early medieval foundations supported first a Tudor building, which was enlarged during the Elizabethan age, as the money rolled in. Later it was given the Queen Anne facade, which was rounded off with Regency finials. I make it sound like a terrible hotchpotch, but the end result was pleasing. The old barns had retained their original Tudor appearance, though they had been repaired many times and their original beams replaced. Their tiles were ancient, and must have been hard to replace, but whoever had authorised the renovations had demonstrated an obsessive eye for historical detail.

The house itself was built on an H shape, like a smaller Hardwick Hall, and fronted with Bath stone, which was unusual for Sussex. The southern part of the H had been filled in to create a bright orangery, faced with the same stone, and aged to look as if it had always been there. From my low vantage point, this was all I could make out.

George, the old boy still aquiver with excitement from spotting his Duke of Burgundy butterfly, was now sufficiently recovered to attempt to pass me. A line was building up behind him and a tetchy voice called out, 'We haven't got all day, you know,' which was a lie as the coach would not return to pick us up until five o'clock, by which time most of its passengers would be exhausted by their exertions and fast asleep.

I made room by stepping onto a second path which intersected with ours and led towards the house (which we had been expressly forbidden to approach) but was, if anything, cut a little deeper than the first. It gave me a restricted view of the house, but that also meant that I could not be observed from any except the very top rooms.

I waited till my entire coach party had moved on. The tour guide called out, 'Keep up, keep up, loo break in ten minutes and then it's morning coffee in the barn.' At the mention of 'loo break' the whole group sped up and followed her out of the meadow. I saw old George, who hadn't managed more than a snail's shuffle up till now, speed up and overtake the others as he hurried on for his first rest stop.

As I waited a peacock butterfly, resplendent in its coat of rusty red with its four blue and yellow eyespots circled in black, settled on a dandelion and flexed its wings. Closed, they resembled a dried brown leaf. Open, they were one of nature's marvels. I paused to study it and, in that brief moment, a large wasp pounced, bit off the butterfly's head with its fearsome mandibles, snipped off its wings with neat precision and carried the still twitching body away to its nest. As I watched it disappear a thought darkened my mind: was I the wasp, the avenging predator, or the helpless butterfly unaware of the dangers surrounding it?

The next coachload would be along in a matter of minutes. I already had my hair hidden under my Hermès *carré* scarf. I slipped on a pair of sunglasses before making my way back down the path and along the side of the house.

I had noticed kitchen staff in white jackets and Croc shoes dumping black bags in the rubbish bins in a small outhouse just to the rear of the house. They smoked handrolled cigarettes and exchanged jokes before sloping back inside.

I made a beeline – a strange expression, bees never fly straight – to the outhouse, walked round the back of it and waited. I peered in through the open rear door of the mansion and saw a large and busy kitchen, resplendent with old-fashioned copper pots and pans in racks on the wall, all run by an efficient housekeeper. She spoke to the staff in two languages, one heavily accented English, the other a sort of bastardised Russian, full of dialect and slang, which I could not entirely follow. However, it was not hard to catch its drift. She was highly displeased with someone on her staff; someone who was liable to lose their job. After about a minute, during which I gathered that someone important was due to arrive shortly, she left the kitchen and went up the back stairs. She had been my biggest obstacle. With her gone, I had a chance.

I emerged from behind the outhouse with my iPhone clamped to my ear as if in the middle of an animated conversation. 'Well you might well say that, but I've been let down before.' My voice raised, I strode past a couple of staff and into the kitchen. Immediately a person I took to be the head cook tried to block me. I shook a finger for her not to disturb me as I carried on my conversation. 'I am warning you, if they do not arrive before one o'clock this afternoon we are cancelling the whole arrangement. You will be seriously out of pocket, especially when we issue proceedings against you for the return of all monies advanced. What?' This last was to the cook, still trying to get my attention and prevent my passage through her domain. Without giving her the chance to interrupt, I returned to the call. 'We were told you were the best in the business, and the cook here agrees with me,' I waved to the cook, who nodded in agreement – what else could she do – as she checked the items on a full English breakfast being plated up and placed into a large dumb waiter. A green button was pressed, the hatch closed and the meal was dispatched to some other floor in the vast mansion. 'And we will, I am warning you now, replace you with another supplier immediately if you fail to perform. Am I making myself clear? Good.' By now I had crossed the kitchen and reached the foot of the stairs. I turned briefly to signal the cook a thumbs-up, to which she responded with a nod, and mounted the back staircase.

I still remembered the old lessons. Always behave as if you have the absolute right to be wherever you are and never back down. That's the only way to convince people that you belong.

There was just one short flight before the stairs divided. Above me to the left I could hear the housekeeper speaking on the telephone in her office. I took the right-hand staircase and headed on upwards, still with my iPhone clamped to my ear as if I were listening to some long string of instructions.

I reached the main floor, emerging from the top of the stairs into a small room which led straight to a grand hall of white marble. It was of double height, taking in two floors, and must have been about forty feet square and the same in height, creating a large white cube. About twenty-five feet up was a balustraded landing, affording a perfect view of any action in the grand hall below. Outside on the terrace, edged with a similar balustrade, stood two men in uniform, dressed like museum guards, watching the day trippers crossing the lawn to the refreshment tent. They were there to keep out the riff-raff, though, up until now, they had missed me. I made my way silently up the carved mahogany staircase to the landing above and found a seat in a richly tapestried chair that gave me a good view of the hall. As long as I sat still I would not be seen.

Behind me two sets of double doors led to what I presumed were bedrooms and ante chambers, probably all linked by interconnecting doors. I could hear the bustle of people cleaning the rooms behind me, and the sound of a vacuum cleaner at work. The area where I sat reeked of fresh polish. I guessed the staff had already scrubbed and cleaned this area and that nobody would disturb me.

I experienced a flash of doubt. How could I justify what I was doing there? What could I hope to achieve? If I found little Alice's parents would they be grateful or wish me harm? I got a grip on myself. If I was discovered I would simply claim to have got separated from my party and taken refuge in the house in the hope of a short lavatory stop. No harm done. I would be escorted out of the house and back to my group and nobody would be any the wiser.

It was a warm day and what with the scent of the butterfly lavender wafting in from the meadows and the faint buzzing of the staff at work I found myself beginning to relax.

I woke suddenly. I cursed myself. All those years on stakeouts, often lasting a whole night, followed by a day and another night, and I had never, ever fallen asleep. And now there I was, only an hour or so into my wait, slumped and drooling, no better than Patrick when I had found him asleep in his car. At the time I had felt superior that I still had all my energy and facilities while he, poor fellow, seemed to be on the verge of losing his.

It occurred to me, too, how if things went wrong now, and I was caught and frogmarched down to the local police station, how humiliating it would be. Not for me, but for

Bernard and Eva, should the press link me to them. I no longer had the service, or the Foreign Office, backing me up. I was doing all this off my own bat, and 'batty old bat' would be exactly how the press would describe me. I removed my tight scarf which was beginning to give me a headache.

I often snore loudly enough to wake myself up, and I was lucky that nobody had heard me now. There were enough noises drifting in from outside – cries of delight from the butterfly enthusiasts, a tractor mowing in the distance – to hide any I might have made. I heard another sound, somewhat muffled, but distinctly that of a car engine, approaching and I saw the guards outside stiffen and stand to attention. At the same time a door below me opened and a butler and two footmen strode out to greet the car's approach. It was a maroon Rolls-Royce, the same one I had seen in Kensington a few days earlier. It pulled up just below the terrace, and I saw the chauffeur get out and hurry to open the rear door.

At that moment one of the guards stepped forward and blocked my view. I edged forward and craned my neck as the car's occupant mounted the stairs to the terrace and entered the great marble hall. Then I saw Igor. He strode ahead of his master, pushing the front door wider. He glanced upwards and I ducked back out of sight. I heard him speak, an ugly voice, rough and strangled, but the voice that answered him was soft, mellifluous, educated and, it seemed in that moment, familiar to me. Where had I heard it before? I risked a step forward and peered over the balcony, but he was already in the house and out of view. All I saw were the butler and the footman, weighed down with luggage and wrapped gifts, disappearing into the house after him.

I can usually connect a face to a voice, and a name to a face, but in this instance I was foxed. The voice was so familiar. I had heard it many times before, I was sure. But where, and in what circumstances? It had been speaking Russian, I recognised that, but I was sure that I had heard that voice speak another language. I just could not place it.

I was in danger if I remained where I was. At any moment the house might fill up with more staff or guests and someone would eventually come out onto my landing, discover me and raise the alarm. I had to accept that I had failed, at first attempt, to discover who was behind Igor and Fashion-Plate. It was time to disappear back into my butterfly group and maybe I would get another chance after lunch. What was it Demosthenes retorted when accused of cowardice and failure? *He who fights and runs away will live to fight another day.* With those thoughts running through my mind, I waited a moment. There was no safety in going back down the mahogany stairs. There were too many people milling about. Instead I approached the closest of the double doors and put my ear against it. I waited until there was silence, then opened the door and stepped through.

I have employed many forms of subterfuge in my time, and I was prepared to use all and any of them to get out through the house, but I had not been expecting to find the butler waiting for me on the other side of the door. As I froze he raised his white gloved hand. It contained a spray canister. Covering his own mouth and nose he sprayed the contents directly into my face. That was the last thing I remembered before I passed out.

33

Bonn, December 1976

Callan contacted me two days later. He apologised for his appalling behaviour, explained that he had been under unbelievable stress, though he went into no details, and asked me to meet him later that night. He sounded desperate. I coldly informed him that I was in deep mourning. A colleague had committed suicide over a lover's betrayal and I was going to evening Mass to pray for her. I did not mention Elsa by name. He could work that out for himself. Though I was again playing hard to get, I eventually agreed to meet him.

When I told Patrick he bristled with excitement. This was our chance to show our worth.

'They'll have gone through the papers you gave them,' he crowed, 'realised they're useless, and come back for the real stuff.'

'And you can alert the BGS to arrest him. He's not under diplomatic protection, unlike your friend Golubstov.'

The BGS were the Bundesgrenzschutz, or Federal Border Guard. They were responsible for the security of the President, the Chancellor, the Foreign Office and the Federal Ministry of the Interior, which is why they had such a heavy presence in Bonn. The arrest and interrogation of foreign spies came under their remit.

'Catching Golubstov red-handed would make it all worthwhile. The Germans would expel him.' Patrick hugged me and gave me an enthusiastic kiss on the cheek. 'It'll be a feather in our caps. A fast track to promotion.'

*

I met Callan in the bar of a hotel that evening. It was busy and noisy, which suited us both. Callan had a bottle of wine and two glasses ready. He started off by again apologising for his boorish behaviour. He was being blackmailed. There were photographs of the two of us exchanging documents (of course there were, he had shown them to me) and his only concern had been to protect me. That was why everything had been so urgent. If he could provide his blackmailer with what he asked, we would both be left alone.

'Who is this blackmailer?' I asked, as if I feared losing my job in the typing pool.

'I can't tell you that. It would be far too dangerous. For you and for me.'

'Have you ever heard of a blackmailer letting his victim off the hook? When there's more information ready to fall in his lap?'

'Believe me, I've considered all the possibilities, but I have a way to get him to stop.'

'Do you want to share it with me?'

'The less you know about it, the better. He wants new information.'

'I am not stealing one more document, not for you nor anyone else.'

Callan sighed. 'Then he will go to the BGS, you will be

arrested and I shall have to leave Bonn. It would not be good for either of us. Believe me, he's ruthless.'

That makes two of you, I thought. 'Do you feel any remorse for Elsa?'

'Elsa?'

'My colleague in the typing pool. She killed herself.'

'That was Elsa?' He looked shocked. 'I had no idea.'

'Did it not occur to you?'

'Why should it?'

'She was very upset when she walked into Maternus and found us together.'

He shook his head. 'I was very fond of Elsa. Oh God, I've really ruined everything.'

If I hadn't known better, I might have felt sorry for him. I had to consider the very real possibility that Elsa had not killed herself. I could imagine how he might have set her up. Callan would have phoned her, told her he had arranged to dine with me at Maternus, but only because I had expressed concerns about Elsa's well-being. He would have brushed aside any queries about how he knew that she and I were work colleagues. He would have arranged to come round to her bedsit and plead to renew his role as her fiancé. The poor young woman, bewildered and confused, with no one else to turn to, would have readily agreed. Perhaps Callan would have promised her happiness and made love to her. And later, while she was asleep, he would have unlocked the door of her little bedsit. Gulobstov, or more likely some of his goons from the *rezidentura*, would have entered and they would have strung her up, planted the photocopies under her floorboards and left her to be discovered on the Monday morning.

'She was less stable than any of us could have imagined.'

I reached out and touched his arm, as if in a gesture of forgiveness. He looked up, a bitter smile on his lips.

'I wish I could go back and undo everything. I'm just in this too deep.' He took my hand and kissed it, his head bowed, his shoulders wracked with well-rehearsed sobs. After what seemed an age he looked up, his eyes red with tears – he could put on a good show, when he needed to – and asked me to help him.

'I can't do that. I have already betrayed my employer.'

'Just one more time. We can set a trap. This is what he wants.'

He handed me a piece of paper, on which were written two words: *Schnez-Truppe*.

I studied them. They meant nothing to me. 'What is this?'

'Just find the dossier and bring it to me. I will have the BGS waiting to arrest him the moment I hand it over. I will never reveal that I got it from you.'

I considered his proposition while he ordered us a second bottle of wine. 'If I do this one last thing—'

'Yes?' he interrupted.

'I want to be there with you.'

'That's crazy, you'd be exposed as my source.'

'The BGS will already know that, won't they? But I want to be there when your blackmailer is arrested. At least give me that satisfaction.'

The wine arrived as he mulled this over. He topped up our drinks. The alcohol and the heat were getting to me. I gave him my most intense, pleading look, and it seemed to make his decision for him.

'If you come, it is an observer, nothing more. I cannot put you in danger. I cannot lose you so soon after Elsa.'

'I'll find what you need. Leave it to me.' I kissed him.

A STING IN HER TALE

Back in my room I washed my mouth out with soap and brushed my teeth thoroughly twice to expunge the taste of him.

34

West Sussex, May 2019

I was wrenched back to consciousness by the slap of water striking my face. Cold water hits you with a force greater than warm – and this water, as it hit me, struck like a hammer blow. I flashed back to my days in convent school, where we girls had to endure a full minute under a cold shower every morning. The water would strike us with such force that we were convinced it must be ice. We would stand there, gasping rapidly to battle the pain, as the water pounded our heads and ran down the nightdresses we were obliged to wear out of modesty. If we were caught leaning away from the torrent to lessen the discomfort we were forced to endure an extra minute of torture and not permitted to dry our nightdresses on the radiators. That meant going to bed damp and cold. I remember two girls contracting pneumonia, but both survived. We were all a lot tougher in those days.

The water ran down my face and into my clothes, stiffening them as it turned to ice. I shivered. I was on the floor of a large freezer, or ice room. Hanging from hooks above me were whole sides of beef, sheep carcasses and a dozen legs of lamb. I struggled to stand, then realised that my hands were bound together, as were my feet. I had been propped in a sitting position, my knees bent up. My breath came out in jets of steam which froze to crystals that fell to the ground. The room hummed with a powerful electrical buzz.

Igor hurled another bucket of water in my face. 'I can keep doing this until your body freezes to the floor,' he said in his thick accent. 'In half an hour your mind will shut down and soon after that, you will be dead.' He popped a wad of gum in his mouth and chewed, his ugly mouth hanging loose.

I realised that what he said was true. Water had run down my back, pooled on the floor and frozen solid.

All large stately homes once contained an ice room, some in a cold dank corner of the estate, others deep in the cellars. In winter, snow and ice would be brought in from frozen lakes and mountains and packed hard to line the walls. Perishable meat and vegetables would be stored there through the winter. In hot summer ice creams and sorbets would be prepared and cooled. The Ashendon house had been adapted and modernised. It now featured a freezer unit, with pipes carrying coolant around the room on one side, and insulated metal walls on the other three sides. I guessed we were below the kitchen, for close to the cooling pipes was the hatch of the dumb waiter, ready to carry frozen items up to the kitchen for thawing.

Igor gave me time to think about what he had said. I shrugged in response.

'My death will bother nobody. In fact, some may even be glad of it. If you are going to threaten a person's life, choose someone for whom life is a precious commodity. The pain will pass quickly and I shall be at peace.' That would have been true a few weeks ago. Now I had a strange urge to live and see little Alice again.

Igor scowled. 'I can make it very painful and very slow.' He looked around for some weapon to back him up, but found none. The place was too tidy. What he was hoping to find was some butcher's cleaver, or tenderising mallet, but these would be kept upstairs. He pulled a clasp knife from the pocket of his puffer jacket – he had had the sense to wrap up warm – unfolded it and set its lock. He lay the blade up against a freezing pipe for a few seconds then held it flat against my throat. The cold blade burnt into my skin as surely as if he had used the sharp edge, and I could not help a flinch of pain. He grinned. 'Just tell me where you are hiding the child.'

'That is what your friend asked when he popped into the police cell pretending to be my lawyer. I would never employ a fellow like that. Flash but hopelessly incompetent.'

'Incompetent?' He was familiar with the word.

'You two are the most unprofessional agents I have ever encountered. You have left your fingerprints wherever you have been, and we have your faces captured on CCTV all over the village. You really should be more careful.' Neither of these were true, but he could not be certain. He reached down and yanked me up off the ground. As he did so my dress tore, gripped by the ice. It took a layer or two of skin with it. He shoved me roughly towards the racks of meat, grabbed hold of my wrists, bound together with cord, lifted me up and slung the cord over a hook. I'm fairly tall but Igor was stronger than he looked. My feet barely touched the floor.

'If you won't talk I shall prolong your pain until you do.'

He filled the bucket with water from a tap. He stepped behind me, held up the bucket and trickled water down my back. I flinched and the movement spun me around to face him. He raised the bucket higher and in that instant I raised my knees as high as I could – I'm not as decrepit as

I look – and kicked with all my might. The bucket struck him hard between the eyes. Freezing water splashed over his face. He staggered back, twisting away from me. As he stumbled, hands rubbing his eyes, he struck the pipes. He let out a scream of agony as his face froze to them. He clawed at the pipes, trying to free himself from their freezing embrace, but his face stuck fast and he risked tearing it off his skull if he persisted.

I stood on tiptoe, managed to unhook my wrists and snatched up his dropped knife. I cut through the cords binding my hands and feet and reached for the door handle.

'No escape,' he rasped. 'It's locked from the outside.'

'In that case I'm going to need this.' I ripped his puffer jacket from him and put it on.

'We'll make you suffer for this.'

'But you won't be around to see it.' The frozen side of his face was turning blue and his breath was turning to frost around his lips and nose.

Wrapped in the puffer jacket I checked the room. He was right: there was no way out except that steel door. But then an idea occurred to me. I opened the hatch of the dumb waiter. It was large enough to hold a side of beef. I clambered inside.

'No!' my tormentor cried out. 'You stay and help me!'

But there was no help coming for him. I reached out, found the green button, pressed it and drew my hand back fast. The hatch closed smoothly and I felt myself rising. I could hear Igor's wails of pain and rage, but there was nothing I could do to help him. Not that I wished to. A few seconds later the machine whirred to a stop, the hatch slid open and I found myself in the kitchen. There was nobody around.

I hurried to the doorway and slipped outside. I looked at my watch. It was almost five o'clock in the afternoon. I strode to the waiting coach, took my seat and was fighting off the remaining effects of the knock-out spray when the first members of our butterfly party arrived back.

'Blimey, aren't you hot in that?' asked one old boy. I realised I was still wearing the puffer jacket, but it was hiding the tear in my wet dress and I was still chilled to the bone.

I slept all the way home.

35

Bonn, December 1976

I approached Frau Müller for permission. She looked up from her desk.

'You want to go down to filing?'

'Yes, Frau Müller.'

'You are making a habit of this. If you simply got things right the first time, there would be no need.'

'So I may go?'

'Make it snappy.' She handed me a pass.

I trotted downstairs and headed for the files. I still had no idea what the words *Schnez-Truppe* meant or what I was expecting to find.

The three filing clerks were hard at work, for once. Mind you, as soon as they had finished their day's allotted tasks they were allowed to go home, so they had incentive. Their presence meant I could not access the vault, so I started by looking for the files under S.

Sometimes you get lucky first time. There it was: a grey box file coated in dust, the words *Schnez-Truppe* written in faded pencil. It was too bulky for me to take back upstairs and contained far too many pages to photocopy, so I brazenly laid it on a desk close to where the filing clerks were working and started to read as fast as I could.

Fortunately, most of the important information was in

the top pages. The Schnez-Truppe, I learned, was a banned paramilitary organisation created by one Albert Schnez, a former colonel in the Wehrmacht during World War II. Its purpose was to resist any Soviet invasion and it was made up of former Nazis and right-wing extremists. As early as 1951 the then Chancellor, Konrad Adenauer, had been made aware of this secret army, as a copy of a letter to him and duly stamped by his office proved. Despite this, no action had been taken to dismantle the *truppe*. Rather, Adenauer had allowed the intelligence services to offer it funds.

Most of the rest of the three hundred odd pages consisted of the names, addresses, occupations and ages of its members. Many were still of fighting age. The list even included Hans Speidel, who had been Supreme Commander of NATO ground forces in Central Europe as recently as 1963.

I had to think quickly. This list was far too dangerous to fall into Callan's or Golubstov's hands. They would be able to pick off the leaders one by one or, and this was far more likely, devise a campaign of disinformation to incite the *truppe* to rise up against its own government. Destabilising nations by insurrection was the Soviet preferred method, and could be employed in this case to incite civil war in West Germany to devastating effect. In such an event, the USSR might march right in on the pretext of bringing stability and order, and then go on to reunify Germany under its own communist control.

I shut the file and strode up to the three filing clerks. I thrust it into the hands of the nearest of them. 'This dossier has been filed incorrectly. It should have been sent to the Bundesnachrichtendienst in Pullach for storage years ago. And marked "declassified". Please see this doesn't happen again, or I shall have to report it upstairs.'

I had no authority to issue orders, of course, but they had seen my pass from Frau Müller and presumed any instruction came from her. The Bundesnachrichtendienst, the intelligence service, was based in Pullach, a suburb of Munich in Bavaria. My guess was that its storage unit was run by people just as muddle-headed as these three, and that they would dutifully file the dossier away without question. (I was right. The declassified *Schnez-Truppe* files were not rediscovered until 2011, more than twenty years after the reunification of Germany, by which time any surviving members of the *truppe* would have been very old men.)

I still needed something to offer Callan, even if it wasn't what he had asked for. I had failed to provide him with an accurate list of NATO nuclear weapons held on German soil, but perhaps I could supply him with something almost as good.

I found something suitable in a row of files marked, conveniently, NATO and, under that, *Nordatlantik-vertragsorganisation*, a guaranteed winner in any game of Scrabble. I flicked through the first three box files and considered filching a few pages from each, but I felt I could do better. The fourth file held exactly what I wanted. I removed the pages relating to Île Longue, the French ballistic missile submarine base. As it was the best defended place in France, I was not overly concerned that I would be handing over dangerous military secrets.

Under the disinterested gaze of the filing clerks I placed the pages in the Xerox machine and waited for the machine to warm up. The girls stopped talking and concentrated on their work. I turned and found Frau Müller standing right behind me. She leant forward, snatched the pages from my hand and studied them.

'Île Longue,' she read. 'Not a suitable place for a summer vacation.' She thrust the papers back in my hand, turned and marched back up the stairs. Did she suspect me? Worse, did she know what I was doing? Did she simply not care, or was she a part of Callan's network? I shook these ideas out of my head and got on with the photocopying.

*

Patrick's plan, which seemed risky at best, was to obtain photographs of the trail of documents: from me to Callan and from Callan to Golubstov. Rather than involve the BGS, Patrick was going to confront Callan himself. Then, with my help, he was going to turn Callan and force him to work for us as a double agent, feeding false information to Golubstov. There was also the possibility that he could deceive the Soviets into believing we had turned the great Golubstov himself. Then they wouldn't know whom to trust. This would be a longer game, but would have far reaching effects. I had little faith in this plan. Hardened KGB or GRU men were idealists, impervious to corruption.

I expressed my doubts about the enterprise, but Patrick confirmed that Chancery had considered the plan in detail.

'It has been approved at the highest level. We can have as many people operating undercover as we need. Though we should manage with just a few. No point blowing the whole year's budget.'

These undercover agents were to be kept in touch via radio, ready to swoop the moment anything went wrong. I continued to express my concerns. If the BGS ever got wind that British agents had exposed a Soviet spy network on West German soil there would be ructions. Patrick, who throughout the operation had been excited and optimistic, was beginning to show the petulant side to his character. We parted at his last words: 'I just wish you'd have a little more faith in me.'

I set up a meeting with Callan in the Baumschulwäldchen park. The Bonn city council had finally splashed a little money on it and the previous week had seen bulldozers flatten some areas and create raised mounds in others. Then landscapers had dug holes and planted young trees and shrubs which, if I knew anything about city councils, would almost certainly be dead from neglect within the year. As a result, the park bench which had been safe from prying eyes only at dead of night was now surrounded by enough greenery to conceal a dozen British agents.

At eight o'clock that chilly evening Patrick and Giles dropped me a few streets from the park. We were shadowed by another car which kept its distance. Patrick studiously ignored it. I guessed that it contained what he called his 'undercover operatives'. As I walked it started to snow hard.

The plan was that I would hand the papers directly to Callan's contact – perhaps Golubstov himself – with Callan present while Giles, hidden in the bushes, would photograph the handover. Then Patrick and I would confront Callan with the evidence. Patrick was convinced Callan would crumble. 'They all do,' he said with confidence. But he had not stared into his cold green eyes, as I had, and seen the onyx-smooth resolve of his obdurate soul.

I made my way through the park. Its paths were now well delineated, strewn with fresh gravel which crunched underfoot. I saw Giles to my right. He stepped off the path onto soft earth already carpeted with snow and took up position behind a thick laurel. Knowing he was safely hidden from view, I took several more paces and found myself facing Callan, seated on the bench and in full view of a lamp whose dull yellow bulb had been replaced by a brighter one, as if purposed to sharpen our evidence.

'Where is your blackmailer?' I asked. I had almost used the word 'handler', which would have given me away. Patrick's nervousness was infecting me.

'Have you brought me what I asked?'

'I found no file on your Schnez-Truppe, whatever that is,' I said. 'But I have something better.' I held out the dossier I had prepared. 'NATO submarine instalments, a list of ballistic missiles.' I wanted to make the dossier sound more appealing. 'That's what you want, isn't it? But you're not getting any of it until I meet your man.'

Callan's eyes flicked to his left. Golubstov stepped out of the shadows. I experienced a moment of smug satisfaction that our plan had drawn him out.

Golubstov's hands were thrust deep inside his coat pockets, as if anything he touched might be contagious. He spoke in a hoarse whisper, the result of an ancient throat wound. 'I am here,' he said in English. 'What do you have for me?'

'Nuclear missiles in NATO bases. Identification numbers, locations.'

'Launch codes?'

I laughed weakly. 'Now you are asking too much.'

'It seems… surprising that you can access so much valuable information so easily.'

'The Bundestag security is lax.'

'Show me what you have.' He held out his left hand, gloved in black leather.

I handed over the pages. Golubstov flicked through them. There was dead silence. Traffic had almost ceased for the night. I listened out for any faint click of Giles taking photographs, but I heard nothing.

I studied Golubstov. I wanted to memorise every detail about him. But there was so little to fix upon. He was quite unremarkable in every way: rather dull little features, neither tall nor short. Average. He was the kind of person you would have trouble picking out in a line-up, which was probably his greatest strength as a spy.

The Russian raised his head, his face disdainful. 'I can find this information in any public library.'

I tensed. Did Patrick have enough evidence to spring his trap?

'I was informed it would be of value.' I glanced at Callan. Was he going to turn on his handler, as he had promised, and Patrick expected? It did not matter, as long as Giles had photographs.

Golubstov edged closer. He withdrew his right hand from his pocket.

It held a Makarov, a bulky soviet pistol based on the Walther PP. Weighing it heavily in his hand, he aimed it at my chest.

'You will come with us,' he rasped.

'Like hell I will.'

Callan rose. Now, I thought. He's turning on Golubstov.

Instead he took hold of my left arm, his grip too powerful to shake off.

'This wasn't what we agreed.' I was getting worried. We were supposed to be exposing Callan and the Russian. Instead, I had walked into their trap.

Golubstov grasped my right arm and together they forced me across the park to where their car was waiting. Its engine started up.

Where the hell was Patrick? What was he playing at?

I dug in my heels and attempted to struggle free.

I yelled out in German. 'Let me go! Help!' in the hope that passing strangers might come to my aid.

There were none.

In desperation I went limp, forcing them to drag me across the gravel path, my tights ripping at the knees, my left ankle boot almost slipping off my foot.

How long would it take them to extract the fact that I was an SIS agent? Perhaps they already knew.

I brought my right knee up to my chest and slammed the heel of my right boot hard against Golubstov's leg. He let out a cry of pain and let go of my arm.

I dropped to my knees. Golubstov, grimacing with pain, raised his hand and I found myself staring down the barrel of his gun.

In the brief moment it took him to pull back the knurled hammer, I heard Giles yell in alarm. A camera flew from the bushes and struck Golubstov hard on the temple. His shot whipped past me into the gravel.

Footsteps running on snow-covered gravel forced him to turn. Giles was rushing him. Golubstov fired his gun three times, the last shot hitting Giles at point-blank range.

Giles was dead before he hit the ground.

'No!' This was Patrick – at last breaking cover – wildly firing his own gun. Golubstov swung around and fired a single round in Patrick's direction – I heard the snap of breaking bone. Patrick fell hard.

Golubstov turned back to me. His gun was aimed low.

'You will die screaming, bitch.'

Callan snatched the gun from his hand.

At last, I thought: he had finally found the courage to do the right thing.

Callan smiled at me – reassuringly, I thought – and shot me in the belly. He turned to Golubstov. I thought he would shoot him too. Instead, he helped Golubstov limp back towards their waiting car.

I looked down and saw an awful lot of blood pumping from my stomach onto the white snow.

I crawled over to Patrick, who lay sobbing on the ground, his left leg stuck out at an odd angle. I snatched up his gun and fired once at the retreating men.

I heard a cry of pain and saw Callan stumble and fall forward. The driver ran from the car, stooped and rolled Callan onto his back. Blood bubbled from his mouth. The driver uttered a single word, '*Mertvykh*'. I spoke no Russian but I recognised the word. It meant 'dead'.

Then the sight of my own lifeblood gushing in a torrent and the searing agony of the bullet which had torn its way through my body sent my head spinning till it struck the ground, my heartbeat faltered and I passed out.

36

West Sussex, May 2019

The trouble with sleeping in the late afternoon is that you do not sleep well at night. The moment I got home I double-locked and bolted the doors and then went up to bed and slept. I set my alarm for an hour. But when it woke me I lay dozing for a while then fell back to sleep and did not wake again till nearly midnight. My ordeal in the freezer had taken a lot out of me. I had a deep frost burn at the base of my throat, across my collarbone, which I could cover with my mother's pearl necklace. I never wore the pearls, except for special occasions, but they would come in useful now.

My other frost burn was harder to deal with. When Igor had wrenched me off the floor of the cold room a part of my skirt had been shredded and, for a while, I thought my scrawny backside had suffered the same fate. A layer of epidermis had ripped away and it smarted like buggery. I got up and found some 'Witchdoctor' antiseptic gel in the bathroom cupboard and applied it liberally. It stung like hell and I had to grit my teeth to stop crying out. My only satisfaction was knowing that, whatever pain I had to endure, Igor would have suffered ten times worse – if he had survived.

I returned to bed, but sleep eluded me. Every little sound, every tap of a tree branch on a window, made me think that they were breaking in to get me and resume their torture. I got up, dressed, and checked the house one more time and then went into the cellar and ran that day's recordings at fast speed. Apart from a family of hedgehogs snuffling in the rear garden, there was no reason to slow the tape. My tormentors had not returned.

I sat at my desk with a hot chocolate. As I sipped it, I thought back to what was really bothering me, the thing that had been keeping me awake.

It was that voice: that caramel, baritone voice. It rang many bells which were now pealing so loudly they overwhelmed all my efforts to recall where I had heard it before.

I finally made it back to bed at three in the morning, by which time a new edition of *The Times* had become available on my iPad. I read the death notices – it's always reassuring to learn one has managed to outlive old school friends and acquaintances – and the obituaries. Then I moved on to the daily quiz and succeeded in getting the answers to fourteen out of the fifteen questions right. I can never answer the sports questions, unless they relate to the 2012 London Olympics. I had enjoyed our two weeks of triumph. Shortly after that I must have fallen asleep, because I was awoken by the persistent ringing of the doorbell.

I did not need to put on my clothes since I had fallen asleep in them, but I wished I had given my hair a quick run through with a brush, or a broom or even a garden rake – it was that untidy – when I opened the door to find Percy, immaculately dressed in a fresh tweed suit and a mustard yellow waistcoat, from which hung his gold watch and chain. He raised his brown homburg. The citrusy spice of Dunhill for Men wafted over me.

'Am I too early?'
'For what?'

'For our date. We have an arrangement. I said I'd pick you up at ten.'

I had no idea what he was talking about. We had made no arrangement, had nothing planned. Or had I been so bound up in my own obsessions that I had completely forgotten that we had fixed a date?

'I'm so sorry, Percy, I seem to have come down with something. Just a cold, I think, but I meant to call you and then I've been on the phone all morning and it just… ' I trailed off. The disappointment in his face was obvious. He recovered well.

'Not to worry, some other time. I should have sent you a text or something to check you were still up for it.' He stepped back, gave me a little bow, turned on his heel and marched smartly away.

It struck me instantly. His scent, the brisk way he marched off, reminded me of someone, provoking a distant memory of a man, taller and more strongly built, turning on his heels. But who?

Fifteen minutes later I was starting the car. As I drove through the village high street I caught sight of Percy, arm in arm with one of the two blonde women who had come to his aid in the café. He caught sight of me at the same time, and his look of disappointment struck me in a place I hadn't felt for many years. I simply stared straight ahead as if I had not seen him.

I drove without subterfuge. If they followed me, I was confident I would see them. I got onto the A27 at Arundel and carried on east to check the traffic and sent a WhatsApp to Patrick to alert him to expect me shortly. I received no reply.

At the Sluice Lane roundabout I ignored the road to Norman's Bay and instead took the road to Pevensey. I carried on all the way to Pevensey Bay and turned left along the coast road back towards Norman's Bay. The ground was open and I would have seen anyone following. But there were no cars except one with an elderly couple who parked up on a concrete stand and struggled to haul their shopping up steep steps to their beachside bungalow.

I stopped the car close to the level crossing, got out and set off walking along the shingle beach. Children were flying kites in the wind and fishermen stood chatting by their rods which had been cast far out beyond the surf. I selected a few flat stones and skimmed them into the water. One bounced nine times before sinking into the waves. I picked up another handful of stones and caught sight of him: a young man of around thirty, tall, slim with glasses. He turned away quickly. Was he the same man I had spotted at the railway station? Had he been watching me or was he just amused to see an old woman playing a child's game on the beach? I tossed the stones away and made a show of collecting slipper limpet shells. He picked up the backpack by his feet, hoisted it on his shoulders and wandered off in the opposite direction, towards the Martello tower.

I reached the lookout, went around to the front door which, typically of Patrick, was round the back of the house. I had to squeeze past his small fishing boat, hauled up by the side of the house and showing signs of neglect, and rang the doorbell. There was no response. I waited a full minute and tried again. Still nothing. Perhaps he had gone to meet me in the lane? I walked around the side of the lookout and, as an afterthought, mounted the white stairs that led to the observation room. Once it had held a gun emplacement, ready for a Nazi invasion. Now it contained sofas and houseplants, insulated with blue-tinted double-glazing.

Patrick was staring out to sea, his mouth hanging open. Music was playing on his Bose professional speakers: the third movement of Beethoven's Ninth Symphony, almost certainly conducted by Karajan. The symphonies were his favourites, and we had enjoyed that von Karajan concert together in Bonn. I could hear its sweet, sentimental chords vibrating through the glass. I tried the handle of the door. It was locked from the inside. I knocked, but he didn't seem to hear, so I knocked harder and louder, rapping my knuckles on the pane, until he turned, his eyes vacant, a small fleck of white spit on his open mouth. Then he saw me, seemed to shake away his reverie, stood to unlock the door and beckoned me in. Without saying anything we both stood and listened to a few more bars of music, then he raised his hand, which held the Bose remote control, pressed a button and the room fell silent except for the muffled sounds of waves lapping on the shingle.

'Sentimental rubbish.'

'I thought you loved Beethoven.'

'Do I?' He thought for a moment. 'Perhaps, but not the symphonies.'

37

Patrick had trouble finding the teabags. He shuffled around the kitchen, opening several cupboards before he found what he was looking for. It was all I could do to stop him dropping them straight into the electric kettle.

'You seem distracted. Is something worrying you?'

'Yes.' He shook his head, as if to clear it, and said no more about the matter. He made tea in a Chinese pot, let it stew a few minutes then poured a dash of milk into each cup and topped them up from the pot. His style was very different from Percy's, but I had a great fondness for Patrick. We had been through so much and, unlike me, he had a shattered left leg to show for it.

'What brings you here?'

'Things have escalated.'

I told him about my 'butterfly trip' the day before, and my incarceration in the ice room. I did not go into any details or mention that I had left Igor with his face frozen to the pipes. Nor did I go into the method of my escape. Patrick and I had eluded more dangerous traps.

'You were very lucky. You're getting on a bit for those sorts of antics.' He leant forward. 'When was the last time you had a bath?'

I hadn't washed since before my ordeal in the freezer. My

backside, which was still raw, had put me off a long soak and I had not had time in the morning, what with Percy. Percy! Had he noticed me stinking like some old bag lady?

'I had a bath last week, if you really want to know. I take regular showers, sometimes twice a day. I have a strong aversion to wallowing in my own filth.'

That changed the subject. We sat sipping our tea. Patrick had not provided any food, but that wasn't what I had come for.

'Another cup?'

'Thank you.' As he poured, I carried on. 'When I was there I heard a voice.'

'What do you mean, "a voice"?'

'A familiar voice, one I've heard before in different circumstances.' And then I played him the recording. I don't think I mentioned this before, it slipped my mind when I was writing my account, but I had taken out my phone and set it to video just as the master of the house had entered. I had not managed to capture his image, but I had recorded his voice, and this I played back to Patrick.

He listened without showing any reaction. I played it again.

'Strange that they didn't take your phone away from you.'

'They did, but I had the presence of forethought to WhatsApp the recording to myself on another number immediately. That's why I still have it. This is a spare phone I keep for eventualities such as this. Does the voice mean anything to you?'

'For what it's worth, my hearing isn't as good as it was. But no, I haven't heard that voice before.' He still seemed very distracted, not himself at all. He got up, went into his study and sat at his desk. I finished my tea and followed him. Patrick was staring at something on the desk before him.

'I thought it might trigger a memory,' I said, still hopeful.

He started, as if he had forgotten I was there. 'No,' he said after a while. 'It means nothing to me.'

Then I saw what he had been staring at. It was a photograph of me in Bonn. It was a cold winter's night and I was wearing a Parka with a fake fur hood. I was with another person, whose back was towards the camera and they were also wearing a hood. I was showing them some documents, presumably to Patrick himself. I had been working undercover, so this had to be a surveillance photograph taken by one of Patrick's team, perhaps his dear friend Giles. But why had he kept it? To remind himself of better times?

I offered to water his plants, which looked sadly neglected. 'I'll do it when you've gone,' he said.

We bid our farewells and Patrick perked up noticeably. He volunteered to walk me to my car.

'You must come by more often,' he said. 'I haven't seen you in ages. It's been far too long.'

I didn't say anything.

He held the door open for me and waited as I got in and started the car. He seemed unconcerned that we might be seen together, despite all my caution. It was as if he were putting on a performance for somebody else's benefit.

I rolled down the window to say a final farewell and, as I did so, I saw the same young man strolling along the beach. He no longer carried his backpack, wore a different jacket and had ditched the glasses, but he was the same man, I was sure of it.

I drove back the way I came, thinking about what Patrick had said and, more importantly, what he hadn't. I wondered if he was on a particularly strong form of medication or in the early stages of dementia. Either way, he might need someone to take care of him. Perhaps I should alert the service. I knew Patrick wouldn't thank me if I did that and decided against it.

It was not until I was passing Charleston, the old home of Vanessa Bell and Duncan Grant, that I slammed on the brakes and almost caused the truck behind to back-end me. The driver sounded his horn loudly and made a big show of driving around my car as I pulled up onto the grass verge. The line of cars behind him honked their horns in support.

I was hardly aware of them. At that moment I knew whose voice I had heard and recorded. It belonged to a man who had been dead for more than forty years.

38

Bonn, December 1976

Thank God for dog walkers. As his spaniel cocked its leg and emptied its bladder over Giles's dead body, the owner ran to summon help while his wife, a doctor, staunched my wound. Drifting in and out of consciousness, I could barely hear Patrick, his sobs for his loss of Giles overwhelming his moans of pain.

An agent was flown over from London to debrief me as I lay in hospital. I had lost more than two litres of blood and the haemorrhagic shock left me delirious for three days, so the poor man had trouble getting much sense out of me. His name was Dennis Osborn. He had been my instructor and mentor when I was first inducted in London. Despite my having gone way beyond my brief, he was surprisingly understanding. He had always had a soft spot for me.

Patrick, his left femur shattered by Golubshov's bullet, was in far more trouble. Despite his assurances to me, he had not kept Chancery fully informed of his operation, nor had he organised any backup in the park. It had been just him, Giles and me. Patrick had hoped to take full credit and glory for the operation and come out of it a hero. Instead, he had got his close colleague (and secret lover) killed. Knowing how much Giles' death was hurting Patrick, I did my best to speak up for him. Golubshov's subsequent expulsion from

West Germany was considered something of a consolation for both of us. Patrick, minus an inch of femur that left him with a permanent limp, was sent back to London in disgrace and relegated to a desk job. He was not back on foreign operations for five years, about the same time that Golubshov reappeared at the Rezidentura in the Soviet Embassy in Cairo. Patrick was eventually given a second chance. He and I were to cross paths again.

Golubshov, a busted flush as far as the West was concerned, was not so lucky. Shortly after Egyptian President Anwar Sadat was assassinated by members of Egyptian Islamic Jihad in October 1981, an attack in which the Cuban ambassador, a Soviet ally, was badly injured, Golubshov himself was killed by a car bomb in a Cairo street. As the Soviet Union had been supporting Egypt against Israel, this was presumed to be an Israeli hit, but Golubshov's protection detail, normally so assiduous in checking the underside of his car, had mysteriously melted away that same morning. The truth of the matter is that it was a covert joint US/UK operation and I may have been involved. I'm not admitting I was, mind you, I'm just saying that I am not beyond taking personal revenge when my own desires coincide with the aims and needs of my country.

Callan was not heard of again. Not officially, at any rate, though there were vague rumours of his survival, all of which proved to be unfounded. My bullet had struck home. Perhaps he had died that night or perhaps I had left him permanently paralysed. That, I confess, is what I would have preferred. He had been directly responsible for Elsa's death. The Bundesgrenzschutz searched his run-down flat and discovered more documents which had been leaked from the West German Chancellery. Security had not been quite as slack as we had supposed. Suspecting that the leaks might come from the typing pool, the BGS had planted faked documents with each typist. If the Soviets, or any other foreign service, were to act on that false information, the Bundesgrenzschutz would know who to arrest. They caught three women this way. Each had been seduced and blackmailed by Callan into betraying her country. They received long sentences, their careers and lives destroyed. What I could not have predicted was that, six months after these events, Frau Müller herself was arrested. She had been working for the Americans. The discovery caused ructions between the US and West German NATO powers that took years to heal. The whole affair was such an embarrassment to each side that it was never reported and the public never got to hear about it.

Dennis escorted me back to Northolt airport in a troop carrier. I was on a hospital gurney all the way, still in pain a week after being shot. I was treated at the Charing Cross Hospital in Fulham Palace Road and a week later I was released into his care. He had made up a bed in his spare room in Gowan Avenue, just a few blocks south of the hospital.

After all my adventures I felt in greater need for human company than I ever had before. One night I stole into Dennis's bedroom and we made love. He was clumsy and came too soon, but I needed the warmth and comfort of a human body. The last person to make love to me had been Callan, and he had been a master of his art. I could not expect Dennis to compete and did not suggest that he try. Every morning he would go off to work, reporting in at Century House, near Waterloo station, before taking a brisk walk to 296 Borough High Street, the non-field training headquarters. I had trained there myself and Dennis had, he now confided, considered me his star pupil, which was why he had asked to be sent to Bonn to bring me home.

After a month of further recuperation – punctuated by bouts of lovemaking – I moved into a ground-floor flat with a fine garden in North Kensington. It was owned by the department. They gave me the option to buy it at any time I wanted to, at a generous discount. I just needed time to muster the funds.

About eight months after getting back to London, and about five months after I had resumed desk work at SIS, I returned to Charing Cross Hospital for a caesarean section. My wounds were such that it was deemed unwise to go to full term and risk the pressure of a natural birth. The operation produced twins, whom I named Bernard and Eva.

As soon as he had heard that I was pregnant, Dennis had offered to marry me.

'You want to make an honest woman of me?'

'I defy anyone to manage that.' He laughed. 'We both know you're beyond redemption.'

I declined his offer as gently as I could. In those days the SIS discouraged married couples from working together. There would be too many emotional complications if a spouse risked danger or died in the field. So I had the babies and hired a full-time nanny to take care of them during the day, while I shared the responsibilities with her and her substitutes during evenings and weekends.

Sometimes I would be away for weeks on end. When the twins were just three years old I was away for four whole months. The children became more familiar with their nannies than they were with me. I told you I was not a good mother. They suffered neglect as did the garden, which became an unruly mess. My experience with Callan and Golubstov had increased my determination to stop whatever they and their ilk were trying to achieve across the world. I wanted to see the Soviet Union fail. I was in Berlin in 1989 when the wall came down. I wish I could say I had a part in that. Well perhaps, in a small way, I did.

When the twins were six I dismissed the nannies, now a rising expense, and sent the children to stay with my mother who, bored rigid in retirement and prone to starting her morning with a triple gin and tonic, offered to improve their education. When I finally went to fetch them back – after nearly twelve months, on and off – they hardly knew me. It was midday and I found my mother in the kitchen, still in her grubby dressing gown, unwashed, her nails black with filth, her hair as unkempt as mine is today, tearing through *The Times* crossword. She usually completed it in under twenty minutes. Even in the fog of alcohol her mind remained sharp to the very end.

This was no way to bring up children, I realised, but I had noticed a change in them. After a whole year under mother's tutelage, they had become remarkably disciplined and self-sufficient, something that has continued all their lives. I cannot take any credit for it, but this resilience in the face of adversity has helped them achieve the stellar careers they enjoy today.

When my mother died she left the children a small inheritance. I was able to use it to buy the lease on the flat and send them early to boarding school. Unlike other children their age, they never wept or felt homesick. I had never provided a home life for them to miss.

Did I regret this? Not at the time. I was too single-minded. But as I got older, when I was eventually forced to retire, I grew to realise what I had missed. I began to understand that, in all aspects of my life apart from the professional, I had totally fucked up.

39

West Sussex, June 2019

It was not until mid-June that the body was found. Again, thank God for dog walkers. A young woman's body had been chopped up, stuffed in a suitcase and tossed into a deep hole in woodland that bordered the Ashendon estate.

Some busybody from the civic society had decided to test the levels of river pollution – the extended heatwave had led to sudden thunderstorms and heavy flooding – and he had taken it upon himself to try out his new membrane filtration test kit, acquired for less than thirty pounds. In an area where the water was filtered by chalk downland he had been shocked to find exceptionally high levels of bacteria.

There was a news item about it on the local radio and an investigation was launched into sewage dumping by the water company. In this instance, the company was entirely innocent. Its illicit dumping was carried out several miles further downstream. A few days later a dog walker lost his pet's ball in thick undergrowth. As he forced his way through the brambles he became aware of an almighty stench. It caused him to gag uncontrollably. The suitcase containing the body had floated to the top of what proved to be a disused well. Its foul contents had leaked into the water table.

Forensics descended on the area. They extracted DNA samples from the mush that remained of the body. My curiosity aroused, as it so easily is, I contacted Ambrose Flynn in Forest Row and asked if there was a chance of acquiring a readout of the woman's DNA.

'Absolutely not,' was his curt reply. There was a pause. 'What do you want it for?'

'Remember that murder in my village a few weeks ago?'

'Of course I do. I understand they still haven't found the perpetrator.'

'I believe the body in the suitcase may be connected.'

'If you have any evidence that might help the police inquiry, I strongly advise you to take it up with them.' He put the phone down.

I stomped into my neglected garden and took my frustration out on the weeds with a scythe. It was hard, thirsty work in the hot sunshine. I telephoned Jamie Cullum and invited him round to help me. Together we bagged three hessian sacks with garden waste, too coarse for my own heap, which the council would take away and compost. In return the council allowed us to buy it back, composted, at twice what it cost in the local garden centre. Even so, I considered it fair recompense for saving me a trip to the dump. Besides, I am a firm advocate of recycling.

After two hours of energetic work we stopped. I brought out two cans of cold lager. Jamie downed his in one and let out a tremendous burp that set the frogs laughing. We were sat by the edge of the small pond which I had dug when I first came to live here. I had planted its edges with aquatic plants acquired from the garden centre. As an added bonus I had found attached to the plants frog spawn which hatched and developed into tadpoles. These were not common frogs, but *rana ridibunda*, the laughing frog. Every time a loud noise sounded or a plane flew over from Gatwick they would burst into a chorus of cackling, prompting Jamie to laugh along with them.

They were laughing so loudly I almost missed the *ping* of the WhatsApp notification. It was Ambrose. He wrote that, while he had not been able to get me a readout of the dead woman's DNA, if I were able to provide him with the sample I wanted tested, he had someone who might be able to compare both samples for me.

I left Jamie to rake up the weeds and climbed the stairs to the spare bedroom. I had kept the small blankets I had bought for Alice. Sometimes I would simply go upstairs to the airing cupboard and smell them before putting them away in a drawer. They had the faintest odour; a whiff like freshly baked cake. I would just sit there and hold one of them to my face, as I tried to puzzle out a problem. And just as often I wondered why I had never done the same with my own babies.

There was still one blanket left in the drawer. I had only handled it with the gloves worn to change Alice's first nappy. As I unfolded it, I noticed that it was slightly soiled. At the time, changing the nappy had absorbed my whole attention and I had folded the blanket away without checking. I popped it into an unused freezer bag. With luck some expert would be able to isolate Alice's DNA.

I called Federal Express, gave them the old account number I had not used since I had sent over a load of documents to the CIA in Langley and, after enduring the tedious process of updating my credit card details, arranged a pickup. Later that day FedEx came for the package. It would be delivered by noon the next day to the laboratory Ambrose had recommended.

I spent the next two days hacking down overgrown shrubs

and ripping ivy off the walls. It was a pointless exercise as the council gave us a maximum allowance of three bags of garden waste and I had already filled those. I needed strenuous activity to occupy my mind and the warm sunshine made the task bearable. Jamie was otherwise occupied. He was learning to drive a tractor on the Langdon estate – he was still going out with Beth, though they hadn't yet informed her father. First he needed to demonstrate that he could hold down a decent job.

On the third day I received another WhatsApp from Ambrose. The lab had managed to isolate Alice's cells on the blanket. They had extracted the DNA, made copies so they had enough to work with, and had run the amplified DNA on a genetic analyser to get a profile. Ambrose adored a preamble before confirming, at the very end of his message, a partial match of the DNA sequence. That was all I needed to know. As I had already suspected, Alice and the murdered woman were closely related.

40

Taking the law into your own hands is actively discouraged in this country. But I believe there are times when an issue becomes so personal that it becomes a duty. As Oscar Wilde said, '*I can resist everything but temptation.*' I knew exactly how he felt.

I locked up the cottage and drove to Ambrose's house near Forest Row. I took the long, circuitous route that I had taken when I first got Alice, but with a couple of variations. I shall not divulge them on these pages. I may need to use them again.

The barn attached to Ambrose's home once housed cattle. They were long gone, victims of foot and mouth disease scares, but evidence of their habitation remained. The floor of the barn was covered in compacted cow dung and straw to a depth of nine inches. Ambrose, carefully avoiding the deepest deposits, tiptoed towards a chain set in the wall and tugged at it. A hidden trapdoor in the floor rose up to reveal stone steps leading to a room beneath. Ambrose waved me down. 'After you.'

I headed down the steps, as I had done many times before.

'Take what you like. I could make some suggestions, but it's best you choose.'

'Nothing too heavy,' I said.

Lights came on in the strongroom. Along one edge were beautifully fitted limed oak cabinets, probably made by Aaron, whose father had been a master carpenter. In the cabinets were a variety of weapons. I recognised many which, in the line of duty, Ambrose or I had removed from people whom we had arrested or despatched in one way or another. None of the weapons was registered in the UK.

I made my selection quickly: a Steyr SSG69 sniper rifle, made in Austria, with a Kahles ZF69 6x42 telescopic sight. As backup I chose a Sterling L34A1 submachine gun, which came with its own suppressor (*not* a silencer, please, guns are never silent) attached. I won't bore you with details of the Sterling, except to say that each round is fired a fraction of a second before it is fully chambered. This, and the lighter bolt, dampens its recoil and makes for a less weighty, more controllable and accurate weapon which, at my advanced age, I needed.

'You'll want these for the job.' Ambrose handed me a box of subsonic ammunition. When fired, the bullets would not produce a loud crack as they left the barrel. The muzzle velocity would be reduced, but that should not pose a problem as I expected to be operating at a distance of less than a hundred feet. The gun's effective range was listed at four hundred feet, so I felt confident of hitting my target. I had brought a large and cumbersome golf bag with me. I concealed both guns and ammunition in the bag, zipped it shut and we headed back up the steps.

Ambrose released the chain. The lights dimmed and went off as the trapdoor closed. He scattered loose clods of dung and straw around. Looking at it, one would believe the floor of the barn had not been disturbed in a decade.

He led me round to the side of the house where he kept a small white model 'e' electric Honda. I had never seen one before. Ambrose explained that it was a pre-production model that he had been given to tinker with. 'False number plates, but they won't attract attention. I shall change them back when you return the vehicle. If anything goes wrong I shall, of course, deny all knowledge of your operation, but it shouldn't come to that. I am loaning you nothing that can be tied to me, not even this phone, and if you do not return that, I shall presume you are dead.'

We swapped phones. Mine would continue to emit signals from his location. Which meant that, contrary to the assertion he had just made, he could be tied to me, but it would take a lot of investigative legwork to do so. Ambrose would have prepared a ready and convincing answer. The phone he gave me, while not registered to his name, had a Bluetooth connection which I would use to operate and lock the car.

I drove on to London and registered at a small, rundown hotel in Earl's Court. I presented a French passport with a somewhat blurred photograph of myself, which would make it hard to identify if the hotel manager were ever asked to produce a copy. In the event, he didn't even look at it, being far too busy playing computer games on his phone to bother with an elderly woman with an impenetrable French accent. He gladly accepted the hundred and forty pounds in cash I handed over in advance. I had parked the car a couple of blocks away. As it was electric there was no need to pay the congestion or Ultra Low Emission Zone fees. And, as I would be up early, I would not need to feed the meter.

The following morning I left the hotel at eight in the morning. I wore a large raincoat over my clothes and did not slip it off until I was inside the Honda. I drove up to St John's Wood to keep my appointment in Avenue Road, which runs north from Regent's Park at a point close to the zoo's entrance. I had made considerable effort over my appearance. I wore a Dior twinset that had once belonged to my mother, along with her best set of pearls. My right knuckle flashed her Burmese sapphire ring with cushion-cut diamonds on the collar, and my habitually scraggly hair was hidden under my Hermès scarf. I wore the obligatory sunglasses, though my disguise was such that I felt confident I did not need them.

The estate agent, a smart young woman who looked as if she had stepped from the cover of *Tatler*, was waiting for me. I drove my little Honda into the front drive. The mansion was on sale for a mouth-watering asking price. A builder's hoarding advertising its refurbishment ran along the front and side of the building and continued around the back into the side street. The woman looked a little put out to be here on a weekend morning, but when your sales commission is likely to run to more than £500,000 you don't mind leaving your partner in bed with the Sunday papers.

'I'm so sorry about the building work,' she said. 'They promised they'd be out by the end of the month, but they've still got a bit of snagging to fix.'

I replied in a well-rehearsed French accent and made a big show of hauling the golf bag out of the car. 'My 'usband, he is crazy about zee golf, but if I looze ze clobs, he will kill me.'

She raised her eyebrows in a brief show of exasperation, then, realising her error, flashed me a big smile. 'If Madame would care to…'

'Countess,' I corrected. I held out my hand, raised as if I expected her to kiss it. She took it awkwardly, jiggling it up and down gingerly, as if it might snap off in her hand.

'You must have a lot of golf courses in the South of France.'

'Belge,' I corrected again. 'I am *Belge*. And don't worry about zee "Countess". My 'usband and I, we 'ave four sons and each of zem is a count, so being a *comtesse* is a little common, *n'est-ce pas*?' It did not come naturally, but I managed a gay laugh.

I followed her into the house, lugging the heavy golf bag. It did not take long to exasperate the poor woman. I asked fatuous and pointless questions about the burglar alarm ('still being installed'), the cooker ('why isn't it 90cm square; whose chef still cooks in a 60cm oven?') and even the light bulbs ('I cannot habide these LED lights'). Every time I turned I swung the bulky golf bag behind me, so there was a danger of destroying the expensive knick-knacks and bibelots artfully arranged around the house. When we reached the upper floor, I begged to put the golf bag down somewhere, 'perhaps *le balcon*?' She agreed and we completed the rest of the viewing in relative comfort. I refused to visit the attic ('I don't 'ave zee right shoes'), but was happy to inspect the staff quarters in the basement. These proved disappointing. 'But where will ze footmen sleep? Ahh, (a sudden flash of inspiration) *pas de problème*, the Count weel be 'appy to buy an extra house for ze staff.'

As she saw me back to the car I suddenly exclaimed, '*Mon Dieu, le golf*!' I insisted the poor woman not escort me back upstairs to fetch the clubs. I would be down again '*toute suite*.'

The golf bag was back in the car and I was away in a flurry of gravel, promising that my 'usband would be calling to make an offer of the full asking price on Monday morning. I could see her mentally totting up the commission on two Avenue Road houses as I disappeared down the road.

I treated myself to an early lunch in Soutine, the brasserie in St John's Wood High Street. It seemed to fit my image as 'ze Countess'. Afterwards I drove down to The Regent's Park, as the royal park is formally known.

I parked the car in the inner circle and made my way to St John's Lodge Gardens. One gains access to the gardens through a single entrance. Normally I avoid places without at least one, preferably two, escape routes. But there are few cameras in the park except around Winfield House, the American Ambassador's residence. There you can find enough cameras to start your own television station.

If you walk to the north east of the inner circle you will find double iron gates which lead to a path shaded by arches of wisteria. At the far end sits an urn in Portland stone. Visitors peer in, think that the path is a dead end, and wander off. But if you reach the end of the path and take the hidden dog leg north, you will find yourself in an enclosed area far from prying eyes.

The first feature to greet you is a circular pond. At its centre is a bronze statue of a young man being supported, it seems, by a mermaid. A woman doing all the real work, as usual. Closer inspection reveals that this is a representation of Hylas, one of Jason's Argonauts from Greek mythology, who was kidnapped by a water nymph and never seen again. In this depiction, Hylas seems somewhat underaged. That would have earned the nymph a visit from the police, though in all probability Jason would never have got the Health and Safety Executive to approve his journey in the first place.

Continue on past the fountain and turn left and you will find another statue, that of a young shepherdess carrying a baby lamb. Inscribed beneath are the words *'To all protectors of the defenceless'*. I thought back to poor Elsa in Bonn. She had been defenceless. But who had been there to protect her? Not I.

In another part of these hidden gardens are four comfortable high-backed benches. I made one of these my resting place, snuggled up under a light rug that I had brought for the purpose and snoozed away the afternoon. I needed to rest up before the night.

I was awake by five o'clock though. To tell the truth, I hadn't really slept. I was too much on edge.

In the distance I could hear music playing. I left the gardens, returned along the inner circle and stopped at the Broad Walk for a pee. To my annoyance the lavatories had been 'modernised' and there was no free entry. I had to swipe a debit card (not in my name, of course) and pay twenty pence to gain access. It was that or popping round the back and peeing in the bushes. I used the card, the automatic gate opened and I stepped into a cubicle and relieved myself. It might be my last chance for many hours.

Afterwards I avoided the grubby-looking taps and used a wet wipe (one of the many left over from my first purchase for Alice) to clean my hands. From the kiosk, a charming little cottage of pale brick with a high roof and chimney, I purchased an ice cream and wandered south towards the source of the music.

Just off the broad walk I found a dozen or more couples dancing a tango to a boom box on the ground. Their instructors – a short South American man and a taller woman from Chicago (if I had identified her accent correctly) moved among them, correcting the odd misstep but otherwise leaving them to find their own rhythms and enjoy themselves and their partners. They danced to 'Por una Cabeza' by Carlos Gardel, a melody that holds within it every expression and emotion of the act of seduction and of love.

As the dancing continued I retreated to a small pavilion – a simple roof held up by slim fluted pillars – and sat there. Eventually the music and the dancing ceased. I checked my watch every so often. I could do nothing until it was truly dark, which would not be for another three hours.

When I felt the time was right I returned to St John's Wood High Street. In a late-night shop I bought a sandwich and some grapes which I ate in the car. Eventually, as its digital clock finally reached 10:00, I listened to the news then drove the few blocks east to Avenue Road.

41

I PARKED A HUNDRED YARDS up the side street and waited to see that all was quiet. A dog foxtrotted past. If he felt it was dark enough, then so did I. Removing my sunglasses – I could not risk tripping over an uneven bit of paving – and with my headscarf hiding my face, I approached the builder's hoarding. It ran all around the side of the garden but did not extend to the next house. That was surrounded by a much lower wall.

I had no trouble clambering over the low wall and then the higher wall separating the two gardens. I dropped down into low shrubs and soft compost. I was not concerned about the cameras set up around the house. I had confirmed that none of them were yet in operation.

Above the mock-Palladian porch jutted the small balcony where I had offloaded the heavy golf bag earlier that morning. I felt around for the nylon filament which I had left dangling over the edge. I could barely see it glinting in the street light. I tugged gently. From above me a rope ladder unspooled to the ground. I climbed, my movements concealed from the street by the hoarding. Only when I reached the base of the parapet was I at risk. Most of the houses were second or third homes. Their owners would already be swanning around on their yachts in the Mediterranean. I struggled up the last few feet, hauled myself up over the balcony and sat down to catch my breath.

Both guns, wrapped in blue plastic, lay where I had left them on the balcony. Had they been spotted by any workman, he might have presumed them to be tools waiting to be collected. I checked and loaded both magazines then sat on the cool marble tiles to wait.

I did not have to wait long. At around ten to eleven the maroon Rolls-Royce I had first seen in Kensington Palace Gardens approached from the direction of Regent's Park. There had been a reception at the Russian Embassy to celebrate 'Russia Day', commemorating the formal declaration of Russian Sovereignty from the Soviet Union in 1991. I had been certain that the man whose voice I had heard only a few days earlier would be in attendance.

Shortly after Patrick had provided the two addresses – Ashendon Park in West Sussex and the mansion in Winnington Road (unoccupied, as I had discovered) – Ambrose had provided me with a third. It was opposite the building where I was now lying in wait in Avenue Road.

The electronic gates opened, the Rolls slid in, and the gates closed behind it. After a few minutes the house lights, already illuminating the ground floor, came on in the floor above. The curtains were open. A maid ran ahead of her master, switching on more lights with a remote control, drawing some of the curtains closed with another. The tall man strode into the bedroom and watched as the maid turned down the bed. He removed his clothes, stripping off while she ran a bath for him in the room beyond. He stood, naked, at the window facing the balcony where I was waiting, ready. I marvelled at the state of his body, still magnificent after all these years. He turned and, through the telescopic sights, I saw the deep hollow of the wound in his back where I had shot him all those years ago. It would have taken a specialist's skills to keep him alive.

As the maid crossed the room Callan, as I still thought of him, grabbed her arm. He twisted her around and forced himself on her. She fought back, clawing at his face, but he tightened his hold and hurled her to the ground. He reached for a baton and raised it to strike her. In the intervening years he had abandoned his highly honed skills of seduction. In his present position, he no longer needed them.

It was then that I squeezed the trigger and loosed off my first shot.

It was aimed to hit him high in the temple and split his skull in two.

Instead it simply left a splatter mark on the glass like a jellyfish. Thin cracks radiated from where it struck. Of course, I should have anticipated that every window in the house would be bullet-proofed. I fired off another three shots in quick succession. All they did was punch opaque patches into the toughened glass, their tight pattern obscuring Callan's face.

At that moment the lights behind me came on. Startled, I spun around, expecting an attack that never came. Some bright spark had set a timer for the upper floor lights to come on at midnight precisely. I was silhouetted clearly against them. I was a sitting target. As the realisation sank in I spun back to face Callan. He was photographing me.

With both guns hanging from my shoulders I shimmied down the ladder and released it with a tug of a second nylon filament. It tumbled at my feet. I snatched it up, ran to the garden wall and hauled myself over with considerable difficulty, weighed down by the heavy guns. I fell hard on the gravel on the far side, picked myself up, got over the low wall and was running as fast as I could back to the car. I slung the guns in the back, got in and drove off at a cautious twenty miles an hour. I had no intention of attracting attention and could hear police sirens approaching from several directions. It didn't matter that I had escaped for now. It was only a matter of time before they tracked me down and killed me.

42

I reached the M25 motorway from Lower Kingswood and hit the accelerator. The little Honda's speedometer climbed to 65 mph and I kept it that way. There were few cars on the road at this hour of night and I could not risk being stopped for speeding.

I headed downhill towards the M23 turnoff. In my rear-view mirror a flashing blue light appeared. Then another. As the police cars sped towards me I heard their sirens screaming. Inside I was screaming too. If only I hadn't used the subsonic ammunition. My bullets would have penetrated the glass and taken that bastard down to hell. I should have followed up with the Steyr submachine gun, with its suppressor. Even toughened glass would have given in under its onslaught. My life was unimportant. Why had I sought to prolong it?

The police cars roared up, their lights almost blinding me in the rear-view mirror. I was on the point of pulling over when they suddenly undertook me, moving onto the slipway taking them onto the M23 towards Gatwick. Either an incident at the airport or a motorway wipeout. My heart thumping, I carried on along the M25 and, eventually, its beat slowed to normal.

I reached Ambrose's house just after one in the morning. He was still up, working late in his study. He came out to reclaim his car and his phone. He returned mine and took away the two weapons. 'I'll give them a thorough clean and oil. In an hour nobody will know either of them have been fired.' I believed I was good at masking my feelings, but it only took one glance for him to know. 'You're in need of a sherry. Just a small one. Don't want you getting pulled over for drink driving.'

We sat in his oak-beamed drawing room. He poured two sherries. 'Harvey's Bristol Cream. You need a sugar boost.'

We sat in silence for a few minutes, taking the occasional sip. Then it all came tumbling out. I told him I had failed. He stood up and, leaning over me, gave me a hug. 'You can't keep a wall around you all your life, you know, Waspy. Eventually something's got to give.'

At the mention of my old code name I felt something well up in my throat. For a moment I thought I was going to vomit, then I recognised the symptoms. I was sobbing: huge sobs that wracked my chest. It had been such a long time since I had felt like this. Ambrose said nothing. He simply held me until I stopped.

I drove home, parked up and was in bed just before three. I shut my eyes and tried to sleep.

They came for me twenty minutes later.

43

At first I thought they were the police. I could hear the siren warbling far off in the distance, then getting closer until it reached the village high street, increasing to a high-pitched shriek as it pulled up outside my gate. By then I was fully dressed. I had been wearing my underwear in bed, a nasty habit which I abhor, but I needed to be ready. I was downstairs and locked in my cellar with its heavy wooden door bolted on the inside before they turned off the engine. I switched off the light and waited in the dark.

On the monitor screen I had several angles of two paramedics hauling out a gurney and wheeling it up the path to my front door. If any doubt remained that they had come to the wrong house it was immediately dispelled by the sight of 'Igor', the left side of his face covered in a white bandage, following them. In his hand he carried a doctor's bag. I could imagine the sorts of surgical instruments and syringes it contained.

The three of them gathered round the door. There was a moment of triumph as one of them found the ring of keys hidden under an upturned flowerpot. This gave way to fury when they realised that not one of the eight keys worked. It's an old trick of mine, guaranteed to give me an extra minute or two: to arm myself, to call for help, to escape. But this time there was no escape.

They set about breaking the lock. By force of habit I always bolt the doors as well as locking them. But this night, exhausted as I was, I had omitted to do so. In under thirty seconds they were inside the house.

I heard boots thump up the stairs and into the bedroom. Did they expect to find me still asleep? I heard hoarsely issued orders – Igor, speaking some Bulgarian dialect, I guessed. I could imagine them clambering the ladder into my draughty attic, and finding nothing. The boots came back down the stairs, softer this time. I heard them approach the cellar door and try the handle. The door didn't budge. I hadn't expected it to. It had been cut from a solid piece of oak, four inches thick and knotted. Just the same, I instinctively stepped two paces back and my jumper caught on a box of loose screws which spilled to the floor, their metal heads ringing on ancient concrete, a clarion call of alarm.

The handle stopped turning. Fresh orders were croaked and, after a few seconds, the gurney was wheeled out of the house, its wheels squeaking. On the screen I could see what appeared to be a body on it, its 'face' covered with a blanket. It took little effort for them to lift the gurney into the back of the ambulance. After all, it was hardly heavier than it was when they had arrived. The 'body' was, in all probability, the duvet off my bed. Any neighbours woken by the siren and watching from their windows would imagine they saw exactly what they were supposed to see: my dead body. The paramedics locked the rear doors, got into the cab and drove off, their blue light still flashing.

I heard nothing for a good five minutes. I did not dare to move. As far as the outside world was concerned, that waspish old woman in the gingerbread cottage was dead. In a few weeks a 'For Sale' sign would appear outside the house and it would be snapped up by some young family moving out of London. Just what the village needed; a bit of young blood. Meanwhile I was trapped in my cellar by the one person who would most relish my agonising death.

Eventually I heard Igor move away from the door. His boots reverberated on the old floorboards as he moved into the kitchen. He was going through my cupboards, opening and closing them quietly, working, I presumed, in the dark, or using the flashlight on his phone. A few minutes later I heard the electric kettle boil. There were clinks as he selected a mug from the shelf and then his footsteps moved towards the fridge. Its aged door squeaked open then closed again with a clunk. I heard the sound of the milk pouring. There was a moment's silence, then a disgusted grunt as he spat the brew onto my carpet. He marched down the old concrete steps to the cellar door.

'Don't you have any fresh milk, you disgusting old sow?' Of course I didn't. I'd been far too busy trying to put an end to his master's life to worry about the state of my fridge. I could hear him more clearly through the floorboards than through the door. He might take many hours to break through the door, but if he had the presence of mind to tear up the floorboards he could reach me in a matter of minutes. With luck he expected the cottage to be built on sturdier foundations than was the fact. The cellar featured an old Belfast sink and a cold tap. I had water. I wished I had a store of biscuits. Then I could have held out for days.

'I can wait here for days,' he said, as if reading my mind. 'But I won't need to. I have your phone, and we've cut the landline. This will soon be over.'

He moved around the kitchen, going through the drawers. I could tell he was working in the dark. The odd curse as he caught his fingertips on sharp objects gave it away. He could not afford to switch on the lights, whereas I, I realised, could. He already knew I was down here, so I had nothing to lose by lighting up the cellar and looking around for a weapon.

The worktable was littered with screwdrivers, some bent and some rusty, two hammers with curved claws for extracting nails, an awl and a heavy spanner. I could do a bit of damage with any of them, but nothing guaranteed to be fatal. Igor would certainly have something much more lethal at his command.

It was Dennis who, after his retirement from the service, had taken pleasure in visiting and carrying out basic repair jobs around the house. Since his death I had hardly ever come down here and had never bothered to tidy up. As I searched around I added to my array of arms: an electric drill, a hedge trimmer – used twice every summer, on the first of May and the first of June – and a little cabinet of drawers containing some of Dennis's odds and sods: drill bits, screws, nuts and bolts, and a whole selection of his little 'treasures' – each of which held a story for him.

I realised that, while I could switch my own lights on in the basement, I could also switch on the main light in the hall. This was a refinement Dennis had wired up for me a couple of years before he died. I reached up and flicked the switch on and off. Three short flashes, three long ones, three short.

'What the fuck are you doing?' Igor growled. I ignored him and continued flashing the hall light. In all likelihood my neighbours would have gone back to bed, excitement over, but there was always the possibility of a night owl, someone irritated by the flashing lights, who might recognise the simple Morse code for SOS.

Igor dragged a kitchen chair over to the hallway. I could hear him climb it. I knew the chair well. It wobbled. Dennis had fixed that wobble for me, but constant use – it was my favourite – had worn down the block of cork glued to its wonky leg.

Igor hit the ground hard, but not hard enough to damage himself. 'You can keep switching on that light as long as you want. It won't make any difference now.' He had removed the light bulb. I stopped flicking the switch. I pulled the small carpet which lay in the centre of the room towards the wall and lay down on it. I might as well get some rest.

44

I AWOKE TO THE SOUND of scratching. I checked my watch. It was after seven in the morning. I had managed to sleep for four hours. My body was stiff and my bones ached. Doesn't time fly when you're having fun?

The scratching came from the other side of the door. Then a few hard taps. Igor was working on one of the larger knots in the door. Knots are created when a branch becomes embedded in the trunk of a tree as it grows. Some knots are tight. I would have preferred that. This one was loose. After about ten minutes of scratching and tapping, the knot dropped forward into the basement and a thin shaft of light pierced the room.

Up until then I had buoyed myself with an unjustified sense of superiority. Thanks to my hidden cameras I could observe anyone coming up the path or moving around the house. I could hear and determine their movements, but they could not observe me. Now all Igor had to do was put his eye up to the hole and he could see where I was lying. With a well-aimed bullet he might kill me.

I sprang across the room and plunged my refuge into darkness.

When I had scouted the cellar earlier I had noticed a powerful flashlight. Now I felt for it in the dark and found it. I stood in the corner, out of the knothole's limited line of sight. The first thing to do was check if the flashlight worked. It did. I switched it off, edged quietly towards the hole, put the flashlight up against it and snapped it back on again. There was a yelp on the other side and I heard Igor stumble back, cursing in his native Bulgarian, as the bright light blinded him. What he uttered was too coarse to merit translation.

The knothole remained dark for the next hour. I guessed Igor had plugged it with something. I sat back down on my carpet and waited. Perhaps someone would come by and check up on me. God knows why I thought that. Apart from Percy, and possibly Jamie Cullum, I had no friends in the village and had never bothered to make any. But I hoped that Percy, at least, might make some enquiries.

There was silence. A silence deeper than any I had ever experienced. Even away from the main road I could usually hear the rumble of lorries, and at night the oestrus-driven barks of vixens and the flutters of birds caught napping by feral cats. Down here there was nothing. Nothing except my own breath, soft, regular, persistent.

At around noon a car drew up in the rear lane behind my cottage. A man got out and approached the back door. It was the man I had nicknamed 'Fashion-Plate' (or Rupert Best-Worthington, Baronet, as he styled himself). He wore a fine tweed suit and carried a cordless drill. He knocked softly on the back door. Getting no reply, he produced his phone. I heard the 'whoop' of a WhatsApp message arriving somewhere about the house. This was followed by silence. Best-Worthington speed-dialled and a phone rang on the far side of the cellar door. Igor's sleepy voice answered. Chair legs scraped across the floorboards as he hurried round to open the back door. I heard angry muffled voices. Best-

Worthington was furious. Igor could have let me escape while he slept. Moments later I saw Igor heading for Best-Worthington's car. Was this a changing of the guard?

I heard a tapping on the door. Best-Worthington spoke.

'So sorry to have kept you waiting down there. I was unavoidably detained.'

I said nothing.

'I know you're in there, so there's no use pretending.' While I was considering a reply, he continued. 'I'm sure you don't want to spend any more time down there than you have to.'

'I can stay here as long as I like. I have ample food' – a lie – 'and a plentiful supply of water.'

From the trunk of the car Igor was hauling heavy wooden planks, a canvas bag and a length of hose.

'Ah yes, water. Well, if you happen to run low I believe we'll be able to top you up.' He had something in mind. Something I was certain I would not enjoy.

'What do you want?'

'What we've always wanted. The return of the little girl.'

'And then you'll let me out and I can get on with my life?'

'Ah, well, now you've gone and complicated matters, haven't you? My employer would insist on guarantees.'

'What sort of guarantees?'

'That you will cease all attempts to harm him, or damage his reputation.'

'If I tell you where the girl is, I will not be harmed?'

'You and little Alisa will be quite safe, believe me.'

Alisa. So that really was her birth name.

'How did you come to lose her?'

'Ah, that was a very unfortunate matter. Her mother had taken the little mite down to the river for a picnic. She had just removed the baby in its carrier from the car. She laid it down on the ground for a moment while she got the hamper from the boot of the car. She was unaware that this was a tidal river and that the water was rising rapidly. She returned just in time to see the baby carrier floating away.'

'The poor woman.'

'She's absolutely distraught.'

'There was nothing about it in the local news.'

'No, we asked it to be kept out of the press, for diplomatic reasons.'

'Your employer must be a very important man.'

'Where he comes from, he is. And we're talking about his only child. The apple of his eye.'

We both sat in silence. Time dragged on.

'This young mother, very distraught, you said?'

'Oh, extremely. Poor thing is out of her mind with worry.'

'But you managed to put her out of her misery.'

'Pardon?' His sophistication was wearing off.

'If you had received a private education, as you pretend, you would know that the proper expression is simply "what?" "Pardon" is considered a little vulgar.'

I had annoyed him. Nobody likes to have their veneer scratched.

'What did you mean by your previous comment?' I could hear the wound in his voice.

'I believe I was referring to you and your friends murdering the baby's mother, chopping her into small pieces, putting them in a suitcase and disposing of them down a well. Not very smart, are you?'

I knew I was sealing my death warrant, but by then I did not care. I could imagine every horrible detail.

A young mistress – no – a young wife, grown sick of the constant exploitation and abuse. Yes, a wife, demanding a divorce under British laws, leading to a possible payout of a half a billion or more. A wife, leaving forever and taking her only child, sedated to keep it silent. The child he craved late in life. For what is the purpose of all the cruelty and ruthlessness, the billions amassed, if not to pass them on to your bloodline? That is how we achieve immortality.

I could imagine the young mother's desperate bid for freedom. How, as his thugs closed in to end her life with a rabbit chop to the neck, or the thrust of a stiletto blade, she entrusted her child to the waters and a better life: a new Moses. What courage that must have taken. And how extraordinary that of all the rivers, she had chosen the one that led her child to me. Her sacrifice deserved to be honoured. Whatever else happened, I would not betray her.

I pictured Best-Worthington's well-polished brogues as he stepped around the kitchen until he was standing just over my head. If I'd had a gun, I would have shot him through the floorboards where he stood. I deeply regretted giving Ambrose back his weapons.

He returned to the door. 'You say you have water. No longer. I've cut you off.'

'I've filled a bucket. I can last ten days here. You are running out of time.'

Something was dragged across the floor. I heard it being pushed up against the top step. A moment later I knew what it was.

Cold water cascaded down the concrete steps like a waterfall. There was nothing I could do to stop it. The thick oak door had never fitted perfectly; there was a gap at the bottom of at least half an inch between it and the step. I had been grateful for this when the washing machine had flooded a couple of years back. Instead of soaking my carpets the water had run straight down into the cellar. This time I was not so happy.

Cold water pooled around my bare feet. I climbed up onto the worktop. Judging the flow, I estimated I would only have ninety minutes at most before it reached me. I would be able to hold out for a while longer, but once the water hit the fuse box, which was at eye level, that would be it.

'I'm leaving now,' he said over the sound of the water. 'If you have anything you want to say, you can say it to my colleague. He is keen to stay and hear your pleas, after what you did to his face.'

His footsteps moved away and I watched him leave through the back door. He got in his car and drove away as the water rose without remorse.

45

I LAY ON THE BENCH, my eyes shut, and listened. Nearly an hour had gone by. Igor was drilling. My thick oak door vibrated as he worked on boarding up the door. The screws he used were of different lengths. Some penetrated the wood by an inch or so, others less. The door would no longer open on my side. I had lost my chance of escaping my cramped tomb. In another half hour I would start to drown. Minutes later I would be dead.

I switched on the flashlight and searched for something I could use to attract help. Dennis had kept an old police whistle down here. Did I still have it? Some neighbour might hear its shrill shriek of alarm. I searched the drawers of the cabinet but could not find it. What I did find were some cartridges from a 303 Lee Enfield rifle. All but one of them were spent.

When struggling with impossible odds in the field, in service to his country, Dennis would reminisce about his time at school. 'Those were terrible days,' he would say. 'By comparison, everything that came later was a doddle.'

One of his grimmest stories was of when he had to go for target practice on the rifle range. The Lee Enfields had been designed for men. Dennis had been only fourteen years old when he was obliged to join the school's Combined

Cadet Force. The sergeant major failed to warn him of the gun's powerful recoil and the first kick had almost broken Dennis's jaw. Seeing the boy hesitate before taking another shot, the sergeant major had struck him across the face with his swagger stick, screamed at him for being a coward and ordered him to fire again. This time the recoil broke a tooth. The sergeant major, devoid of sympathy, instructed him to tuck the rifle's stock into his shoulder. Dennis loosed off the rest of his magazine, but each round felt like he was being struck in the shoulder with a sledgehammer.

'Reload,' shouted the sergeant major. Dennis reloaded, but slipped one live round into his pocket. He was saving it for the back of the sergeant major's head.

He never got a chance to fire that bullet but in due course he developed into an excellent shot, winning the all-schools cup two years in succession. He always kept that live cartridge to remind him. And now here it was in my hand.

As my index finger ran over the tip of the bullet an idea began to develop in my head. Gradually the idea took form. I would have to get into the water, which was already at chest height. I thanked my stars it wasn't winter. The water was cold, but not so cold as to stop me putting my plan into action.

In the dark, I felt for the knothole in the door. It was approximately the diameter of my index finger. It narrowed towards the far side of the door. Would it be too tight for my purpose?

I inserted the cartridge into the hole. It slid in and stopped at the obstruction which blocked it. The obstruction felt soft – probably a wad of Igor's chewing gum. The base of the cartridge protruded. A standard 303 cartridge, including the actual bullet which is fired from the rifle, measures around two and a quarter inches in length. The door was nearly four inches of solid oak. Even with Igor's obstruction removed, the cartridge would fit snugly and the bullet head would not show on his side.

I needed something to hold the cartridge firmly in place. There were washers of varying sizes in the cabinet's bottom drawer. I found one that fitted neatly around the base of the cartridge and tried it in the knothole. It would hold.

The water had now reached my shoulders. If I was to act, I would have to be quick about it. I picked up a hammer and searched for Dennis's awl. It had been on the bench earlier. Now I couldn't find it.

I was shivering with cold. I placed the flashlight on a high shelf, angled towards the door. As I did so, I felt something bob against me. The awl. I snatched at it and missed in the shadows. I got it on the second attempt. I was ready.

The drilling ceased. I removed the cartridge and washer from the knothole and prayed (to whom I had no idea) that Igor had not yet boarded over it. I hammered on the door. There was no response. I hammered again and that little shaft of light returned.

'You feeling wet enough?' his hoarse voice asked.

'I'm cold,' I said through chattering teeth. 'You win. I'll tell you where the baby is.'

'I'm listening.'

I looked through the hole. He was standing a few feet back, wary. Above the bandage poked the blackened tip of his frostbitten ear.

'Turn off the tap first.'

'Tell me, then I'll turn it off.'

'I'm so cold,' I murmured softly, as if I were already fading.

'I can't hear you.'

I mumbled something in response.

'Come on, out with it.'

Through the hole I could see him move forward, lean in and put his ear to the hole. I heard a soft splash and he cursed. Water had got into his shoes.

As silently as I could I lined up the cartridge. My hands were shaking with cold as I eased it back into the knothole.

It slipped from my fingers and dropped into the water.

I had lost my chance. My plan was futile.

I was never one to give up, however, not even with everything stacked against me. Those cartridges are made to be watertight. Though more than fifty years old, it stood a good chance of remaining dry. I took a deep breath, ducked down and felt blindly around on the concrete floor. Nothing. I had to come up for air.

How long would Igor remain with his ear to the door?

'I'm drowning!'

'Tell me, and I'll free you!' he shouted back. I did not believe him. He would relish leaving me here to drown, just as I had been happy to leave him to freeze to death.

I ducked back down in the water. Bent double, I spread my palms wide. I moved them forward in a sweeping motion, but the air in my lungs kept pulling me back to the surface. My fingers touched something and I felt it roll out of reach. I kicked forward as I felt my mind numbing, my resolve waning as my brain became starved of oxygen. Then my hands closed around the cold metal cartridge. I burst out of the water, gasping for air.

'Are you still there?' I spluttered.

'Yes,' he grunted. 'Tell me. If you want to live.'

The shaft of light disappeared again. He was listening at the door. This was my last chance.

I slipped the cartridge and washer into the hole and it held fast. The wood was already starting to swell.

I placed the point of the awl against the primer cap, raised the hammer and struck.

The shock as the primer ignited the propellant to drive the bullet into Igor's brain made my hands ring. I dropped the hammer into the water and removed the spent and smoking cartridge, almost gagging from the stench of cordite. I put my eye to the hole. There was no sign of Igor – he must have dropped below my line of sight – but I could see blood and brain splattered across the top of the concrete steps.

For a moment I felt exultation. It did not last. I was treading water. There only remained a gap of a few inches above my head. Very soon I would have no more air.

46

I UNBOLTED THE DOOR AND pushed. I could get no leverage and the swollen door wouldn't budge. The long screws were enough to stop a charging buffalo. My strength was spent. Soon I would be dead. My only consolation was that I had not surrendered Alice.

I shut my eyes and wondered if I should simply exhale and let my body sink into the cold water. That was what I had intended only a few short weeks ago. But now I wanted to live. Should I hold on till the very last second in the vain hope of rescue? Which would be worse? What was left of my consciousness kicked in with a new awareness. I realised that the water had ceased to rise.

How could that be? The tap was still running. Water continued to gush from the hose outside the door. I scrambled forward, reached for the fading flashlight, held it above the water and swept it in a wide arc around my little refuge.

The rear of the cellar was faced in brick which, I had always assumed, was backed with a concrete damp course. As the water reached the upper levels of brick, it rose no higher. I kicked out to bring myself up against the wall. I could hear water splashing behind it. That meant there was a gap beyond the wall, a gap which could prevent me from drowning. But I felt no relief. I had already resigned myself to death, and the glimmer of hope that I might prolong my life just a little longer was unwelcome. I was simply exchanging death by drowning for death by hypothermia.

The drive to keep on living surpasses all others. I hooked the flashlight onto a protruding nail and duck-dived down to the cellar floor – I could get no colder than I already was – and found the hammer. I swam back up to the wall, raised the hammer high and smashed it against the bricks. The top three rows gave way instantly, crashing into the void beyond. I swung again and the next two rows toppled. Water spilled over and I saw that I had made a space large enough to crawl through.

I unhooked the flashlight – its beam pathetically dim now – pushed it through the gap and peered in. I had uncovered an underground passage. It led away from the house. The beam was too weak to illuminate more than the first twenty or thirty feet. Even as I watched, it flickered as the battery failed. I tossed the flashlight aside, crawled through the space and dropped onto hard flagstones.

The passage had appeared low and mean in the flashlight's beam. I had anticipated having to crawl, but I found I could just about stand up in it, as long as I kept my head down. I staggered forward in the dark, hoping that it would not lead into some disused well. Dying in a dank well would be far worse than dying in the cold cellar of my own home. Even in death we wish to be found, to be mourned and remembered by our loved ones. As I walked on I realised that, in truth, I had no loved ones to mourn me.

As I moved along, one hand on the brick roof, the other thrust ahead of me, I noticed that the flagstones were dry. The passage sloped gently upwards. I had walked through a black tunnel more than once before, most spectacularly in a *levada* on the island of Madeira, but each time I knew that the tunnel led somewhere. In this case, I was not so sure.

After what felt like a hundred yards my shin struck sharp metal. I stifled a yelp, sat and clasped my leg in the dark, somehow controlling the excruciating pain. I found myself sitting on some sort of platform at the end of the tunnel. I felt around and realised I had struck the iron step of a spiral staircase. I had no option but to head up it. After a dozen or so steps my raised palm struck a steel plate. I shoved upwards with all my remaining strength and it swung open. As silently as possible, I clambered out and found myself in a hexagonal room with slit embrasures for a machine gun. The stone floor was littered with cigarette butts and used condoms. Jamie Cullum had been making good use of the pillbox in my paddock.

Unsteady on my feet, my shin still smarting and my clothes and hair sopping wet, I stumbled across the paddock, straddled the fence, crossed the gravel where my car was parked and staggered to the back door. My hands were shaking so badly I could hardly twist the smooth doorknob but I managed. The door was unlocked. I stepped inside and nearly collapsed with exhaustion. I carried on to the hall, determined to see what damage I had wrought on Igor.

He was scarcely recognisable, unidentifiable on a mortuary slab except for the blackened tip of his ear. He must have suspected something at the last moment and leapt back. The bullet had hit him in the weakest part of the skull, the point where the bones knit. Maori warriors understood how vulnerable this point was. In close combat against the British they had been invincible. With a *mere pounamu*, a jade hand axe, a Maori could strike his opponent's temple just above the ear and, with a jerk of his wrist, flip off the top of his victim's skull. Igor's skull had shattered into pieces. His brain was no more than a slush of pink and grey spread over my floor. His eyes, no longer held in place by bone and cartilage, hung loose from their sockets.

I collapsed, no longer able to bear my own weight.

It was then that I heard the footsteps. Someone was standing over me. Reluctantly, I raised my eyes.

It was Best-Worthington. He nodded his head in weary relief.

'I was wondering where you had got to.'

47

As far as I was concerned Rupert Best-Worthington, Bart, could kill me. I just hoped he would make it quick.

'Very unfortunate, all this,' he said. 'Josef was so very good at these difficult jobs. I would go so far as to say he relished them. I don't know how I can possibly replace him. Stay where you are a moment, if you would oblige.'

He strode into the kitchen. I let my eyes drop and, in that moment, saw the butt of a pistol protruding from the pocket of the body that used to be Josef, as I thought of the man whom up until now I had been calling Igor. In death, we all deserve to be named.

Best-Worthington turned off the kitchen tap. The water ceased to flow into the cellar. He returned with two knives.

'Let's not waste any more time. I told Josef his silly water torture wouldn't work. An old bird like you won't crack.' He studied the knives. One was newish, thick bladed, sharp, good for cutting vegetables. The other was an old carving knife of my father's, so worn by constant sharpening that its blade was as thin as a filleting knife, but terrifyingly sharp. Best-Worthington held the horn handle lightly and slashed the carver's blade towards me. I instinctively raised my right hand in defence. The blade struck my little finger. It happened so fast I felt no pain, but the last joint of my little finger was severed and flew into a corner.

'Sorry, didn't mean to do that,' he apologised with a smile. 'Too quick. The next will be much slower.'

That was when I shot him. I had eased the pistol out of Josef's trouser pocket. I had meant the shot as a warning, aimed at the ceiling, but it caught Best-Worthington's arm, running up his triceps into his deltoid muscle. He dropped the knives.

'Oww! That fucking hurt!' He cradled his arm like a petulant little boy who'd been punished unjustly. 'I'm bloody bleeding!' Perhaps he had been privately educated after all.

He hurled his bulk at me, knocking the gun from my hand. His hands flew around my throat and he squeezed with all his might.

'Interfering old bitch. You've been nothing but trouble from the start. You're dead. That child can rot as far as I care.'

I thought I heard another voice in my ears, but perhaps it was my own blood throbbing. I was passing out. No air to the lungs, no blood to the brain. A darkness fell over my eyes.

An almighty gunshot echoed around the hall. Best-Worthington let out a cry of pain and rolled off me.

'Are you all right, my dear?'

The darkness lifted, I opened my eyes and, as I blinked myself back to life, the figure standing over me came into focus.

'Percy!'

He hauled me up and sat me in the chair where, a half hour or so before, Josef had been seated. In his hand he held a Glock 19. He gave Best-Worthington a kick. 'You, get up.'

'How can I fucking stand up? You've shot me in the fucking arse,' whimpered Best-Worthington.

'You'll get its twin in your other cheek if you don't.'

The big man levered himself up off the floor, a pantomime of pain: gasps, groans and wild rolling eyes.

'Justin?' called Percy. A young man, the one I had noticed days earlier on the beach at Pevensey Bay, stepped forward.

'Sir?'

'You and this man will remove the body and put it in the trunk of his car. Then report back.'

'Yes, sir.'

Best-Worthington and Justin picked up what was left of Josef – he was small and thin and, with half his head gone, relatively easy to lift – and shuffled towards the garden door.

'Don't forget that,' Percy said. He pointed to the top of Joseph's skull, lying under a radiator. Best-Worthington dropped Joseph's legs – he had taken the lighter end, of course. He limped to my waste bin, removed the plastic bag that lined it and used it to gather up the skull and whatever bits of brain he could.

'You can go,' Percy said.

I moved to the rear window and watched as they carried Josef to Best-Worthington's car. It had been parked behind an overgrown laurel, which was why I hadn't noticed it on my struggle back to the house. They rolled the body into the trunk and slammed it shut. Justin left Best-Worthington standing by the car as he returned to the house. Seeing his chance, Best-Worthington got into the car, started it up and drove away at speed.

'You're letting him get away.'

'Yes, my dear,' said Percy. 'But he'll only get a few hundred yards. He'll be met by some nice gentlemen from Special Branch who, when they search his car, will find one dead body and, where his spare tyre should be, the wrench with

Mrs Price's blood all over it. The evidence they intended to use to frame you.'

'You've saved me twice, Percy,' I said.

'Yes I have, haven't I?' he replied with a grin. 'Justin's got a couple of agency ladies coming over to help him clean up. And dry out that basement. Some of these old houses can get awfully damp.'

Justin stooped to pick something up off the floor. It was the top joint of my little finger.

'I'll have that,' I said.

'I think it might be too late to sew it back on,' said Percy.

'That's all right, I have other plans for it.'

48

Percy's house put mine to shame. It was a late Georgian masterpiece in miniature. Well-proportioned rooms, nicely framed military prints and drawings: a couple of Egyptian sketches by Edward Lear and an early watercolour of the walls of Rome by J M W Turner.

I was concerned about dripping blood over his fine wool carpets but he told me not to worry. In any case the handkerchief he had confiscated from Best-Worthington – finest monogrammed silk of course – did a good job of stemming the bleeding.

Percy led me upstairs to the bedrooms. 'This one's mine,' he pointed to the right. 'And this one's yours, on the left, for as long as you need it.' He led me into a warm, cosy room. A little too chintzy for me, but I could see why women would like it. A copy of Singer Sargent's 'Carnation, Lily, Lily, Rose' was framed above the fireplace, which was stacked with dry wood, though it was too warm an evening to merit lighting a fire.

'You have your own bathroom. I am going to draw your bath, hot, and add some restorative magnesium flakes. Good for relaxing the muscles. If the water's too hot, you can wait till it cools a little. I'll leave you to get out of those wet clothes. The ladies will be round in a while with a fresh change from your wardrobe.'

'Ladies?'

'Dottie and Lottie. Very capable couple. You must have seen them in the village.' He meant the two blondes from the tea room who had placed the video camera in my front wall. 'They'll know what to bring. I shall go downstairs and warm up dinner. It's a sort of stew, so it'll be ready any time you are.'

I could have stayed in that big bath all night, but I did not want to keep Percy waiting long. I came down in silk pyjamas (his?) and a big white fluffy bathrobe. Not my thing at all, but it was very comfortable just the same. I don't know what Percy put in his stew, but it was the most delicious thing I had eaten in years. The base was ox cheeks, which he had slow-cooked for several hours, but he had added any number of herbs and wines to bring out the flavours of the meat. With the wine from his cellar – a Château Talbot 1982 he had picked up for a hundred pounds a case when first bottled, but which he said we must drink now (it was delicious) – I was, eventually, able to put some of the day's events behind me. My little finger smarted like the blazes, but Percy had arranged for a district nurse (how had he got her at such short notice?) to attend to it. She had, despite my protestations, administered a local anaesthetic before putting in a couple of stitches and covering the stump with a bandaged pad. It would soon heal over.

'How long have you been watching over me, Percy?' I asked as I finished my second glass of claret.

'Since shortly after you went to see your son, Sir Bernard.'

'"Sir" Bernard?'

'Oops, birthday honours list, hasn't been announced yet. Forget I said it.'

'So you work for…?'

'You and I have both signed the Official Secrets Act. Let's not break our vows.'

'You have quite a reputation in the village. As a ladies' man.'

'Rightly deserved, I'm afraid to say. Makes an excellent cover.' He refilled my glass. 'What's the expression? Hiding in plain sight. Except I'm not really hiding, am I? Simply masquerading.'

'And doing a bloody good job of it. You had me fooled, and I'm pretty good at sniffing out a fraud.'

Percy reached into the pocket of his jacket which was draped over the back of a Chippendale chair. 'I think you might want this.' He placed an envelope before me.

It was addressed in my hand: *To whom it may concern*. I had written it the morning I had gone down to the river. That same morning that I had found Alice. As a suicide note it was brief and to the point.

Percy had taken it from my escritoire at the same time he removed the bloodied tyre jack. The envelope had not been sealed. Had he read its contents? I looked up, but his warm eyes gave nothing away.

We said no more about the matter. Percy removed our dirty dishes to the kitchen and returned with two lemon possets.

'Delicious. Did you make them?' I asked as I polished mine off.

'In this instance the credit goes to Sally Clarke in Notting Hill. I find her puddings and soufflés beyond compare.' He looked me in the eyes. 'Will you be able to sleep? I have a couple of sedatives if they'll help.'

'I think I'll sleep very well without them, thank you.'

I was wrong. Relaxed from the bath and the wine, I got into bed and was dead to the world within minutes. But around one o'clock I was awake, and restless. The anaesthetic had worn off and my finger hurt like the blazes. The pain, and my memories of the previous twenty-four hours' events came (forgive the pun) flooding back, and I spent most of the rest of the night fully awake, plotting my revenge.

In the morning I woke to the smell of frying bacon. I showered, made myself presentable and came down in a blouse, jumper and skirt that Lottie and Dottie had brought over during the night and laid, neatly folded, on a chair outside my bedroom door.

Over breakfast I confided the broad outlines of my plan to Percy. He disapproved.

'Far too dangerous. And if you tell anyone else about it, I shall deny all knowledge.'

After our relaxed mood the previous night, I had expected him to be more receptive. But Percy, in the bright light of day, was all practical efficiency. So different from the twinkly-eyed old-fashioned seducer I had taken him to be. But not so different from me. We were both professionals.

'Don't take this the wrong way,' he said. 'I want to see the man expelled from the UK and sanctioned, but we are talking about the finer points of diplomacy. No matter how much we may hate it, we cannot afford to cut all ties with a country or even one of its citizens, no matter how unwelcome.'

'I was merely suggesting a confrontation in a safe and open place, under scrutiny. Nothing more.'

Percy fixed me with those hazel eyes of his and, for a moment, they twinkled. 'You've got something else in mind.'

'Nothing that would embarrass the UK, I promise.'

'Well, it's not as if I can stop you. My remit was to see you didn't get yourself killed. I think we can safely say I've managed that so far. I should apologise for arriving so late yesterday. I was summoned to London in the early hours. It seems that someone had made an attempt on the life of a Belarusian diplomat in St John's Wood and it was suspected that I might know something about it. But I managed to put minds to rest, for the time being, at any rate.'

After my second cup of coffee (Colombia el Carmen No.50 beans, for your information – Percy had high standards) I decided to go home and sort out the house. Percy was reluctant to let me go. 'You need time to recuperate. I know you think of yourself as an old warhorse but, as I've said before, none of us are getting any younger. Stay here a few more days, at least.'

'If I stayed here any longer I would never want to leave.'

'That wouldn't be such a bad thing, would it?' The old twinkle was back.

Lottie, Dottie and his men had made good on Percy's promise. You would never have known that less than twenty-four hours earlier there had been blood and brains splattered all over the hallway. Every brick, every tile had been scrubbed clean. There remained a faint odour of ammonia – excellent for destroying tell-tale DNA – and a few areas, damaged by bone or bullet fragments, had been freshly painted. It reminded me of that old joke about the royals: their world smells of fresh paint, as every blemish is touched up the day before their visit.

The ladies had done their best to tidy up the bedroom. Both Josef and Best-Worthington had turned it over searching for clues to Alice's whereabouts and had left a trail of destruction. The other rooms, which were mostly bare, had hardly been touched.

I went through the drawers and found all my clothes neatly folded and put away. Rather more neatly than I was accustomed to, if truth be told. A rail in my wardrobe, which had come loose over the years, had been screwed back on and tightened.

The one area where they had not been able to do much work was my cellar. There was no masking the musty smell. They had removed Josef's attempts to board up my cellar door and prevent my escape. But the water had swollen the door and they had had to remove part of the frame to access the room where I had been entombed. The floor was still damp, as was the shelving and the various bits of junk I had never bothered to tidy away. The fuse box had, fortunately, remained just above the rising water, but the monitor, so well installed by Aaron, had not. I phoned Ambrose and booked a fresh visit.

Around tea time Aaron arrived, cheerfully reassuring me that he would be able to replace the monitor and get everything back up and running promptly. There was still the man with the moles on his face to consider. He might try to come back at any time.

I went into the kitchen and extracted my little finger joint from the freezer. I explained what I needed while Aaron listened attentively. Once I had boxed it up with ice packs in a polystyrene box to keep it at sub-zero temperature, he took it away. He assured me the job could easily be done overnight.

49

Bernard picked me up from Tregunter Road. Silvana had offered me a room for the night and Eva, to my surprise, had readily agreed. I thought they might want me to take Alice off their hands. Quite the opposite. Eva had softened since Alice's arrival. She had become prone to making all sorts of daft baby noises, cooing like a dove over her brood, a habit she detested in others.

Eva had even helped me with my make-up, while Silvana attended to my hair, giving it a blow-dry and snipping my split ends so that, for once in a very long while, I looked quite presentable. I had dug out those old black stilettos from the back of my wardrobe. I knew I would find a use for them someday. Getting them on was a squeeze, what with my bunions. For backup, I carried a pair of low-heeled roll-up pumps in my handbag. As a finishing touch, Eva loaned me a beautiful antique stole with an Erté design which must have set her back a few thousand pounds. I made a mental note not to spill any wine on it.

The doorbell rang at a quarter to six. Eva answered, gave her brother a quick peck on the cheek, and ushered me out. Bernard stared at me. 'Mother, you've actually made an effort.' I resisted comment and followed him down the steps to where his official car was waiting. He held open the door, I slipped in and he walked round to the other door and got in beside me. His driver started the car. We drove into The Boltons and carried on to Cromwell Road, turned up Queen's Gate, where Eva had been schooled, past the Royal College of Music, then up the West Carriage Drive through Hyde Park and across the Serpentine.

There we waited for a string of ponies to cross the road. It was a warm evening and the driver had his window open. As we stopped to let a group of children cross the road, a wasp flew in. It buzzed angrily against the windscreen. Bernard's driver swatted at it with a printed invitation.

'Leave it,' I said. 'It just needs to find a way out.'

He opened the far window. The wasp flew out and went off to bother somebody else.

'What is that?' Bernard asked. He was referring to the tip of my little finger.

'It's a prosthetic,' I told him. 'Rather smarter than a raw stump when I'm socialising.'

'Looks very convincing.'

'It's supposed to.'

Aaron had taken a cast of my severed finger joint and made a silicone reproduction that slipped over my stump. He had taken pains to colour it realistically. Not just any skin colour, but *my* skin colour: a garden tan with light liver spots. The prosthetic was hollow. If I depressed it, it would collapse. Otherwise it was good enough to fool anyone up close.

We came out of the park at Lancaster Gate and turned left. As we passed the Bayswater Euro Car Park we slowed and stopped outside the building I recalled from the 1970s as a private residence once owned by Jimmy, of Jimmy's Wine Bar, which had been housed in the old royal barracks in Kensington Church Street. Because of its close proximity to Kensington Palace Gardens and the Russian and Czech embassies, we had spent much of our 'down' time, between surveillance duties, hanging out at Jimmy's bar. They cooked excellent steaks, partly subsidised by our expenses.

Bernard got out, walked round and opened the car door for me.

'I really don't know why you want to come to this thing. It's all diplomatic tosh, just the sort of thing you hate.' In response to my shrug he added, 'Well, at least it means Bridget can have a night in with the children.' Bridget was his wife. According to Eva, who had suddenly become a source of indiscreet gossip, the couple were going through something of a *crise*. Bridget was a very successful divorce lawyer who earned more in one year than Bernard did in five. She was rumoured to be having an affair with the American boss of her international law firm. But Bernard's elevation to knighthood and her becoming a 'Lady' was something she was unwilling to sacrifice, even for marginally better sex.

Bernard accepted the printed invitation from his driver and we both headed into the cream building. In the late sixties and early seventies its large ballroom had been a venue for 'coming out' balls. I had attended several, at my mother's suggestion. I mostly stuck with my old school friends, if there were any present, while trying to avoid the soi-disant 'deb's delights' who prowled the dance floors, sniffing out unwise virgins to deflower. Sometime around 1980 Jimmy had sold the building to the Russian Embassy for a great deal of money and, as far as I know, disappeared to some sunny paradise. The Russians used the building for consular purposes, but the ballroom and the other large room off it were still used for embassy functions.

Bernard handed his invitation to a heavily built usher or bouncer, which for all intents and purposes he was, not that anyone would be foolish enough to gatecrash such an event. He looked us up and down and in a loud voice announced in Russian: 'The British Secretary of State for Defence and' – a pregnant pause here – 'his wife.' I laughed, but managed to turn it into a discreet cough. Bernard frowned, but got the joke once the announcement was repeated in English.

'Well that's a first for me,' he said. 'Now let's meet the ambassador and get some drinks. I've only got an hour, then I'm due at the theatre.' Percy had provided Bernard with 'comps' for his latest theatrical investment. I had not been surprised to learn they knew each other.

The ambassador proved harder to find than Bernard had anticipated – he had been 'unavoidably detained' – so I left Bernard and wandered around a bit on my own. The ballroom opened up onto a raised terrace overlooking the garden. I remembered spotty young men fumbling under petticoats once the sun had gone down; young women hoping to look sophisticated by lighting up cigars, only to be discovered later throwing up in the bushes, victims of nicotine poisoning. Nowadays nobody ever smoked, unless you were rich, in which case you would draw on an expensive cigar, nauseating your fellow guests, and attempt to relight it when it went out, which it did if you neglected to keep puffing.

On the terrace a whispered conversation was going on between three dour-looking Russians. As I approached, one of them looked up, made a signal, and they all went silent. They checked me out, seeing if I posed a threat. I smiled graciously, nodded and retired. Their conversation resumed.

I went back through the French windows into the vast ballroom, searching for one face in particular. Over in one corner I saw Bernard deep in conversation with a figure I recognised from the French Mission – an impossibly self-important type lampooned weekly in the British press and in the French, monthly. Diplomatic wives huddled together in groups, cold shouldering those who, for Byzantine reasons of state, were arbitrarily no longer part of their coteries. The one person I had come here to find was missing.

Then I saw him, making a grand entrance, preceded by a waft of cigar smoke. His name was announced – a name I had read many times in relation to multi-billion dollar deals, massive corruption and strange, unexplained deaths, but had never associated with the man himself, the man I had once known as Callan. Two men walked behind him, powerful thugs with only the thinnest veneer of domestication. He stepped forward, letting his cashmere coat drop behind him. It was caught before it hit the floor.

The Russian Ambassador – moments earlier too busy even to attend his own function – appeared through a door, went straight over to him and planted a kiss on each cheek in a singular show of obeisance.

They exchanged some words and then 'Callan' stepped away, moving around the room like a czar expecting tribute from his trembling subjects. Once I had found his features attractive, his eyes capable of feigning empathy and compassion. But even then I knew that the compassion was pure deception. Now the mask was gone, the truth revealed: cruelty and entitlement in their darkest forms.

I pushed through the crowd towards him. I was elbowed back, my presence unwelcome, my perceived supplication undeserved. I circled around the crowd and took up a position by the door, knowing that his stately procession would eventually bring him back to me.

He accepted a flute of champagne from a waiter with his left hand, leaving his right free to shake hands with his admirers, those who believed that just touching the sleeve of his jacket would confer on them enough power and influence to set them up for life. He completed his tour of the room, turned to view his supplicants and I saw my chance, stepping forward with my right hand outstretched, taking his and shaking it before he could react.

'So good to meet you again, after all this time.'

His shock of recognition was such that, as he tore his hand away, he failed to sense the tiny prick of the needle protruding from my prosthetic fingertip.

'You!' He searched around for his thugs. It would have been a simple matter for them to deal with me. Back home he would have had me taken out and shot, but in front of all these people, the cream of London's diplomatic corps, that was impossible. Instead, he leaned in to me.

'This is not over. You will not deprive me of my daughter.'

'Oh, I think I shall. You see, it *is* over for you. All over.' I spoke just loud enough for him to hear me over the babble of conversation. He gave me a puzzled look and backed away. I watched him as the crowd parted like the Red Sea before Moses, all eyes upon him. I opened my purse, threw in the redundant prosthetic and sealed it in the toughened glass case Ambrose had provided, along with the few drops of toxin he said would be sufficient for my task. I dropped the case into my handbag.

There was a communal gasp from across the room. I edged forward to see Callan stagger and slump back on one of the wide sofas that faced the garden.

'Get a doctor!' someone shouted. People looked around in hope and expectation. I saw a gap and strode forward, reaching the sofa and taking a seat beside him, as if about to administer some life-saving treatment.

In the hub-bub I studied his face. Paralysis was taking effect. In a few moments he would be frothing at the mouth. I spoke clearly, so that he would not miss a word. 'All the power you have acquired, by deceit, manipulation and corruption, will evaporate in a few moments. And who will inherit? Not your children.' His eyes, the only part of him he was still able to control, swivelled round to me. 'Yes, you have children,' I continued. 'Twins: a boy and a girl. Yours and mine. One of them is here tonight with me. But you and your like will never have them. And you shall never have Alice.'

At that moment Bernard came over. 'Mother, we should go.'

Callan raised his eyes. They met Bernard's own green eyes with their hazel flecks, took in his son's strong jaw, his noble nose, his proud bearing, and knew that what I had told him was the truth.

I don't know if it was the first spasm of death, or whether, by some supreme effort, he could still control a part of himself, but his look turned to one of such unutterable hatred that I drew back, as if it could take form and throttle me.

'This man is having a stroke,' I said loudly, rose and took Bernard's arm.

'You're not a doctor,' he said.

'Yes I am. I'm a Doctor of Philosophy,' which was true, but Bernard did not appreciate the joke.

'Let's get out of here,' he said. 'The party's over. I'll drop you at Hyde Park Corner and you can take the tube back.'

'Thank God. These heels are killing me.'

50

Ambrose and I met up at Norman's Bay. It was early afternoon. Ambrose carried a doctor's bag, much like the one Josef had brought to my cottage. I had a fair idea of what it might contain. We trudged up the shingle beach. When we reached Patrick's house we edged past the rusty hulk he kept for fishing. It was filled with water and green slime. We made our way round to the door. It was ajar. Ambrose glanced at me. I shrugged. He pushed it open and we went inside.

We found Patrick staring out to sea. He moved away from the window, went into another room then, as if he had forgotten something of importance, returned to the first room. Again he seemed to have forgotten something. He went back into the other room, stopped and turned again. How long had he been doing this? It was two weeks since I had last visited and his mind had deteriorated far faster than I could have imagined.

He saw us. There was no sense of recognition. He had no idea who we were.

Ambrose opened his case. Set in formed foam rubber was a subcompact Glock 26, taken from his hidden arsenal. Beside it were three syringes. They would contain the same toxin I had administered to 'Callan'. It was virtually undetectable.

As Ambrose reached into the case I took his hand and held it.

'Look at him.' We both watched Patrick, confused, lost to the world. 'He's no threat.'

'Then decide what you want to do. It's your call.' Ambrose waited while I struggled with my best and worst instincts.

'What if I called social services?'

'Very decent of you, considering the circumstances.' He clicked his case shut.

'It looks like he hasn't eaten in days.' I was putting off making my decision.

'When did you first realise it was Patrick who betrayed you?'

'When you gave me the address on Avenue Road, in St John's Wood, the one Patrick had omitted to give me. But perhaps I've always suspected it. As early as when, in that restaurant in Bonn, he let slip that he recognised Callan from somewhere. And later, when he was angry I had given Callan faked documents. He set me up. He sacrificed me as a hostage to Callan and Golubshov, to be tortured until I gave them everything I knew. Because he was in love with Giles, his friend and colleague, and Callan was blackmailing him. In those days it would have got him thrown out of the service. Times have changed.'

'He will never be held to account, never be punished.'

'Look at him now. Isn't that punishment enough?'

Ambrose was not convinced. He went over to Patrick's untidy desk. He found the photograph that Patrick had kept. Now I looked again it was clearly of me with Callan, tall and broad shouldered. I had thought that Patrick had kept it as a reminder of our time together. But now I think it was a permanent reminder of his betrayal, of me and of Giles, who had taken the photograph.

Ambrose swept it up together with the papers referring to our time in Bonn. Most of them should have been destroyed a long time ago.

'You told me Patrick had an incinerator.'

I took the papers to the incinerator. A pilot light burned brightly. I threw in the papers. The last thing to go was the photograph. I closed the steel door, pressed the red button and heard the 'whump' of igniting gas. At the same time I heard the muffled report of a pistol shot. Ambrose had made my choice for me.

Afterwards we changed into smarter clothes: he into a light lounge suit, I into my mother's twinset. We headed back down the A27 to Glyndebourne Opera for a dress rehearsal. The other attendees were dressed casually. Only one poor fellow, a television personality, stood out in evening dress. Black tie is for the opera proper. Rehearsals are more relaxed, and the tickets less expensive. More affordable for a couple of old retirees.

During the interval we sat on the lawn enjoying the picnic Ambrose had arranged: rare roast beef with horseradish sauce, roast chicken drumsticks and a Russian salad. With a *macédoine de fruits* to finish.

'You're taking the piss, Ambrose, aren't you?'

'What do you mean?'

'The Russian salad.'

'Belarusian salad might have been pushing it, but I think we're okay with Russian.'

I provided the champagne, Taittinger Comtes de Champagne Blanc de Blancs. We were celebrating, after all.

We resumed our seats. Fifth row, centre. My treat, but Ambrose had chosen the opera. I might have preferred something lighter, perhaps Mozart's *Marriage of Figaro* with its beautiful arias and its theme of ultimate redemption. But Ambrose had preferred *Don Giovanni*, with its tale of murder, deceit, betrayal and ultimate damnation. In the end, I felt it was more fitting.

51

The leaves on Eva's *acer palmatum dissectum* were already curling and turning brown. It was a few days after the first downpours and the lawn had at last greened up after the long hot summer. We had placed a plastic sheet under the tartan rug to prevent worm casts sullying it.

The rug had been intended to be Alice's playground, but none of the coloured wooden bricks and soft toys held her attention. Instead she was determined to crawl off the lawn and into the flower beds, where she could seek out beetles and worms. My job was to ensure she did not eat any.

'Oh, Mum!' Eva exclaimed. 'You're supposed to be minding her!'

I put down my gin and tonic, reclaimed Alice and deposited her back on the rug.

'I'm in training,' I said. 'I missed out on your childhood, so don't expect too much of me.'

'Well whose fault was that?' Once Eva would have thrown the accusation at me with a scowl, but not today.

Silvana came out of the kitchen door, stood at the top of the steps and called, 'Your brother is here. Can you get the door?'

Eva harrumphed, but she did it happily. She ran in through the basement then upstairs to the door. A moment later she reappeared from the kitchen.

'Look who's here.' She moved aside as Bridget and Bernard appeared, laden with birthday presents, at the top of the external steps. Bernard's knighthood had, as I had suspected it would, improved marital relations. We had all agreed on a date for Alice's birthday and today was our chosen day to celebrate.

We watched as Alice tore the coloured wrapping off her presents and then proceeded to play with the wrapping paper and ignore her gifts inside. Silvana emerged from the kitchen, carrying a cake with a single lit candle. We joined in singing 'Happy Birthday' as she made her way down the steps. Rowdy Chelsea football supporters, returning to their low rent housing estates nearby, joined in with a second verse from beyond the garden wall. An empty beer can flew over the wall and landed in an hibiscus bush. I expected Eva to storm outside and challenge the thrower, but she ignored it. I exchanged a look with Silvana, who smiled. She placed the cake before Alice. When she failed to show much interest, we blew the candle out for her.

Afterwards Bernard came over to my deckchair and knelt down beside me.

'How's the adoption going?' I asked, topping up the tonic on my gin: an inch of tonic to two of gin. Bernard had taken it upon himself to help with Eva and Silvana's adoption of Alice. He had influence in all the right places.

'Surprisingly well, as it happens,' he said. 'But there's something puzzling me.'

'Don't let it.' I swigged a large glug of my G&T. I felt I was going to need it.

'It seems that the DNA test you got Eva to take has produced surprising results.'

'Really?

'Yes,' he lowered his voice to a whisper. The Chelsea fans, singing at the tops of their voices: *'Carefree, wherever you may be, we are the famous CFC'*, almost drowned out his next words. 'It seems that Eva and Alice share rather a lot of their DNA. Do you know anything about that?'

'Maybe I do and maybe I don't. Now go away and mind your own business.' Bernard gave me a hug. The first I had ever received from him without having to ask first. 'Mum, you are a wonder. A difficult, sometimes impossible wonder, but a wonder nevertheless.' He moved back to Bridget and she put her arm around him.

'No!' yelled Silvana. A wasp had settled on Alice's hand.

'Swat it!' said Eva.

'Leave her be,' I said. 'Alice will be all right.'

We watched a while as the large wasp, perhaps a new Queen, sat brushing her antennae and stroking her wings. Alice chuckled as if this was her best birthday present.

The wasp flew away. She might die in hibernation or she might live to make another nest. Either way, her offspring would live on.

Acknowledgements

Thanks to my terrific agent, Jason Bartholomew, for taking me on, and to my lovely publisher, Carolyn Mays, for her impressive and diligent editing. Also to freelance editor Kitty Walker, who made excellent suggestions for restructuring the middle of my book, and to Marcelle D'Argy Smith, former editor of *Cosmopolitan* magazine, who got me to keep my sentences short and to the point. Also to Marc Blake, who led an entertaining set of classes on writing your novel in a month. And most importantly to my wonderful wife Jenny, who read my manuscript first and inspired new ideas and better lines.